Mine

By

Casey Kelleher

Other titles by Casey Kelleher

Rotten to the Core

Rise and Fall

Heartless

Bad Blood

The Taken

The Promise

The Betrayed

The Broken

The Forgotten

For more details, please visit <u>Casey's Amazon Page</u>

In loving memory of my beautiful Aunt Sandie x

Prologue

You never anticipate how your world can completely change in just a short space of seconds.

How one tiny movement, one slight jerk of the steering wheel, one split decision can change everything.

And it does change everything, forever more.

That was the thought that flashed through my mind, as we glided through mid-air, in slow motion, our heads whipping back and forth with every jolt.

BANG.

Your body catapults from the chair beside me. I see your skull crashing against the windscreen, decorating the glass with a newly formed web of jagged cracks. A web that is speckled with fragments of your bloody scalp and clumps of your hair.

My body slams backwards, hard against the leather. The seat belt, saving my life, holding me in, as shards of shattered glass rain in around us both.

A deafening sound of metal crunching against wood and earth roars inside my ears as the car starts spinning weightlessly through the air, then crashes suddenly into the ground. We flip over and over, our limp, broken bodies cocooned in the crushed metal as the wreckage folds in around us.

I black out.

Maybe for just a few seconds, or minutes. I don't know. But when I come back around my head is throbbing and I'm dazed, my head feels fuzzy.

I panic, opening my eyes wider, only I can't see properly. Instead I'm blinded by a bright, brilliant white until I realise with relief that my head is buried in the airbag.

My nose has exploded with the force of the impact and I can taste the acrid metallic trickle of blood as it slides down the back of my throat.

I turn my head, my vision blurred and hazy as a stream of blood runs down my face and into my eyes. I reach up and touch the deep gouge in the flesh of my forehead lightly with my fingertips.

Disorientated, I realise that I'm hanging upside down in my seat.

The car is on its roof, the metal shell folded in around me. The seat belt is the only thing keeping me from falling.

I feel claustrophobic, I can't breathe. I need to get out.

I'm panicking, pulling frantically at the seat belt and pushing the release button, but it doesn't budge. My body weight is pushing too much tension onto it.

I don't want to look, but I do.

I turn my head, staring ahead at the windscreen, the glass missing now, I see you.

Your twisted, broken body, hanging half in, half out of the window. And I know that you are dead, as you hang there, limp and lifeless, dangling from the car.

For a few moments it's like time has stood still, the world so deafeningly silent that for a second I wonder if perhaps I'm dead too?

That my heart has given up?

That I'm not really here?

Instinctively, I place my hand on my chest, embracing the dull thumping beat that pulsates beneath my fingertips, still so persistent, so obstinate.

I wince. Wishing to God that my heart had stopped.

Because I know that there's worse still to come.

Chapter One

'I now pronounce you husband and wife.' The registrar's voice jolted Rebecca back from her daydream.

She shakes her head, still in disbelief. As if in denial. But the tiny movement is futile. *This is real*, she realises as the registrar's announcement echoes within the walls of the huge, sparse ceremony room.

'Mrs Rebecca Dawson,' Jamie Dawson says, leaning in close and kissing his new wife tentatively on the mouth, to make it official, before whispering in her ear, 'That has a lovely ring to it.'

Rebecca laughs then, finds herself repeating the words out loud.

'Rebecca Dawson. I like it, it suits me.'

He's right, she thinks. It sounds perfect, each letter rolling slickly from her tongue as she allows Jamie to wrap himself around her. The broadness of his arms and shoulders cocooning her into the warmth of his embrace. As if he's shielding everyone else in the room, so they can have this one last intimate moment all to themselves.

They kiss.

For a few seconds it feels as if there's no one else in the room. Only the two of them in a world of their own.

Though it wasn't hard to pretend they were alone, when they were accompanied today only by their two witnesses.

But Jamie had insisted on a small, intimate ceremony, and Rebecca knew why.

He'd done all of this for her.

He'd sacrificed his chance of a lavish white wedding just so it wouldn't magnify any wounds for Rebecca. So she wouldn't have to walk into a room full of strangers and see her side of the church sitting empty.

Another reminder of the loss she'd endured in her life. A past filled with so much pain.

He'd listened when she'd told him about losing her parents at such a young age, how she'd suffered a lonely upbringing in care with no other real family in her life to speak of.

She knew this was his gift to her. This wedding, with just the two of them and their witnesses.

He hadn't even invited his own mother. He did that for her, broken his mother's heart no doubt, to help protect hers.

Even so, when she'd first walked in and seen Jamie standing at the end of the short make-do aisle, she'd faltered for a few seconds.

Her feet stuck to the floor, unmoving as her eyes swept across the brightly lit ceremony room. The huge earthy fireplace that lined one wall, and the rows of bookshelves at either side of her.

The room seated twenty people at most, but only two chairs were taken up by their witnesses, Lisa and Michael. The sight of so many empty, undressed seats made her flinch.

She second guessed herself, just for a split second, wondering if they were doing the right thing.

Because as much as Rebecca had hoped for this, as much as she'd prayed for this, the haste of Jamie's proposal had actually caught her off guard.

She'd never expected it all to happen so quickly.

A whirlwind of a romance some would say, marrying merely three months after they'd met. Others, more cynical, might say a whole lot more. They might think Rebecca was a gold-digger. Or that Jamie was blinded by lust. Or that perhaps she was pregnant, and this was a shotgun wedding.

But it didn't matter what others thought, Jamie had said the day he'd surprised her with an engagement ring, down on one knee.

Because this was different. *They* were different.

She hadn't thought twice about saying yes, throwing her arms around him. Kissing him hard and crying tears of happiness before joking that they might as well do it quickly, before he changed his mind.

Just weeks later, here they were, standing in the Mayfair Marylebone room at the library, as husband and wife.

'I'm your family now,' Jamie said softly, taking Rebecca's hand and holding it to his lips which made Rebecca want to weep, because she knew he meant it. That Jamie would be true to his promise.

That he would look after her.

That this time it would be different.

It was all so perfect that even now there were moments she just wanted to pinch herself. To check this wasn't all just some cruel dream that she'd awake from at any moment, finding herself back there. Back in the darkest depths of despair from which she'd fled.

How life could change so quickly, so dramatically, in such a short space of time.

Rebecca Dawson.

She was someone else now, and she couldn't wait to start their new life together.

In Jamie's home. *Their home*, she reminds herself, thinking of Jamie's constant reassurances.

Staring down at the white gold band on her finger, the sparkling diamond glistening there next to it, she smiled to herself.

This was all real. This was happening.

No more living out of hotel rooms. No more having to hide away from the world. She could leave all that darkness behind her now.

This was the fresh start she'd been longing for.

And the day just proceeded to get better and better. Their wedding breakfast was at Claridge's, of course. *Nothing but the best for my beautiful wife,* Jamie had declared as they'd sat in the beautifully decorated restaurant, Rebecca's dress dazzling in the light from the striking Chihuly glass chandelier that hung down above them as they toasted their good fortune with the finest champagne. They guzzled it down greedily, both giddy with happiness.

Rebecca stared around the room in awe, glad that despite their ceremony being small, the day was still special. *The venue was stunning,* Rebecca thought as she eyed her reflection in the vast splay of shimmering mirrors that adorned every wall, her ears homing in on the sound of the grand piano, as the notes drifted around them all, just loud enough to hear over the chatter in the room.

'Are you not hungry?' Jamie asked, watching Rebecca staring into space as she pushed the salmon around on her plate, picking at the odd morsel now and again.

He grinned then, before she answered, realising that he'd been doing exactly the same. Nibbling at the food just for the sake of it, both their appetites gone, they were both too excited, both only hungry for each other.

'We could always make our excuses to leave…' Jamie said, his hand working its way up Rebecca's thigh, concealed by the cloth draping the table. His fingers pulled at the lace fabric of her wedding dress, tracing the soft outline of her silk lingerie underneath, which made her think about the Royal suite, upstairs, that Jamie had booked them into for the night.

'Well, we are newlyweds after all…' Rebecca said, raising her brow with a mischievous smile as their two guests, Lisa and Michael, Jamie's sister and trusted colleague from the office, continued eating their food, caught up in their own conversation, oblivious to the simmering heat at the table. 'I'm sure they'd forgive us for running out, just this once…'

And they did. Of course.

'Oh, no need to apologise, mate. I'm sure you've got better things to do than wait around for your dessert!' Michael winked as Jamie and Rebecca both stood up, thanking their guests for attending the ceremony before making their excuses for the swift exit from the table. 'I'm sure myself and Lisa won't let any of the champagne go to waste.'

'Oh, absolutely,' Lisa agreed, raising her glass. 'I'll drink to that! And congratulations once again to you both,' Lisa said, getting up from her seat and kissing Rebecca on the cheek. 'My brother is a very lucky man.'

Rebecca smiled, hoping that Lisa's words were sincere now that she'd officially become her sister-in-law.

Rebecca hadn't let it slip Jamie had told her Lisa's concerns of him marrying too quickly. How she'd warned her brother that he might live to regret marrying someone he barely knew.

Instead of heeding her warning, Jamie had simply laughed it off as he relayed the conversation to Rebecca. 'Who really knows anyone though? Isn't that part of the fun, that we can spend our lives getting to know each other?' He hadn't even considered his sister's concerns, brushing it off by saying that she was a worrier. That she was too sensible. That Lisa let her head rule her life and sometimes he wished she'd loosen up a bit, to stop being so serious all the time.

'Christ, sometimes I have to remind myself that I'm the eldest. She's supposed to be the one who needs looking after, not me.'

Lisa's negativity had rattled Rebecca at first. But she hadn't confessed that to Jamie; instead Rebecca had played along and told Jamie that perhaps his sister had a point. Maybe it did feel a little rushed. Maybe it was too soon?

It had been a test that Jamie had passed – immediately insisting that they were doing the right thing, that he was certain. That had been enough for Rebecca to convince her of his love.

So, she'd dropped it, and ended the conversation saying that he was lucky to have someone who cared for him so much, who had his wellbeing at heart.

'You look absolutely exquisite, Rebecca,' Lisa said to her, smiling.

It was true; Rebecca had never looked more breathtaking. Her long red hair was pinned high on her head in an elegant chignon and decorated with pearl embellishments, matching the same delicate pearls that adorned the lace Vera Wang dress hugging her slim figure. The dress was a bold choice, even Rebecca was aware of that. Extreme for a simple registry office wedding, and if she was honest, the dress wasn't really her at all. But Jamie had insisted that money was no object, and had sent her to an exclusive bridal shop to find the perfect dress, and the shop assistant had been so lovely to her, especially after Rebecca had told her that the wedding was going to be an intimate affair and that she had no real family of friends of her own attending. The lady in the shop had pulled out her most breathtaking gown then and insisted that Rebecca try it on, and she almost didn't recognise the reflection that stared back at her in the dressing room mirror. She looked so elegant, so demure, that for a few seconds, the beautiful dress had taken her breath away.

Even today, even now, it still didn't feel as if it was really hers. It felt as if it belonged to someone else, that she was just borrowing it. A beautiful princess, playing dress up just for the day.

But she'd chosen well – when she'd seen the look of pure delight on Jamie's face as she'd walked down the aisle towards him, she knew the dress had been worth every penny and every pearl.

'*Exquisite*. That you are, Mrs Dawson!' Jamie had teased once they were both tucked away in the Royal suite, as he unzipped her dress and let it fall at her feet, before they'd made love, their bodies entwined, lost together inside the gigantic four-poster bed.

Jamie had fallen asleep soon after. Rebecca looked at him now, his head lolled to one side, his mouth gaping open as he snored gently. Spent from sex and too much champagne.

But she can't sleep.

Lifting his arm carefully, so she doesn't wake him, she slides from the bed. Stepping over her dress, the fine silk and pearls wrinkled in a heap on the floor, she wraps her robe around her naked body and makes her way to the lounge at the opposite end of the suite.

She runs her hand across the top of the espresso machine, craving caffeine, something strong to keep the edge off the excitement that's still fizzing away inside of her. She decides against it, not wanting to chance waking Jamie with the noise.

Let him sleep, she thinks, so she can have a few moments to get her head straight. To take all this in. Settling for the dregs of the champagne they'd abandoned on the coffee table earlier, she takes a seat on the chaise lounge by the window. She folds her legs beneath her before pulling back the curtains, just enough to allow her to stare out into the brightly lit night skies of London.

The breathtaking panoramic view of Mayfair's shimmering lights dance back at her through the windowpane, and for a few minutes it's all she can do to stop herself from opening the window and shouting out so all of London can hear her.

She'd done it.

She'd escaped.

Replaying the vows back inside her head as she finished the last gulp of champagne, Rebecca closed her eyes and leaned back on the

11

cushion behind her, Jamie's words whirling around inside her head. *'Til death do us part.*

You know what, Jamie Dawson, I believe you, she thinks.

Because he is her lifeline. Her second chance.

He has no idea how lost and broken she was before him. But she knows that she is safe now.

I am forever yours and you are mine.

Chapter Two

'She looks just like her mummy!' The nurse beamed, placing the swaddled baby down on Rebecca's chest.

'I can't believe she's here,' Rebecca said, a loud sob escaping her mouth, finally relaxing as she sunk back into the pillows behind her. Overwhelmed and completely exhausted, the twenty-three hours of labour she'd just endured had almost beaten her. *But it had all been worth it*, she thought as she stared down at her precious baby daughter, every minute of excruciating pain that had violently ripped through her.

Even the pregnancy had taken it out of her.

It was all lies, what they told you about the pregnancy glow; she'd found that out the hard way. All those magazine articles about women blooming in pregnancy.

Rebecca hadn't bloomed. Not one little bit. Instead she'd felt out of control, as if her body had been taken over by a tiny, greedy alien who was sucking all the energy and vigour from her.

But none of that mattered now as she held her child in her arms.

Looking down at her daughter's face she tried to work out who she looked like more, her or Jamie? Either way she was perfect, and Rebecca had never felt such a rush of love.

'She's so tiny. She looks so fragile.'

'Don't be fooled, Rebecca. She's a lot stronger than she looks, just like her mum!' The midwife reassured her as Jamie stepped forward, beaming proudly and placing a kiss on Rebecca's forehead as he stared down at his daughter.

'I couldn't agree more. You did amazingly. I'm so proud of you. She's perfect.'

Jamie was in complete awe of Rebecca and how she'd managed to keep her cool throughout the entire process of giving birth. Guided by the midwife, she'd concentrated on the breathing techniques they'd been shown in their antenatal classes. Slow and steady. Breathe through the contractions.

Though all they'd been told had been wasted on him, it seemed.

Because in the moment, Jamie had panicked. Fretting and worrying every time Rebecca screamed out in pain, or the monitor bleeped loudly. He'd felt powerless, seeing his wife in so much agony and knowing that there was nothing he could do to help her. So he'd done what little he could, placing a cool flannel on her forehead and massaging her back, all the while telling her how well she was doing.

Because she really had. Rebecca had taken it all in her stride and just breathed her way through it and just when Jamie had thought she physically couldn't go on any longer, somehow, she did. It was as if she went inside herself, closing her eyes and searching for the last reserve of strength buried there, before delivering their child out into the world with one final, agonising push.

'She is perfect, isn't she,' Rebecca cooed, besotted by the little life that had been placed in her arms. She stared down at her daughter's mop of red hair, her plump pink skin, wondering what it was she'd been so worried about her entire pregnancy. Staring at her daughter, feeling the waves of overwhelming love, she instantly dismissed the pent-up feelings that had consumed her throughout her pregnancy, the constant fear whether she would be capable of loving this child inside of her.

She'd never wanted children. They'd never factored into any of her plans. Only Jamie was adamant that he wanted to start a family as soon as possible after they'd married, and Rebecca wanted to give him the world, no matter the cost.

She wanted them to be perfect. And maybe now it really would be. Because she'd been wrong to think that she wasn't capable of loving a child of her own. Not after what happened before. But she didn't want to think about any of that.

She truly knew that now.

The second the delicate little life had been placed in her arms, it was as if something had been ignited deep within her, an instant connection, like nothing Rebecca had ever experienced before. And something more than that, a fierce protectiveness swelled inside her.

'I'm going to be the best mummy you could ever wish for, my darling,' Rebecca said, kissing the top of her child's head.

'You guys!' Lisa's voice cracked with emotion as she walked into the delivery room and saw the three of them. Embracing the sight of her brother and his new little family. 'Jamie told the nurse that I could pop in and see you? Is that okay, I don't want to disturb you... Ahh! It's a girl?' Lisa said, unable to hold back her tears as she spotted the blush pink blanket in which the tiny new-born baby was swaddled.

'It is indeed!' Jamie nodded proudly. 'Come and meet your new niece,' he beamed, holding out his arm to invite Lisa over.

'Oh, she's just beautiful,' Lisa said, wiping a tear that ran down her cheek. 'Oh God, what am I like, eh? I just can't believe how perfect she is.'

Jamie laughed.

'This is your Auntie Lisa,' Jamie said to the baby, 'and as much as she makes out she's a tough nut, I think we've just found her weak spot, little lady.'

Lisa playfully elbowed her brother in the ribs, then she smiled at Rebecca.

'Congratulations to you both. Do you need anything? Can I do anything for you?'

'Nope, your brother's got it all covered. I think he was in more of a panic throughout all of this than me.'

'Jamie? Flapping around in a panic?' Lisa said, feigning shock. Teasing her brother. They all knew Jamie was normally so calm and organised. Becoming a new father had set him on edge. Lisa knew it was only because he wanted to do a good job. 'I don't believe you!'

The two women both laughed then as Jamie rolled his eyes.

'I couldn't help myself. Seriously, I really don't know how she did it,' Jamie said, eager to hold his daughter now. 'Can I?'

Rebecca nodded her head, allowing Jamie to take the baby from her arms. Seeing that the sleeves of her hospital gown had pulled up as she handed over the baby to her husband, Rebecca quickly tugged them back down.

But she caught the look on Lisa's face, at the concern etched there, as she caught sight of the raised white scars that zigzagged their way up Rebecca's arms.

Seeing the uncomfortable look on Rebecca's face, Lisa tried to spare the woman any awkwardness, immediately looking away and pretending she hadn't seen. Instead, she stood with her brother, cooing and laughing at Jamie acting so besotted with his newborn daughter.

Rebecca thought of Mark then, rubbing her arms self-consciously, as if to soothe the old scars that had been sliced into her skin with sharp, jagged glass. The small circular cigarette burns that were dotted between them.

Tears suddenly stung her eyes as she realised she'd never completely be free of him.

Because he was always there, haunting her, in the back of her mind.

Even now, in moments like this, where everything should be so perfect. She had her new life, her new family. But she would always have constant memories of the pain she went through.

The memories of him and what he'd done to her.

'Hey!' Jamie said, interrupting Rebecca's thoughts and mistaking the pained look on her face for her feeling bereft at not holding their daughter. 'She's right here, honey. She's not going anywhere.'

Rebecca took a steady breath and plastered a smile to her face.

'It's the hormones. Sorry. It's all just been so overwhelming.'

'Do you have a name for her yet?' Lisa asked.

'Well, we spoke about a few, but nothing definite as yet...' Jamie trailed off, shaking his head.

'Ella,' Rebecca announced, looking at Jamie hopefully, her eyes pleading with him to agree. 'I want to call her Ella.'

Jamie grinned, unable to refuse his wife anything after what she'd just been through.

'Ella?' he said, tentatively, as if testing how the name sounded out loud. As he handed his daughter back to his wife, he said, 'It's perfect. Welcome to the world, gorgeous Ella.'

Chapter Three

'I don't know if she's eating enough? She can't be, can she? If she doesn't settle for very long after a feed?' Rebecca asks the health visitor, hoping that the woman will be able to give her the magic answer so that she can settle Ella's crying. 'I've tried everything. I've fed her. Winded her. Changed her bum… she's like this all the time. I don't know how to settle her?' Rebecca says, rocking Ella frantically in her arms, frustrated now because Ella is still fractious, and Rebecca was hoping to have her more settled for the health visitor's visit this morning.

So far, her morning couldn't have gone any worse. She'd been awake all night after having another bad dream, and the second she'd fallen asleep, Ella had woken and demanded her feed. Somehow, they'd both overslept, waking just minutes before the appointment. Rebecca had barely had time to make herself look presentable, let alone do all the chores that she'd promised herself would be done by the time the health visitor had arrived.

She'd wanted to show the health visitor that she knew what she was doing. That she was coping. Authority figures always set her on edge, and she wanted to prove to this woman that she was strong and capable. Even if right now she felt anything but. Her top was covered in baby sick, where Ella had brought up the last bit of her feed, the sickly milky smell lingering in the air, and the house looked like a bombsite. Not that Kerry Day mentioned that, of course.

'Some babies are just naturally harder to settle, Rebecca. I'm sure it's nothing to be concerned about,' Kerry says kindly, trying to reassure Rebecca. She'd had similar conversations with umpteen new mothers this week. 'What you're going through is all part of the process. Ella is only a few weeks old… you'll still be finding your feet. Here. Can I?' Kerry asks, holding her arms out in an offer to take the baby from Rebecca, not only to give the woman a break from the incessant crying but also so she could give Ella a once over and double check that there wasn't something more obvious they were both missing.

Taking Ella, Kerry cocoons the child in her arms, patting the child's bottom rhythmically through her padded nappy, rocking her back and forth. All the while cooing at the tiny baby.

'She's such a pretty little thing, isn't she. And look at all that lovely red hair. You must be so in love with her.'

Rebecca nods, then shakes her head in dismay as Ella starts to settle with the combination of the rocking motion and the health visitor's soothing voice.

Instead of feeling relief that Ella is finally going to sleep, she feels stricken, worried that she is showing up her shortcomings as a mother. Trying to distract herself from saying anything, Rebecca bites at her nails, but she's so fuelled by her own anger and bitterness that she can't help herself.

'Is it me? Am I doing something wrong? Doesn't she like me?' She blurts the words out. Kerry sees the tears forming in her eyes, so she shakes her head with certainty.

'Absolutely not, Rebecca.' She gives Rebecca a small smile of reassurance. 'This is all perfectly normal. You are stressed, Rebecca. Fretting and worrying so much about her, and babies can pick up on that kind of thing. She's absolutely fine though, and I'm sure you're doing a sterling job. You just need to have more faith in yourself.'

Rebecca bites her lip, part of her believing that the health visitor is trying to appease her. Lying to her to make her feel better. *She probably thinks she's an awful mum.*

She's doing it again, Rebecca realises, feeling angry with herself for letting the feeling of not being good enough overwhelm her. But she can't help feel like a failure. Not when she's been trying to comfort her daughter for the past half hour, but Ella seems more comfortable in the arms of a complete stranger than she does with her own mother.

'Would you like me to lay her down in her crib, I think she's ready to go off?' Kerry says, keeping her voice low.

'There's no point putting her down, she'll wake as soon as you do. Trust me,' Rebecca replies with a shrug, but doubting her own prediction, because already Ella was settling. Already she was proving her wrong in front of the health visitor.

'She needs her blankie on her face. I place it on her right cheek,' Rebecca says, but before she reaches the Moses basket, she stops, surprised to see Ella's eyes already closed. She's fallen straight to sleep.

Rebecca stands there numbly, doubting her own motherhood skills once more. She feels suddenly redundant, as if Ella is doing this all on purpose today to make her look bad.

The atmosphere in the room is suddenly broken up by Jamie's entrance. As usual he is dressed in a designer suit, his laptop case in his hand.

'Hello, ladies,' he says cheerily, not picking up on the tension, and greets the health visitor with a smile, before kissing Rebecca on the head.

'You're back early?' Rebecca says, surprised to see him here at all during the day. He'd been so busy at work the past week that he'd barely made it home in time for dinner.

'Well, I didn't have anything scheduled in the diary, so I thought I could work from home this afternoon. I forgot you had the health visitor coming.' Jamie gives an apologetic look to Kerry, not wanting to offend her.

Rebecca frowns. She'd always been able to read Jamie so well and she could tell something was troubling him. Only, she didn't know what.

'I was just saying to Rebecca how well Ella is doing. She's a nice healthy weight. And a gorgeous wee thing.' Kerry grins. 'But I've been hearing she hasn't been sleeping all too well, so while she's down, I'm going to get off and leave you two to it. Hopefully you'll get a bit of peace and quiet for a while.' Kerry winks at Rebecca. 'You're both doing a great job, really. But if there's anything you need, please don't hesitate in giving me a call. Otherwise I'll see you next month for Ella's eight-week check.'

Rebecca mutters her thanks, putting on a fake smile, though she doubts Kerry's efforts to get her child off to sleep would last very long. Ella will be awake and crying again soon, she's certain of it.

'Here, let me see you out,' Jamie offers, walking Kerry to the front door.

Only when they reach the door, Jamie steps outside too, closing the door behind him.

'Is everything all right?' Kerry asks, catching the apprehensive look on Jamie's face as he glances in the living room window to check that Rebecca is still there, and not trying to listen in to their conversation.

'Well, actually, I was hoping that you'd be able to tell me that,' Jamie replies, shifting uncomfortably on his feet. 'I feel disloyal even just asking. I mean, I'm not checking up on her or anything.' He shakes his head. 'Shit, who am I kidding. I am. But I'm worried about her...'

'About Rebecca?' Kerry says, surprised by the genuine concern she can hear in the man's voice.

Jamie nods, his eyes going to the front door again.

'Don't get me wrong, she's a fantastic mother. I just worry that she might be doing too much.'

'Too much?' It was Kerry's turn to look confused.

'She's barely put Ella down for five minutes since she's been born. And if she does leave her in her crib, she's constantly checking on her...'

Kerry nods and smiles, guessing that this was the real reason Jamie had come home early. He had concerns of his own. He'd wanted to speak to her too.

'The other night, I found Rebecca sleeping on the floor of the nursery. She said she was worried about Ella's breathing. She was a little bit snuffly but nothing to warrant that kind of worry...'

'She's just anxious, Jamie. And you'll be pleased to hear that we did speak about this. In fact, it was Rebecca who brought it up. She worries that she's not doing a good enough job, but as I said to her, she is. And worrying is to be expected. It's perfectly natural for her to still be finding her way. But she's doing just fine. Being a new mum is a huge responsibility and Rebecca just wants to do the best she can. It can take a while for some mothers to adjust to such a big change.'

'Yes, of course,' Jamie says, lost for words, as he stared down at the pavement, but Kerry could sense that there were words he wasn't saying.

'Is there something else?' she asks, gently coaxing the man for whatever it was still bothering him. Only Jamie didn't elaborate any further. He just continued to look at the floor.

Kerry guessed this was all a struggle for Jamie too. 'Some new fathers can feel a bit pushed out at first. That's normal too,' she says, guessing rightly that things were stressful for all of them right now, Jamie being no exception.

'In fact, sometimes men have it even harder when it comes to parenting. Because everything is geared up toward the mother, isn't it? The pregnancy, the antenatal classes, the birth is all about the woman and the baby. Men barely get a look in.' Kerry smiles, letting Jamie know she understands exactly where he's coming from, that he's important too.

'It's like Rebecca doesn't even see me anymore. All she sees is Ella.' The health visitor gives Jamie a knowing smile, and squeezing his arm, leans in.

'She's focused. And maybe for a little while you won't be the centre of her time and attention. That's another factor for you and your family to have to adjust to. But it doesn't last forever. You just have to give things time. Especially with the first baby. They take over your whole life. You might feel as if you lose yourself for a bit, Rebecca might too. So, it's important that you still make time for each other. Keep talking. Don't shut each other out,' Kerry says, putting Jamie's mind to rest once and for all. 'It's a big change for you all. That little girl in there is doing just fine. And so is her mother. And like I said, if there's anything I can help with, just give me a call.'

Jamie nodded his head, grateful to the woman for taking the time to hear him out.

He wanted so badly to believe what she was saying, that he was probably worrying over nothing and Rebecca was coping just fine.

But still Jamie couldn't shake the feeling that something more serious was wrong and Rebecca's fears and actions went way beyond that of a 'normal' new mum.

Chapter Four

'Finally, I get you all to myself. Well, it's never completely to myself anymore. Is it?' Jamie says, knowing full well he shouldn't be guilt tripping Rebecca, but the alcohol has loosened his tongue.

Not bothering to hide his sarcasm, he raises his brow as Rebecca places the baby monitor down in the centre of the coffee table, as if to prove the point that he's making.

'She's not been herself today. I just want to keep an eye on her,' Rebecca says, trying to avoid the same argument they'd been having for weeks now. She knew what Jamie was implying; that in the eight weeks since Ella had been born, she couldn't seem to leave Ella out of her sight, not even for a minute.

Ignoring his glare, she eyes the baby monitor as she sits down on the sofa, chewing at her short, jagged nails, as her child stares back at her on the screen. She knows exactly what Jamie is thinking. Because she's thinking it too.

'I'm sure she'll settle soon enough,' Rebecca says, but that's a lie, because despite being exhausted, Ella is still wide awake, wriggling and cooing alone in her cot, showing no signs of giving in to sleep anytime soon.

Rebecca can't help but feel on edge again. It must be her, mustn't it? She must be doing something wrong? Because she's really trying her hardest to be a good mum to Ella, but nothing she does seems to be good enough. Ella is constantly fractious and unhappy.

'At least she's stopped crying...' she says, more for her own benefit than anything else. The words sounding hollow even as she tries to keep positive. Ella had been grizzling all day, the dull constant sound grating on Rebecca's nerves as she'd tried so desperately to block it out.

'Well, sitting here staring at the monitor isn't going to make her fall asleep any faster, Rebecca. You need to chill out a bit. She's probably picking up on you constantly fretting about her.'

'I'm not fretting, Jamie...' Rebecca snaps, unable to stop herself, catching the fleeting look of annoyance on Jamie's face and the deliberate edge to his tone before he purposely turns his attention back to the pile of paperwork he'd brought home from the office. He immerses himself back in his work, but he'd made his point.

'And yet again, you're lost in your work,' Rebecca says, unable to stop herself.

She'd promised herself that tonight she wasn't going to bite at any more of his cutting remarks, because she didn't have the energy to argue with him. Not again. The two of them are going round and round in circles, bringing up the same old argument that they'd been having for weeks.

Rebecca bit her lip, the words he used the last time they'd fought still spiralling around her mind.

Obsessive and neurotic.

Wasn't that what he'd called her, annoyed yet again that Rebecca was unable to leave her child alone for even a minute. That the real problem here wasn't Ella at all, it was all her, he'd shouted.

It wasn't supposed to be this way. She'd thought it would be easier, that Jamie would support her, not berate her at his every chance. He was the one who'd wanted Ella so badly. When she'd first told him she was pregnant, he'd said he would be hands on, that he'd help her. Yet sometimes she felt as if she was doing it all by herself.

Wrinkling her nose, she sees the wine glass on the table, the bottle beside it almost empty. She'd smelt the strong bitter smell of whisky on him earlier when he'd first walked through the front door. Bending his head towards Ella to greet her.

Rebecca had turned her head, the smell of whisky always repulsed her. Instantly propelling her back to her childhood. A time she tried her hardest to block from her memory completely.

Now he was drinking wine, which meant it wouldn't take much to cause an argument and then they'd both go to bed in silence again. And tomorrow morning, Jamie would leave for the office early.

It was all right for Jamie, she thought bitterly. How easily he could just switch off from Ella. He could get lost in his work. He could leave each day and spend ten straight hours at the office. He could come home at night and drink until he passed out.

But Rebecca couldn't do that. She wouldn't do that.

Ella was her priority now, and Rebecca was consumed by the overpowering feeling of needing to protect her daughter, almost as if it was beyond her control. Her natural maternal instincts had just taken over since Ella came along and the force of Rebecca's love for her child had knocked her for six.

Rebecca couldn't leave Ella alone. But that was her job, she told herself. Wasn't that what a mother should do? Wasn't that normal – to feel anguish and uncertainty? To constantly check on the child and make sure that she was okay?

Maybe her behaviour was a bit over the top, Rebecca told herself. Tiptoeing into her room at all hours of the day and night, just to watch Ella, so she could see that she was still physically breathing. Taking her temperature at least five times a day, paranoid that Ella might be too hot, or too cold. Or that she may become ill. Carrying Ella around everywhere she went. And if the baby wasn't in the room with her, Rebecca didn't leave the baby monitor out of her sight.

But she'd rather be overly cautious than not, because just the thought of something happening to Ella, of her not being there to shield her from harm, made her feel physically sick inside.

Ella coming along had changed everything for Rebecca.

'I don't want to keep fighting, Jamie…' she said then, softly, hoping that he'd listen to her, that he'd understand. There was so much she wanted to say to him, but she just couldn't find the words. What he saw as neurotic and paranoid was really just Rebecca trying to do her best by her child.

But she was failing miserably, it seemed. Her best wasn't good enough.

Her fractious mood always seemed to put her on edge. Ella cried so much, and so often it was hard for Rebecca to believe deep down that her daughter was really okay.

'I know you think I'm being too much, Jamie. But I just worry. I can't help it. She cries so much…' Rebecca admitted. 'And I worry that what if I'm doing something wrong? That she's not just crying because she was overtired or hungry. That her tears weren't just because she was teething or sick? What if there was something really wrong with her?'

Placing down his laptop, Jamie lets out a long sigh. He was tired of all the arguing too.

'Look, I'm just finishing up with some figures before the meeting tomorrow,' he said, gathering all the loose bits of paper into a neat pile, his attention back on her. 'She's okay, Rebecca. Wide awake maybe, but she's not in any distress, and she's not crying now.' He nodded over to the bottle of wine on the table. 'Have a drink with me?' Jamie insisted, getting up and getting another glass from the kitchen. 'You look like you could do with one.'

About to refuse and say no, she stopped herself. This was an olive branch, she knew, Jamie's way of making amends. Maybe he was right. She probably could do with a drink.

'I shouldn't,' Rebecca said, pursing her lips. 'Ella might start up again.'

'So what? One drink won't hurt you!' Jamie tutted, clearly annoyed that Rebecca's every decision, every thought was totally reliant on how it would affect Ella. 'For Christ's sake, Rebecca. It's not a crime to relax for five minutes and have a glass of wine with your husband.'

She faltered, knowing the truth in what he was saying, and sitting down on the chair next to him, poured herself a glass of wine. She'd expressed enough milk for Ella's next feed. Jamie was right, one drink wouldn't hurt her.

Taking a large gulp, she immediately feels the familiar warmth spread through her. She hadn't had a drink since she found out that she was pregnant. She'd missed this.

'Sorry,' she says, relenting. Jamie was right. They needed some time together. On their own, without Ella. To properly talk. 'It's been one of those days.'

'It's been one of those days a lot lately,' Jamie spat, bitterly, rubbing his brow in frustration.

The past few weeks hadn't been easy for either of them, Rebecca knew that. The confident, strong, sexy woman he'd married had quickly been replaced with this hot, neurotic mess she knew she'd become.

It was as if she'd changed completely, overnight. Rebecca no longer cared about her appearance, willingly trading in her usual make-up, regular blow dries, and designer clothes for a more comfortable tracksuit, no make-up, and a messy bun.

Jamie had commented that she'd lost herself, but she hadn't at all. She'd found a new self. A self she hadn't known was ever capable of existing. Being a mother was her only focus and she knew that's what Jamie was really struggling with.

She hadn't lost herself in the process, but she realised Jamie felt as if he'd lost his wife. That's why he seemed so permanently angry with her, she knew it. That's what Jamie was really struggling with. Since Ella had been born, Jamie had acted like she'd pushed him out, but if the truth be told, she was starting to resent him for acting so jealous of Ella, annoyed at the attention Rebecca gave their daughter, attention she used to give solely to him.'

Some men struggled with that, according to an article she'd read in a baby magazine. Shortly after having their first child, when suddenly, the dynamics in a relationship rapidly change. Protesting at no longer being the centre of attention, they start to act like a petulant spoilt child.

'We need to get back to how we were,' Rebecca says, sliding her hand onto his. Desperate to make things right again between them. To fix this marriage and get them both back on track, to how things used to be. But even as she said the words, her daughter was on her mind. Ella deserved a loving family. She deserved parents who at least tried to get along.

'It's been a pretty stressful time around here lately,' Rebecca says, trying to find her courage to tell him the truth about how she was feeling. How overwhelming everything had become. How she wasn't coping... But just as she is building up the strength to speak, Jamie interrupts her.

'Stressful? Oh, you could say that! Though it's to be expected, I guess, with the team expanding. I've got more meetings in my diary than I have hours.' He knocks back his glass of wine, before massaging the deep furrowed lines etched on his forehead.

'Still, I shouldn't complain. It's almost done. This contract could take the company to the next level. And it will be, without a doubt, worth every ounce of hassle.'

Rebecca feigns a smile. He'd thought she was talking about him. Of course, he did. Yet again, it was all about Jamie. He had no idea that she was trying to reach out to him, to tell him how much she was struggling. How empty her days had become, roaming around this big old house on her own, for days at a time, with only a tiny baby for company. A baby that screamed and cried all day long.

Since Ella had arrived, everything had quickly unravelled around them and this wasn't the life Jamie had promised her. Was it any wonder that she was starting to feel as if she was going out of her mind?

'Anyway, how was your day?' he asked her finally.

She nodded slowly, only the words she wanted to say were caught in the back of her throat. Suddenly she couldn't bear to see the disappointment on his face, knowing how many times she'd repeated how difficult it was to spend all day with their daughter. So she danced around it.

'Ella hasn't really been herself the past few days. She's been a bit cranky, you know? Crying a lot...' She shrugged, playing down her concerns. Instantly she regretted her words as Jamie's eyes glazed over.

'Oh? She's seems okay now?' Jamie says, boredom in his tone as he eyed the monitor.

She knew what he was thinking. Ella, again. She is obsessed with the baby.

Rebecca bristles, holding her wine glass just a fraction too tight. Imagining for a second the glass crushing inside her firm grasp. That delicious feeling of white-hot pain as the blood seeped out from the deep cuts.

She purses her lips, then, shrugging her shoulders, quickly composes her thoughts. How she'd been about to tell him about her visit to the doctors today. About how he'd prescribed her antidepressants.

33

Even though she was sure she wasn't depressed, she'd gone along with it and picked up her prescription from the chemist afterwards. How she'd taken the first tablets.

But suddenly she was conscious of ruining the mood. Of Jamie's hand slipping from hers. So, she drank some more wine, told herself that she'd tell him when things were better between them, when things weren't so fragile.

'I took her for a walk in the park in her buggy. It was nice to get out of the house. I think the fresh air did us both good.' *More lies.* 'I think she was just overtired.'

She was trying too hard now to play down her concerns and sound upbeat, but Jamie didn't seem to notice.

And the wine was already working its magic, mixing with the antidepressants, making her feel lightheaded. Unburdened, almost. Free for a few minutes of the dark thoughts that had consumed her day.

Jamie must have felt her relaxing too, because his mood softened suddenly. Placing his arm around her shoulder, they both laid their heads back against the sofa, the first bit of affection between them in weeks.

It was nice, the two of them sitting silently for a few minutes, staring at the crackling fire.

Rebecca leaned her head on Jamie's shoulder. Her touch igniting the response in Jamie that she knew it would.

He kissed her.

He wanted sex. Of course he did. It had been months. And even though the last thing she wanted right now was to have sex, she knew she couldn't put it off any longer.

So, she kissed him back with all the passion and effort than she could summon. Hoping that this would help bring them back together somehow, that this could forge an intimacy between them once more. But the tenderness wasn't there.

Jamie was drunk. She could still smell the acrid bitterness of whisky on his breath as he forced his mouth on hers, moving her head back forcefully when she tried to turn her head away from him. Tugging roughly at her clothes, he moved himself on top of her, inside of her in just seconds.

The pain was excruciating.

She'd thought Jamie would be more considerate seeing as it was the first time they'd had sex since Ella, but he was selfish and greedy and seemed so fuelled with anger… as if this was his right.

Then she heard it.

Jenna.

Another woman's name entangled in the earthy groan that escaped from the back of his throat.

Though he seemed completely oblivious, so caught up in his moment, that he didn't notice her body tensing rigidly beneath him, flinching as if she'd just been punched.

Startled, Rebecca just lay there as he continued to grunt away on top of her, willing it all to be over as quickly as it started. Fighting back her tears, along with the bile that threatened to rise from the back of her throat.

He was here in body, but his mind was somewhere else.

Had he already been with her, this Jenna? Dark thoughts swirled violently around inside her head as she tried to piece it all together.

All those late nights at the office recently. The business dinners out. The way Jamie suddenly always went for a shower the second he came through the door, no matter what time of the night it was. The tiny smear of make-up she'd spotted on his shirt collar.

It was all such a cliché.

The distracted wife, struggling with a newborn. The lying cheat of a husband.

How could he do this to her? To Ella?

Ella.

The sound of her child crying echoed from the baby monitor, just as Jamie let out one last groan, shuddering to a halt on top of her.

She'd never been so grateful to hear that sound. For Ella to give her a reason to quickly slide herself out from under him and make a rapid getaway.

Because she needed to think straight. To get her head around what just happened.

One word. One moment. It changed everything it.

Taking the stairs, she held on to the banister tightly to steady herself as she walked.

Jamie had betrayed her. She was certain of it.

He'd taken the one good thing in her life, her perfect little family, and he'd destroyed it.

Chapter Five

I was just seven years old when I realised we weren't like other families.

That we weren't normal.

To mistake honesty for the truth leaves you wide open for deception.

My mother had lived and breathed that phrase, which I only really understand now that I'm that much older. If you say something with enough conviction, you believe it eventually. But that doesn't make it the truth.

And my mother always believed her own bullshit. She was one of the greatest of actresses, our mother. So great, that deep down I think she'd even convinced herself that her lies were true. A woman capable of delivering Oscar-worthy performances without any kind of dress rehearsal. Although she wasn't ever on the screen or stage.

The only starring role she played out was that of a wife and mother, inside the four cold and decrepit walls of the house we all lived in.

I say 'house', because it was far from a *home*. But it was all we had, and we'd never known any different.

My parents had everyone around us fooled.

The police. The social workers. The teachers at school.

No one must ever know.

We must never tell, they drilled us repeatedly.

We were just kids. My sister, two years younger than me.

So, of course, we did what we were told. Going innocently about our days, aware that everything we said and did played some part in covering up the big lie we all kept, but no one actually articulated that fact.

Instead, we concentrated everything we had into showing everyone around us only what we wanted them to see.

But people around us actually wanted to believe it, fooling themselves that the façade we created was the truth. People around us actually wanted to believe it.

Sometimes though, when I think back, I'm certain someone must have known the truth.

And that cuts me deeply. Because if they did know what was going on, what was really happening in our house, no one ever offered us any kind of help. No one ever even so much as tried.

They let us suffer.

Ignorance is bliss was another of my mother's favourite sayings.

And for a while back then, I really was oblivious to how fucked up my family were. Because it was all so normal to me. That life I'd been born into was the only life I'd ever known. I had nothing to compare it to, nothing to make me question that anything was wrong.

Not until I was seven years old; the first time I went to a friend's house for tea.

My mother had actually encouraged the arrangement, which itself was a rarity. Because our mother had always refused to allow us to attend anything outside of school. No birthday parties, no after-school clubs. No visits to friend's houses.

But that day had been different.

My mother had been laid up in the darkness and solitude of her bedroom for days. Much longer than she usually hid away for, so I knew something really bad had happened. This was far worse than all the other times, because even my father had made himself scarce. Normally, he'd skulk around the house, as if hiding among the shadows, not saying a word, not even looking at us.

This time, he'd left, had been missing for days. Not the usual few hours until things had calmed down. And he must have taken what little money we had, because the house had turned an icy cold and there had been no food in the cupboards. Me and my sister had been left to our own devices, forced to fend for ourselves.

Normally, when they'd gone too far and their arguments had turned to physical violence or after the anger had been taken out on us, my mother would do her bit of collateral damage. Plying us with bowls of hot cornflakes the next morning, making a special effort to warm the milk up for us. To do what mothers do for their children. Sitting there, among the mess and clutter of the filthy, sticky kitchen table, the nourishment was more an unspoken reward for not telling anyone what had happened than an apology for what we'd endured the night before.

And we always lapped it up. Knowing that this was as good as it was ever going to get.

But this time was worse. This time, things had changed forever. Because Mother hadn't left her room for days and there weren't any cornflakes. There was no milk. There was no anything. The cupboards were bare. Our shrunken stomachs ached so violently, and we were so weak and dizzy that we were forced to steal another child's lunch box at school one morning. We were caught red handed, hiding under the coats in the cloakroom, devouring the contents by our teacher and of course, she rang my mother.

We anticipated the punishment we'd receive when we got home. Not for stealing the food though, only for getting caught. Our crime would be for bringing attention and shame to our door.

So, when my mother called me into her bedroom, I stood close to her bed, bracing myself for a slap or her scream to rip though the darkness at me.

Only what I got was something far scarier. Her voice was tiny. Quiet. Unnerving, as she whispered her instructions to me. I was to ask one of my friend's mothers at the school gate tomorrow if me and my sister could go around there for tea. I was to tell them that my mother was sick.

Which I guess, now I look back, wasn't a lie. Though back then, I had no idea how just how sick my mother was.

I didn't want to ask my friend's mother, but I was seven years old and we were starving, and I knew what would happen if I disobeyed my mother, so I did what I was told. Brazenly putting the woman on the spot at the school gate the next day, tears of humiliation filling my eyes.

Looking back, I think she simply took pity on me. And even though me and my sister were welcomed into their home, I remember overhearing the hushed whispers about us, the look of disdain as we entered their pristine home, so unlike our own. The hushed conversation between my friend's mother and father as they stood huddled together in the kitchen, talking about us, about how skinny we looked, how feral. I didn't know what that meant at the time, but I guess they judged us fairly, because we were unwashed, and we stunk. Our hair matted from where it was so very rarely brushed. Our clothes caked with dirt and stains and the acrid stench of piss from where we rarely washed. But they made us feel welcome to our faces and I'd never sat at another family's dinner table until that day. It caught me off guard. Sitting there, like a stranger peering in from outside, at this weird family all laughing and chatting among each other as they ate their food. As if they were friends. As if they liked each other. The room so full of noise and chaos and something else that I'd not felt in our house. Warmth.

It should have filled me with joy I guess, to be part of this household, even if only for a short while, but in that moment, I'd never felt more as if I didn't belong.

Part of me wondered if maybe these people were acting too, pretending that their lives were perfect in the way that our mother lied about the reality of our existence behind closed doors.

Maybe none of this was real, I quietly observed, waiting patiently for one of them to slip up and give the game away. But they didn't. They kept talking and laughing and smiling until the meal was finished.

Sitting at that kitchen able, eating a hot, home-cooked meal, the likes of which I'd never tasted in my short life, I just knew.

This was how other families lived.

This was how other families behaved.

There was love, laughter, chaos, mess. But mostly love. A stark contrast from how we lived.

It left me feeling cheated. I vowed that one day, when I had children, I'd do things differently. I'd be better than the parents I was given.

And later, when the police came, they promised we'd be okay. That we'd be safe. That they would help us.

But they were wrong.

We wouldn't be okay, and they couldn't help us.

Nobody could.

Chapter Six

The medication the doctor gave her isn't working.

It can't be, Rebecca thinks as she grips the cot with both hands and stares down at Ella, whose face is bright puce as she screams loudly, huge droplets of tears streaming down her face as she lays there, kicking her legs defiantly.

She's already taken two antidepressants, double the recommended dose, and two paracetamols on top, but her mood is still sombre. It hasn't lifted. If anything, she feels as if she's only sinking down further. She's losing it. The tablets haven't even so much as taken the edge off the dull constant thudding inside her head.

And Ella isn't helping.

She's roaring, the noise of her high-pitched sobbing crippling Rebecca. She's squealing so loudly that Rebecca is convinced the sound has gotten inside her skull and penetrated her brain. So much so she can't think straight anymore.

'Please stop,' she begs, but Ella just continues, selfishly oblivious to the distress she's causing Rebecca. She screams at the top of her lungs and nothing Rebecca says or does will calm her.

She's worked herself up into such a state it's as if she doesn't even see Rebecca now, it's like there's no one there behind her eyes.

'Please, Ella. For Mummy, please stop.'

Rebecca can feel herself losing control.

She can feel that bubbling heat spreading through her.

The familiar rage she'd felt before.

'SHUT UP!' she screams back. Defeated, she lets her body slide down the bedroom wall. Burying her head in her hands, joining in with her daughter, she screams too. Over and over again. Weak and dizzy and completely exhausted, Rebecca feels as if she might pass out. Or throw up.

Breathless now, it's like she's suffocating, unable to breathe, and suddenly the walls are closing in around her.

Ella is still crying. Louder and louder, and Rebecca can feel her temper swelling inside of her. The fury that she's been fighting to subdue the past few days is starting to win.

She needs help.

She needs to get the fuck out of here, to get the fuck away from Ella before she does something she knows she shouldn't.

Dragging herself up from the nursery floor, she runs through her bedroom and into the en suite.

Locking the door behind her, she runs the bath. Sitting on the edge, she embraces the loud gush of water that flows from the taps, the sound instantly blocking out the noise that Ella is making. She can't resist the urge to just get in. To sink down into the water and let all her worries and fears float away. Rebecca undresses quickly, letting her clothes fall to the floor before stepping into the bath, forcing her feet to stay cocooned as the scorching hot water laps up around her ankles.

She needs to feel the pain. The heat. Anything to stop another panic attack from trying to take her over.

And finally, she can breathe again. Sitting down in the water, Rebecca lays her head back against the bathtub, closes her eyes, and she thinks about before. The woman she used to be.

It all seems so long ago. Like it's just a dream now. No longer real.

Within minutes all the noise has gone.

It's silent and she's back there again.

Hanging upside down inside the car, her body rigid with terror as she strains to hear a sound. A whisper, a murmur, anything other than the harrowing silence that descends upon her.

Because silence can only mean one thing.

Don't look, she tells herself, only she knows that she has to. She needs to look, so she knows for certain it's true.

She turns her head and flinches as all her worst fears are confirmed. And then, there's a noise. A godawful wailing screech, full of pain and anguish, like nothing of this earth, like nothing human. It quickly pulls her from her trance-like state.

It's me, she realises. The heart-wrenching scream is coming from her. From her mouth. She's sobbing uncontrollably, as her body convulses violently, wiping the stream of blood that drips down her face, before biting back strangled sobs. Her left leg is searing with pain, trapped in the concaved metal shell, the roof partially crushed, cocooning her inside.

And that's when she sees the smoke.

A thin plume of black pouring out from the bonnet, slowly at first. Then faster, thicker.

A sickening hot bile rises from the back of her throat.

I need to get out, *she thinks.*

Lying in the bath, thinking back to her darkest time, the panic Rebecca feels jolts her awake and she's back in the en suite.

She must have fallen asleep. Though she has no idea how long she's been there for. Long enough for her body to be trembling and her skin to turn a pale shade of blue, prickled with goosebumps.

Ella? she thinks with a start as she clambers from the bath with urgency, only to hear a noise that stops her in her tracks.

Someone's angry. They're shouting.

Jamie's home.

Chapter Seven

'Rebecca? You've got a visitor,' shouting over the sound of his daughter's loud cries that were carrying throughout the house, Jamie Dawson led the health visitor through to the lounge.

'I'm so sorry about this, sounds like madam is having a bit of a moment. At least now we know why Rebecca couldn't hear you at the front door. I'm so sorry you were kept waiting.'

Jamie apologised again as he eyed the state the house was in. The lounge curtains were still drawn, a cluster of discarded, half-full cups of coffee on the coffee table that had clearly gone cold before Rebecca had a chance to finish them. Picking up an empty cereal bowl that had tipped up on the floor, a pool of milk and muesli spread across the carpet, Jamie bent down and wiped the mess with one of Ella's muslin cloths that had been left on the sofa.

It was the middle of the afternoon and the place was a mess. Jamie was mortified. Before Ella had been born the house had been like a show home. Every room perfectly decorated and dressed with designer accessories. Jamie remembered Rebecca's face when he'd first brought her back here. How impressed she'd seemed with how he was such a perfectionist. Only these days it was if Rebecca didn't see, or care about, the mess and dirt she and Ella created.

'Honestly, it's not a problem.' Kerry Day smiled back reassuringly. 'I've seen and heard it all in my time, I can tell you. You should have seen the state of my house when mine were little, life just takes over.'

He nodded to appease the woman, but Jamie wasn't convinced. The place had been immaculate when he'd left this morning, but now, just a few hours later, it was unrecognisable and there was no sign of Rebecca.

Hearing Ella crying loudly, Jamie assumed that Rebecca was changing her upstairs and that she'd be down shortly now she'd heard them both come in.

'What is that godawful smell?' Jamie said, wrinkling his nose, as he tried to work out where the putrid stench was coming from. Spotting the soiled nappy, folded up and left in the middle of the front room floor, Jamie quickly scooped it up before opening the lounge window to let some air in.

'The place isn't normally like this. I mean, we're coping. It just gets a bit hectic sometimes, you know. We're still trying to work out our routine,' Jamie said, his cheeks flushing with red. Though judging by the sympathetic look on the health visitor's face, his anger was mistaken for embarrassment.

'I'll just clear some of these bits out of the way. Please, take a seat.' Grabbing the discarded blankets and Ella's changing bag from the sofa, Jamie offered Kerry Day a seat.

'I expect she's just upstairs changing Ella's clothes or something. Probably had another nappy explosion again. It's never-ending glamour around here.' He forced a smile for the health visitor, nodding to the nappy as if making light of the situation. But he wasn't happy with

Rebecca. Not one bit. Surely it wasn't too much to ask that the house be kept clean and tidy? How hard could it be to pick up a dirty nappy and stick it in the bin? All Ella seemed to do when Jamie was home was eat and sleep. It was hardly hard work. What in the hell was Rebecca playing at?

'Can I get you a cup of tea or coffee?' Jamie asked, doing his best to contain his temper as he tried to read the woman's expression. So far Kerry hadn't given away any of her private thoughts on the state of the place; if she noticed all the mess or the bad smell that lingered in the air, she was too polite and professional to let on.

'No, I'm fine, thank you,' Kerry replied, folding a muslin cloth that she'd found on the arm of the chair.

'I'll go and see if Rebecca is okay,' Jamie said, concerned now that she hadn't replied to him calling out to her and that Ella was still screaming the place down. Surely Rebecca should have managed to calm her down by now?

'Rebecca?' he shouted again, taking the stairs and awaiting a reply.

When he didn't get one, an awful thought crossed his mind.

What if something had happened to her? What if that's why she wasn't answering?

Hurrying then, a ripple of panic cutting right through him, he followed the sound of Ella's hysterical cries. Going straight to the nursery, he breathed a sigh of relief to see his daughter sprawled out in her cot, her face red with frustration, big fat tears cascading down her little chubby cheeks.

She quietened the second her father leaned over and scooped her up into his arms. Jamie breathed her in, his sudden presence immediately placating the child as he kissed her reassuringly on the forehead.

'It's okay, baby, Daddy's here,' Jamie said softly, feeling Ella relax inside his firm hold, grimacing as he felt the wetness leaking out from her soiled nappy and covering his hand.

Not wanting to upset Ella further, he tried to contain his temper, but felt his annoyance build that she'd been left alone to cry herself into hysterics and that her nappy was so full. Jamie was aware that the health visitor was probably downstairs taking notes; God knows what she was already thinking about them both as parents, turning up to this mess.

'It's okay, darling. Shall we go and find Mummy?' he said tightly. 'Rebecca?' he shouted again, but there was still no answer.

Marching into their bedroom, Jamie stopped in his tracks as Rebecca opened the door of the en suite, a towel wrapped tightly around her hair, her dressing gown on. She looked startled at Jamie's sudden presence in the bedroom.

'You're home? Is everything all right?' Rebecca gasped, her eyes going to Ella. Her daughter's eyes were red and puffy, much like the rest of her face. She wondered how long Jamie had been here for, and was glad that Ella had finally stopped crying, but felt the familiar annoyance that it was Jamie who always managed to appease her. Of course, he had. Ella was such a little daddy's girl.

'You were in the bath?' Jamie said through gritted teeth, seeing the wrinkly, pink skin of Rebecca's fingers, as if she'd lain in the water too long. Like she didn't have a care in the world. Leaving poor Ella to scream the place down. 'Did you not hear Ella crying?' Jamie was unable to keep the accusation from his tone. 'Because the rest of the bloody street could hear her!'

'I'm sorry, no. I didn't hear a thing? She must have just started. She was fine a few minutes ago,' Rebecca lied, mortified that Jamie had come home early and caught her out, thinking about how she'd left the house in a such a state this morning. She'd planned on doing what she normally did lately and getting the house straight just before Jamie came home, so at least it looked as if she was coping. But this morning, Rebecca hadn't done a thing. Remembering the soiled nappy she'd left on the living room floor along with her empty breakfast bowl.

She knew that Jamie would be judging her now. Questioning whether she could cope.

'I was washing my hair. My head must have been under the water.' *Not technically a lie*, she thought. Her head *had* been under the water. Intentionally, so she could block out all the noise. The water had helped, but the irony wasn't lost on her – even before she'd got into the water, she felt as if she'd already been drowning. Trapped here in this house, listening to Ella's cries all morning, she'd felt as if she was submerged… out of her depth.

'She's soaked through, Rebecca? How long did you leave her for?' Jamie spat, furious that Rebecca had let Ella get into such a state. He paced the room, gathering the fresh nappy and baby grow he'd brought through from the nursery, before placing Ella down on the bed and changing her nappy.

51

'Kerry's downstairs,' he hissed. Then, seeing the puzzled look on Rebecca's face, he forced a whisper, 'The health visitor! Christ knows how long she stood on the doorstep listening to Ella screaming the place down.'

Rebecca shook her head, confused.

'You had an appointment? Ella's eight-week check?'

'No, that's not today. It's next week,' Rebecca said with certainty, trying to gain back some control and at least look as if she knew what she was doing. Making her way over to the bed, she picked up her phone, scrolling through her calendar to show him the entry she'd made just a few days ago. Rebecca frowned as she saw the appointment scheduled in for today.

1 p.m. Kerry Day. Ella's 8-week check.

'Shit! I'm sure it said next week. I must have misread it…' Rebecca said, embarrassed under Jamie's watchful eye as she tried to make excuses. 'I checked my diary this morning? There was nothing there, I thought we had nothing planned today?'

'Clearly,' Jamie muttered quietly; his expression full of disgust as he buttoned up Ella's clean baby grow. 'You seem to be making a habit of forgetting things lately.'

There it was again. That condescending tone. Jamie really did have no idea.

Biting her lip, scared of what might come out of her mouth if she dared to speak, Rebecca let Jamie's words hang awkwardly in the air between them before he spoke again.

'Well, you better get dressed and make yourself look half decent. Christ knows what she's already written in her notes about us. And I need to get back to the office. I only came back to pick up some paperwork' – Jamie paused – 'unless, of course, you can't manage?'

Rebecca winced at Jamie's insinuation, part of her wanting to scream at him, to make him realise that yes, she was struggling. But why would she reach out to him when he always responded with such anger? Constantly putting her down and making digs at her, making out she wasn't a good mother. As if she wasn't trying. When the truth was, she was trying her damn hardest, all the time.

She hadn't left Ella on her own because she was neglecting her.

She'd left Ella on her own for her own protection.

Because she was scared of what she might do if she was pushed to the edge.

'Look, I'm sorry, Jamie. Really, I am. I must have forgot about the appointment, and as for Ella, I didn't hear her. I was in the bath. I just needed a few minutes to get my head straight...' she said, willing herself to be brave enough and ask him who Jenna was. Maybe then she'd get his attention. Maybe then he'd realise she had other things on her mind.

Only she didn't get a chance. Instead, she was met with Jamie rolling his eyes at her.

'And our daughter just needed her mother to change her soiled nappy. Jesus, Rebecca. You need to sort yourself out. You're a fucking mess!' Jamie said shaking his head, his parting words ringing in Rebecca's ears as she stood and watched him scoop Ella up and take her downstairs.

Standing at the top of the stairs, she listened as Jamie walked back into the room, recognised the false joviality in his voice as he charmed the health visitor. Just like he charmed everyone else around him.

God, how he used to charm her.

Jamie could turn it on and off like a running tap.

But he was right. She needed to pull herself together, for the health visitor's sake if nothing else. Doing as she was told, Rebecca quickly threw on some clothes while fighting back her tears, before going downstairs and trying to salvage the meeting as best as she could.

Chapter Eight

'Are you all right, Becks? You don't look so good.' Placing the coffees down on the table, Lisa stared over at Rebecca with genuine concern as her sister-in-law stifled another yawn.

She'd guessed from the long text Rebecca had sent late last night, asking to meet for a coffee, that Rebecca wanted to talk to her about something.

Rebecca had tried to play it down and say that she just needed a friendly ear. Now, picking up on Rebecca's dark mood and the exhausted look in her eyes, Lisa was almost certain that this wasn't just a general catch-up.

'I'm so sorry I haven't been around so much this past week to stop by and see you guys. I mean, Christ! I live next door, I should be popping in and pestering you both for a hug with this one every five minutes.' Lisa smiled over to her adorable niece and feeling guilty for not being around more than she had. 'But I've barely had a minute to myself. Work's been so manic that I've hardly had a chance to breathe. I wish I could help out more…' she said, realising that Rebecca was struggling. It had evident the second she'd set eyes on her wrestling the buggy in through the narrow doorway of the coffee shop. Rebecca's voice sounded fractious as she tried to soothe Ella's cries that immediately filled the room, announcing their arrival.

Lisa had been shocked at the sight of Rebecca. Bedraggled, devoid of her usually heavy make-up, her complexion pale, and her expression withdrawn. She looked sickly, almost, nothing like the vivacious woman she'd been just a couple of weeks ago, when Lisa had last seen her. Unless of course, she'd just been putting on a front?

'Is she okay? I mean, don't take this the wrong way, but you look exhausted, Becks. Has Ella been keeping you up?' Lisa said sympathetically.

Flustered and preoccupied since she'd sat down, Rebecca had barely looked Lisa in the eye. Instead, she constantly fussed over Ella, who in turn repeatedly rejected her mother's every attempt to soothe her incessant cries.

'I've been up with her all night. I just don't know what's wrong with her?' Rebecca shrugged. 'She won't settle. Nothing I do works. Maybe we should have stayed at home, but I thought the fresh air might do her good. I thought she might sleep in the buggy...' The tremor in Rebecca's voice was clear to them both.

'Well she certainly has a set of lungs on her, I'll give her that. I can't believe such a dinky little thing like her would be capable of making such a racket.' Lisa grinned and affectionately stroked her tiny niece's cheek, to see if she could deter the child from her angry cries.

'Come on, Ella, darling. Try your bottle,' Rebecca said, aware of the people at the tables around them who were disgruntled by the noise, wanting to enjoy their coffee in peace.

Rebecca forced the teat of the bottle into Ella's mouth, but the baby pursed her lips tightly, spitting the bottle back out. Turning her head away, she screamed louder.

'I think that's a firm no,' Lisa said with a smile. 'Jeez! She certainly knows her own mind.'

'Come on, Ella…' The plea was clear in her voice as Rebecca tried the dummy instead. 'This will help you sleep.'

'Here, do you want me to have a go?' Holding out her arms, Lisa offered to take Ella from Rebecca, so that her sister-in-law could drink her coffee before it went stone cold.

'No, it's fine. I can manage.'

'Oh, I have no doubt about that,' Lisa said softly, catching the defensive tone in her voice and seeing tears of frustration forming in her eyes. 'Honestly, Becks, stubbornness is a Dawson family trait. I bet my mum would say that Jamie was the same as a baby… in fact, he's probably even worse now as a grown man. Is he helping you?'

'Yeah, he does what he can,' Rebecca said tightly. 'He's just got a lot going on right now, you know how it is. Work's super busy. He's stressed out. It's hard.'

'Always a workaholic. I guess nothing changes, eh?' Lisa nodded, making a mental note to make more effort to help out with her niece. She'd have a word with her brother too. Knowing Jamie, he'd be near on useless with the day-to-day care of his daughter. Of course he adored her, but Jamie's number one priority would always be his business. By the looks of it, it had taken Rebecca a whole year and a newborn baby before she found out the hard way that she'd be left to her own devices when it came to looking after Ella. She hated seeing Rebecca struggling.

Lisa had been dubious at first about Rebecca's intentions, but had quickly realised she'd been wrong to judge her. Rebecca didn't want anything from Jamie except love, and a family, she presumed. And Lisa could see that she was doing everything in her power to make the relationship work.

'Nothing I do seems to be right,' Rebecca said, shaking her head. 'I've taken her to the doctors twice this week, and both times they've said she's fine. But I just don't know. It can't be right her crying this much, can it?'

'Do you think she might be teething?' Lisa offered before laughing at her words of advice. 'Fuck, we're all in trouble if you start taking baby advice from me. I only know what I hear from the two women in my office who have recently become mothers. Baby talk is the only talk going on right now, and trust me, some of the stories they've told me about childbirth has honestly put me off for life!'

'Teething? Do you think? She's only two months old…?' Rebecca said, running her finger across Ella's pink firm gums checking for signs of a tooth poking through. 'Nope. Nothing there. Unless they haven't broken through the skin yet,' Rebecca said, a hint of relief in her voice that it wasn't another thing she'd simply missed. Another thing she'd not noticed that she could add to her ever-growing list of failures so far as a mother.

'What if she's sick? What if there's something wrong with her? What if the doctors weren't thorough enough with her?' Rebecca said, her voice rising. Rubbing the child's back rhythmically. She was self-conscious that the other customers in the small coffee shop were glancing over at her now, irritated by the loud wailing noise. She felt they were silently judging her for not being capable of making the noise stop, all of them thinking the same as Jamie, that she didn't know what she was doing.

Putting the dummy back down on the table, Rebecca's hand shook. Knocking her cup of coffee over, she jumped to her feet, lifting Ella up to avoid the spillage but not quickly enough to stop the pool of hot coffee from spreading across the table and trickling down her legs.

'Here, give Ella to me,' Lisa said, standing up and reaching out her arms for Ella. She rocked the child gently in her arms while Rebecca patted her trousers with a paper napkin.

A waitress joining them, helping to mop up the mess with a handful of cloths.

'Can you bring a fresh cappuccino, please?' Lisa asked, handing the waitress some money, before the two women sat back down again.

'Becks, it's a cup of coffee, not the end of the world,' Lisa said, shocked to see her friend openly crying after the waitress returned a few moments later and placed a fresh cup in front of her.

Lisa had guessed rightly that this had nothing to do with a spilt coffee, or Ella being fractious and difficult. There was something much bigger on Rebecca's mind and whatever it was would have to be coaxed out of her.

'What is it, Becks? You know you can tell me anything…'

'I don't even know where to start,' Rebecca said, her words coming out in sporadic bursts between sobs. 'It's everything. I'm just so bloody tired. I haven't been sleeping very well and when I do finally go to sleep, I keep having these awful nightmares. They seem so real, so terrifying that I've been suffering with panic attacks. When I wake up,

I'm just physically exhausted. And I'm trying my best to keep on top of everything, and to keep it all together, but I'm failing miserably. I keep forgetting things,' Rebecca said quietly, before adding, 'Important things. Like Ella's doctor's appointments. I think the surgery think I'm losing my mind. I turned up there the other day only to be told that they'd received a text from me to say to cancel it. I felt so stupid. I don't even remember sending it. Then yesterday, the health visitor turned up to do Ella's eight-week check. I don't know how I missed it. It was in my diary on my phone, but I'm sure when I checked it that morning there'd been nothing pencilled in. And typically, Jamie had come home early. He'd forgotten something he needed for work, and he found the health visitor out on the doorstep waiting. The house was such a mess, I was a mess, and Ella was crying and he just looked so disappointed in me...' Rebecca shook her head, cringing at the memory of how angry Jamie had been that she couldn't seem to manage the most basic of tasks.

'I'm sure he's not disappointed at all. He's probably just worried about you, that's all. So what if you forget a few things? That's normal, isn't it? They don't call it *baby brain* for nothing, you know. Sarah, one of the new mums I was telling you about in my office, told me that she once put a pile of clean towels in the dishwasher and a pile of dirty plates in the airing cupboard. Can you imagine! She found it bloody hysterical though. Especially when her husband got out of the shower and found them. She said her brain's been like a sieve since she had her son. It happens.' Lisa laughed, trying to make light of the situation.

'I think the health visitor thinks it's a bit more than that. She left me this.' Grabbing her bag from under the table, Rebecca reluctantly slid the leaflet across to Lisa.

'Home Start? What's that then?'

'It's some charity organisation. They send volunteers around to help you. Cleaning, helping out with the baby… She didn't say it, but she mustn't think I'm coping very well either, must she? Otherwise why would she leave it for me?'

'Oh, I don't know, Becks. Maybe that's a good thing? I mean, if you think it will ease the pressure a bit?' Lisa picked up the leaflet and read the information on there, before tapping the back of it. 'It's also got details of local mother and baby groups listed here. Maybe that's more what she was advising. That you should get out more and meet up with other new mothers? Build yourself a bit of a support network? I mean, a messy house and a tired mother is hardly the sign of not being able to cope. In fact, I think it's actually part of the job description.' Seeing the look on Rebecca's face, she could sense that her sister-in-law was holding something back from her.

'What is it, Becks? There's something else, isn't there?'

Rebecca considered telling Lisa how she'd felt paranoid the whole way here to the café today. Turning every few minutes as she'd pushed Ella in the pram, convinced someone was following close behind her. Only every time she turned to look there was no one there.

She knew how crazy it would sound, saying that out loud. And maybe she was a bit crazy right now?

'I've been diagnosed with postnatal depression.'

61

'Oh, hunny! I'm sorry!' Lisa said, even more annoyed at herself now for not making more time for Rebecca now. She needed help. No wonder she looked so tired. Now that Rebecca had said it, it was obvious this was what was going on. She could have kicked herself for not realising sooner.

'Can I ask you something?' Lisa said, cautiously, not wanting to say anything out of turn, but wanting to learn more about what she'd seen that day in the hospital delivery suite.

'The scars on your arms? Have you…? Did you…?'

'Oh God, no.' Rebecca shook her head at what Lisa was implying, that she'd been hurting herself. 'That was… before. Before Jamie. I was in a bad relationship. Mark… he did things…' Rebecca paused.

'This Mark, he hurt you?'

Rebecca shrugged her shoulders. Then pursing her mouth, she clearly stopped herself from saying anymore.

'I don't want to talk about any of that now. It's not my life anymore. This is different.'

'I'm so sorry, Becks. I had to ask. And I'm sorry that you're going through this now. I had no idea,' Lisa said, feeling sad that her friend had obviously been on the receiving end of an abusive relationship, but relieved that she'd moved on and left all that in the past. What she needed help with was *now*. She was reaching out to Lisa for help, and Lisa was going to make sure that she gave it to her. 'You know you can talk to me, anytime. About anything.'

Rebecca nodded her head.

'How's Jamie been about it all? Can he take some time off work, to help you out a bit more?'

'I haven't told him.'

'Why not?'

'Because I don't even know where to start, Lisa. He already thinks I'm a failure, I can tell. For not coping, for forgetting everything. And he's right. Some days, I can't even think straight. I barely manage to get out of bed and look after Ella, let alone look after myself. And as much as your brother may love me, he didn't sign up for that.'

'Oh, Becks, stop beating yourself up, you are not a failure. You're suffering with postnatal depression,' Lisa said. 'You need to tell him, he will understand. He will help you. You need to reach out and ask for help. You don't have to do any of this alone. You know that don't you?'

'Oh, bugger. I better take this.' Hearing her phone go off in her pocket, Lisa stood up and passed Ella back to Rebecca. 'More office dramas. It's a nightmare at the moment. We're having to make some redundancies, and it's just been decided that muggins here has the pleasure of breaking the horrendous bloody news to the staff we're letting go.'

Lisa took the call, a frown on her face the entire conversation, before ending it a few minutes later.

'I'm so sorry, babe, I'd love to stay and chat some more with you, but I'm going to have to go. Honestly, I don't know how they survive without me there telling them all what to do.'

Taking one final swig of her cappuccino, Lisa stood up and hugged Rebecca tightly to her and peered down at Ella, who had finally given in fighting her tiredness and fallen asleep in Rebecca's arms.

'At least she's sleeping now. She must have worn herself out, bless her. Anyone can see you're doing a great job with Ella, look at her, Becks. Seriously, stop beating yourself up. And talk to that brother of mine, please. He'll understand. I promise. Try to get some rest, yeah?'

'Thank you.' Rebecca nodded, kissing Lisa goodbye before placing Ella down gently in her pushchair, careful not to wake her.

Maybe Lisa was right.

Maybe reaching out and asking for a bit of help wouldn't be such a bad thing.

It was decided. She'd go home and get some sleep and tonight she'd tell Jamie everything.

Making her way out of the café, shortly behind Lisa, Rebecca wished she'd been brave enough to open up to her friend and tell her the other things that were taunting her too.

How her mother had suffered from depression too, and how they'd all suffered in the hands of it.

Rebecca had to get better. For Ella's sake.

She could never turn out like her.

Chapter Nine

'What's all this crying about, my little darling, your poor mummy must be frazzled listening to you. Can I get you a cup of coffee, Rebecca? You look like you could do with one.' Maggie Fisher smiled down at Ella who lay in her pram crying hysterically, before placing her arm affectionately on Rebecca's. 'It's bloody hard work sometimes, isn't it?'

Rebecca nodded her head.

In her late fifties, Maggie was the backbone of Jamie's company. He'd said it often enough. How the woman had been with him right from the very start. How her ideas and input in the company had been paramount to his success. And though her official title was the company receptionist, Maggie was far more than that.

The woman could run this place with her eyes closed. Jamie freely admitted that he'd be lost without her.

'Jamie's just in his office, darling, f… Finishing up in a meeting with his PA. He shouldn't be much longer. Are you sure I can't get you a drink? Some water at least? You look all hot and bothered, Rebecca.'

'Some water would be good.' Rebecca smiled but narrowed her eyes, convinced that she just caught a slight pause in Maggie's sentence, an edge to her wording as she made excuses for Jamie.

Rebecca watched as Maggie made her way over to the water machine, her back to Rebecca now.

So that she wouldn't have to look her in the eye?

Was Jamie up to no good?

Rebecca closed her eyes then, silently berating herself for doing it again. For acting paranoid and overthinking everything. For creating problems that weren't really there.

Of course Jamie had meetings with his PA. He had meetings with a lot of people. Maggie wouldn't cover for Jamie if he was doing anything he shouldn't be doing. The woman was too honest for that. It was one of the things Rebecca liked the most about her, that she always spoke her mind. That, and the fact that she wasn't scared to give Jamie a much needed reality check when it was called for, unlike the rest of his staff who constantly ran around the place sucking up to him and singing his praises, just to get their foot higher up on the ladder. Jamie was a self-made man. He'd pulled himself up from the bottom and created a recruitment empire that was doing exceptionally well.

He was used to people pandering to his every whim, but what he respected more than ever were people who could be straight with him. And with Maggie, there was no pretence. The woman was always as honest as she was brutal. And she was always kind to Rebecca.

'I thought getting her out of the house would help, but I guess I was wrong.' Rebecca sighed as Ella continued to scream, rubbing her head to ease the headache she now had. Ella's incessant crying had been ringing in her ears since the moment she'd left home, echoing through her skull as she'd traipsed halfway across London to Jamie's Mayfair offices. The journey had taken almost an hour in the end, zapping all her energy and patience as she'd dragged the pushchair through the overcrowded maze of the underground.

Tucking the loose strands of hair that had fallen out of her clip behind her ears, she wiped the beads of perspiration that had formed on her forehead. Her swollen feet throbbed inside the ridiculously high shoes she'd forced on because they went with the dress she'd decided would seduce Jamie into finding her attractive again. Only the whole outfit felt too tight now, the extra baby weight she'd gained making the fabric cling to her body, sticking to the thin film of sweat. She could only imagine what a sight she must look.

And Ella was worse now. Fractious and due her next feed. Rebecca suspected she needed her nappy changing too.

It was all going wrong. *She shouldn't have come,* she thought as she looked around the immaculate reception area and suddenly it didn't seem like such a good idea to just turn up at Jamie's office unannounced, with Ella in such a state.

But she was trying. *Wasn't that the entire point of today?* After her chat with Lisa yesterday, she'd vowed to make more of an effort, to try to get back on track with Jamie. If they were going to talk, properly, then they needed to start spending some time together.

'Do you know what, Maggie, if it's just finishing up, I'm sure he won't mind me and this little one interrupting the meeting. I was hoping to surprise him anyway…' she said, holding up the little picnic of Jamie's favourite foods she'd packed neatly into a cool bag. 'I bought him some lunch.'

She'd come this far. She needed to go and see Jamie before she lost her nerve completely.

'I should really give him a call… he did say that he didn't want to be interrupted…'

'Oh, right,' Rebecca said, eyeing the woman suspiciously. She wasn't imagining it, was she? Maggie was acting cagey. The look of panic crossing her face as she reached over the desk for the phone.

'Don't,' Rebecca said, her voice too hard, her tone too sharp. 'I want to surprise him,' she added, her tone shocking them both. It wasn't a request it was an order.

Maggie wavered for a few seconds, as if considering what she should do for the best, before placing the phone back down on the receiver.

'You know what, that sounds like a wonderful idea. I'm sure he'll be thrilled to see you both.' Maggie winked, quickly trying to disguise the hesitancy in her voice as she plastered a smile on her face. 'And this little poppet will probably be all the better for seeing her daddy. Though he might hear you both coming before he sees you.' Maggie grinned, her eyes on Ella, whose loud cries filled the reception area.

'Thank you,' Rebecca said politely, before making her way down the corridor towards Jamie's office. Shaking the pushchair rhythmically as she went, in a last-ditch attempt to get Ella to quieten down, she'd guessed that was exactly what Maggie was counting on – Ella's cries announcing their arrival before Rebecca did, giving Jamie a few minutes' warning before they interrupted whatever was going on in his office. Unless, of course, she was just being paranoid again. Lately she really didn't know what to think or believe.

Reaching the office door, Rebecca paused, her hand visibly shaking as she reached for the handle. Scared of what she might see on the other side. She took a deep breath and flung the door open.

'Surprise!' Composing herself, Rebecca forced a smile, despite the pang of jealousy that she felt ripping through her as she eyed Jamie and the younger, attractive woman sitting next to him at his desk. So close to each other it felt almost intimate. *It's more of a cosy little lunch date than a meeting*, she thought as she took in the takeaway boxes that sat on the desk. A selection of fancy looking tapas along with a bottle of wine.

'Shit!' she said, wincing then as the buggy smacked hard against the door frame, only for it to spring back and whack her shin, the sudden jolt sending Ella's already deafening sobs into near on hysteria.

Their surprise arrival was nothing like the grand entrance she'd envisaged in her head.

'Rebecca? I didn't know you were going to drop in. You've met Jenna?' Jamie said, awkwardly standing up. Awkward now. But nowhere near as awkward as Rebecca felt standing self-consciously in the doorway. There was practically a crackling charge running through the airwaves around her.

Jenna.

The name Jamie called out when they were having sex. This was her.

'No. I definitely haven't. I'm sure I would remember...' Rebecca put on a fake smile and shook her head.

Jamie would have made sure of that.

69

Because the girl was simply stunning. Even from here, Rebecca felt mesmerised by her sultry blue eyes. She was a perfect size ten, Rebecca guessed, taking in the younger woman's tiny, toned figure. Her long blond hair trailing down past her waist. The type of woman that most wives wouldn't want working in such close proximity of their husbands.

'I've made you egg mayonnaise sandwiches,' Rebecca said, instantly regretting the lame sentence escaping her lips, before silently wishing for the ground to swallow her up. Catching the younger woman's eyes, she recognised the look she gave her. Full of sympathy. No, something else.

Something worse.

Pity.

As she quickly looked away, fixing her gaze on the floor, Rebecca caught her smirk. It ripped through her as she knows it was intended.

'Right, well, I'll get that all typed up and emailed over as soon as possible. Thank you for lunch,' Jenna said, her tone professional as she gathered up her things.

Rebecca's glad that this woman at least has the decency to get up from her seat and make her excuses to leave, only Jamie misses the beat. His puzzled expression lingers on Jenna's face as he tried to work out what Jenna was talking about.

'Right. Yes,' he said. Flustered. Playing along, only he's a few fractions of a second too late.

Rebecca sees it.

Because you can't bullshit a bullshitter and Rebecca has always known an actress when she sees one.

Stepping aside as Jenna walks towards her, she can't help but compare herself to the girl, aware that in contrast she's tried too hard and hasn't quite pulled it off.

She's wearing too much make-up. Her perfume too strong, too overpowering. Her clothes too tight. She feels cheap and frumpy.

Ella is screaming now. Louder than Rebecca has ever heard her cry before. Embarrassed, she picks her up to comfort her, glad of the distraction. Grateful of something to do, only the sudden movement dislodges what's been bothering Ella the past few days, and Ella projectile vomits all over her. The last strand of dignity she possessed slips from her grasp. Her plans ruined, she catches the look on Jamie's face. Instead of concern, she just sees anger as he visibly cringes with embarrassment. Saint Jenna quickly rushes to her aid, leaning over the desk in her bum skimming dress before passing Rebecca a wad of tissues along with an apologetic glance, before rapidly fleeing the room. Leaving Rebecca and Jamie finally alone.

Jamie doesn't have to say anything because she can tell by the stilted expression on his face that's he's beyond angry with her.

And her emotions get the better of her then.

All the effort she went to. For what?

She starts to cry. Huge wracking sobs that rip through her body, making her shake.

'Jesus, Rebecca. What's got into you?' Jamie said, taking Ella from her. He holds her awkwardly, away from his body so that he doesn't get

71

his suit covered in vomit, before bending down and grabbing a spare blanket from the bottom of the pushchair and wrapping it around her.

'I brought you some lunch. I thought it would be nice. The three of us. I just wanted to surprise you,' she said, wiping her running nose. Her tears subsiding as she watched Jamie lay Ella down on the office sofa and change her out of her puke-sodden clothes.

And she feels it again, the jealousy that wells up inside of her as Jamie deals with Ella so attentively. Giving their daughter the time and attention he no longer has for her. Hot flushes of shame wash over her, because despite herself she can't control it. She's tried so hard to make everything right, but once again she's messed everything up.

When he's done cleaning her up, Jamie kisses Ella on her forehead before placing her back in her buggy. Ella seems a bit better now. No longer crying. Quieter, more settled.

But Jamie is still as cold as ice.

'She's not well. You better take her home. I'll have Maggie call you a cab.'

Rebecca bristles.

He's dismissing her.

Suddenly she feels so hurt, so humiliated that she can't find her voice, so instead she simply nods in agreement and allows Jamie to usher her from his office as if she's a scolded child.

Back at the reception desk, Rebecca can barely look at Maggie as the woman shoots her a sympathetic look. Because she knows Maggie tried to stop her from going to the office. And she knows now that when

Maggie suggested calling ahead, she hadn't been trying to cover for Jamie, she'd been trying to protect her and Ella.

'Can you call Rebecca a cab please? Ella's not well,' Jamie says, as Rebecca eyes the other staff that walk by and look at them, convinced that Jenna has already told her colleagues about Jamie's emotional wreck of a wife turning up unexpectedly and catching them both in his office together.

She can already imagine the Chinese whispers. The rumours.

She bet everyone knew.

'Don't worry about the cab,' Rebecca said, pushing the buggy towards the main doors, before Jamie or Maggie could insist otherwise. 'I'll walk. The air will do Ella good.'

'I'll be late tonight,' Jamie said curtly, still visibly annoyed as he walked Rebecca out. 'I'll see you later.'

Rebecca was left standing on the street then, staring at Jamie's silhouette as he walked back into the tall glass building. Alone amid the chaos of the busy Mayfair road with its queues of traffic in complete gridlock. The bustling sound of people in their droves as they stepped around her, as if she wasn't even there.

As if she was invisible.

As Rebecca pushed the pram down the footpath, almost in a trance as she headed for home, that was exactly how she felt.

Chapter Ten

Wiping the rain from her face, Rebecca had been in such a trance with her thoughts she hadn't realised the heavens had opened. *She should have got the Tube*, she thought as she looked up at the bleak, grey sky noting the dark clouds that loomed above her, droplets of rain pelting down on her and the pushchair.

However, she couldn't face the hordes of people, so she'd wandered the streets of London, preferring to walk the hour journey back to their home in Kensington instead. Unable to get thoughts of Jamie cheating on her with that little tramp, Jenna.

'Shit!' she said, as the sky above her opened up, the rain heavy now.

Bending down to the basket underneath the pushchair, she searched for the rain cover, cursing loudly when she realised it wasn't there, that she'd forgotten to bring it out with her.

Who did that? What kind of mother forgot something so important? Another thing to add to the endless list of her being a crap mother. She was useless.

Taking her coat off, Rebecca draped it over the pushchair to ensure that Ella kept dry at least; she didn't care about herself.

They weren't far from home now. Another mile or so, and they'd get there quicker if she cut through Hyde Park. Crossing the road opposite the parade of shops, Rebecca picked up her pace. The last thing she needed right now was for Ella to come down with a cold or chest infection because of her forgetfulness.

Another thing that Jamie could get pissed off about.

'Oh, this is just great!' she mumbled, as the rain began to pour down, the clouds above her opening up, followed by a huge clap of thunder. Within seconds she was soaked through, her hair and dress clinging to her skin. Her carefully done make-up now running down her face. She was walking so fast that she'd given herself a stitch. She'd gone from a hot sweaty mess to a drowned rat. Not exactly what she'd planned.

She was the only idiot out in it, the bad weather seemingly driving anyone with a decent amount of common sense away and into the warm somewhere.

Hyde Park felt eerie without the usual bustle of people walking around. Bleak and depressing, just like her mood.

Steering the buggy along the crooked pathway, Rebecca replayed the conversation she and Lisa had. She'd been wrong about her brother; it wasn't a case of just talking to Jamie. He wouldn't just understand.

It wasn't as simple as that.

Becoming a parent changes you. And having Ella had changed Rebecca completely.

She wasn't the same person anymore, she knew that. Some days she didn't know who she was at all.

Fatherhood had changed Jamie too. He'd become so bitter and resentful that Rebecca's focus had completely been on Ella. That she always seemed so preoccupied with making sure their tiny daughter had everything she needed. In Jamie's eyes, Rebecca making Ella her priority meant she was neglecting her husband.

Rebecca took a deep breath, wiping the rain from her face again. She was irritated now; it angered her that men could be so pathetic and weak, and she was annoyed with herself for ever believing that Jamie would be any different. That he was better.

He clearly wasn't. Instead of trying to fix what was broken, he'd looked for solace in the nearest, easiest option. Jenna was Jamie's easy option.

Though she had no proof, Rebecca had seen it with her own eyes when she'd walked into his office earlier. The intimacy between them as they'd exchanged awkward looks. The fact he'd called out *her* name while they'd been having sex.

She knew he'd betrayed her.

Rebecca winced, tasting blood on her tongue as she realised she'd been biting her lip. Looking down at her hands as she steered the pushchair through the narrow pathway at the park's edge, she noted how white her knuckles were as her hands locked in a grip around the handle.

She could feel the rage building inside at the thought of her husband's infidelity.

How could Jamie do this to her? To Ella? They had only been together for less than eighteen months and already Jamie was ready to trade her in for an easy fuck with a girl half his age?

He had shattered whatever hope she'd had for them and broken them both completely.

She was crying now, her feet burning in pain as she continued to walk in her uncomfortable high heels. The park felt as if it went on for miles and the heavy rainfall mixed with her tears and blurred her vision as she walked towards the exit.

She didn't bother to turn when she heard someone behind her on the pathway, the heavy thud of footsteps pounding the pavement, she just stepped to the side to let them pass, keeping her head down, her face hidden. Embarrassed that she was crying, the last thing she needed right now was sympathy from a random stranger.

Only, whoever was behind her didn't pass, instead matching her pace, walking close behind her, so close it felt like it was deliberate.

Curiosity getting the better of her, Rebecca turned, jumping with fright at the sight of the tall man not even a foot away from her, almost touching her. Dressed all in black, his hood pulled tightly around his face so she couldn't see his features.

Startled by his proximity, Rebecca was filled with a sense of dread.

Her intuition was never wrong. She'd lived her life guided by it and there had been many times it had saved her.

Now, she knew wasn't safe.

She could feel it.

She tried to quell the rising panic in a last-ditch attempt to make herself believe she was just being paranoid again.

This man had his hood done up tightly around his face because it's raining. He's walking fast to get out of the rain. Just like you are.

But she knew that wasn't true.

And despite not being able to see his eyes properly as he approached, she could feel his stare burning into her.

The shove came from nowhere, a scream leaving her mouth as she lost her balance and sailed through the air, her body slamming hard against the faded grey fence that lined the pathway. Putting her hands out for protection to no avail, her face scraped down the coarse, splintered panel.

Dazed and confused as she lay helplessly on the ground.

Ella.

Pulling herself back up onto her feet, Rebecca rushed to check that Ella was okay, limping as the pain in her knee shot up her thigh. She must have twisted it in the fall.

Lifting up her coat, she sighed with relief to see Ella still sleeping soundly, completely oblivious to anything going on around her.

'Thank God!' Rebecca murmured to herself, shaking now, in shock, as she looked back towards the park's exit. Watching in dismay as the man continued walking as if nothing had happened, as if he hadn't just attacked her. As if he hadn't even seen her splayed out on the floor, the pushchair just a few feet away from her as she cowered in shock, her clothes and hands covered in mud.

Rebecca scanned the park in the vain hope of finding a passer-by who might come to her aid. But the park is still empty, the rain acting like a deterrent. She could see a figure on the opposite side of the playing fields, sheltered from the rainfall underneath a row of trees. It's a woman walking her dog, but she has her back to Rebecca. And just the at the park's entrance, there's a man jogging in, but both are too far away to even hear her.

She'd be better off just getting home. She needed to get Ella indoors. They'd both be safe then.

Grabbing the pushchair with two trembling hands, Rebecca hobbled down the path, her head spinning as she tried to make sense of what had just happened.

She'd been attacked? Deliberately pushed?

But the man hadn't spoken a word to her, and Rebecca hadn't seen his face.

And then he was gone. Just like that.

Stepping out on to the busy main road, she felt safer now that there were other people around. Rebecca walked as fast as she could despite the pain in her knee and her throbbing head, reaching her street just a few minutes later. At her front door, she made a quick inventory of the street, nothing appeared out of place.

There's no one there. But she can't shake the feeling that someone *is* out there. That they *are* watching her.

What if the man has followed her home?

Shivering, she twisted the key in the lock and dragged the pushchair inside, slamming the door shut before double locking it behind her. Leaning up against the wall, she closed her eyes, frozen with fear of what could have happened to her and Ella.

Just the thought of someone wanting to harm her, or Ella, makes her feel physically sick.

Her fear of being hurt, of being abused, bringing forth all those buried, suppressed memories that she had stored away, deep inside her mind.

Picking up the phone, her hand shaking as she finds the number. Bursting into tears when the phone is finally answered, she manages just one sentence between her loud, wracking sobs.

'Jamie. Something bad's happened. You need to come home!'

Chapter Eleven

'Rebecca! I can't get in.' Shouting through the letter box, Jamie had tried twisting his key in the lock before pushing at the front door, only it wouldn't budge.

'It's double locked,' Jamie said, eyeing Rebecca's bare feet through the tiny slit in the door, as they padded down the stairs towards him.

'Oh, thank God you're home.' Opening the door, Rebecca threw herself into his arms.

'Are you okay? Is Ella okay?' Jamie asked. He'd been in a meeting with an important client when Rebecca had called, and he'd barely been able to make out what she'd been saying between her anguished sobs. The only words he'd heard clearly were 'attacked' and 'hurt'. He vaguely remembered her begging him to come home but Jamie didn't need to be asked twice.

He'd never moved so fast in his life, racing across London in record time.

'She's asleep, I just put her in her cot. We're fine. I was just so scared, Jamie. All I kept thinking was, what if something happened to Ella?'

Unable to make out what Rebecca was saying through her sobs, Jamie let out a sigh of relief, just glad that she was okay. Hugging Rebecca to him, he could see how distraught she was, as her body violently shook in his arms. He was glad he'd got here so quickly.

'You're safe now. You're home. Whatever happened, no one can hurt you here.' Stepping inside the house, Jamie closed the door behind him.

'Lock it,' Rebecca insisted, before stepping forward and twisting the key in the lock herself and yanking down the handle to make sure it was done properly.

'What about the police? Are they on their way?'

'No. Not yet,' Rebecca answered, making her way into the kitchen as Jamie followed her, watching as she double checked that the patio door was locked too.

'*Not yet?* What are you waiting for?' Jamie said, taking in the streaks of mud across Rebecca's knees and dress, the sore looking pink graze across her left cheek. 'You're hurt. You need to call them.'

'There's no point. It will just be a waste of their time,' Rebecca said resolutely. She wasn't going to tell Jamie that she'd already decided not to involve them. 'It all happened so quickly, I didn't even get a look at him and there was no one else around. There's not a single witness. I've got nothing to tell them except that I was pushed.'

'Fuck that, Rebecca. Call them. Whether or not you saw him properly or there are any witnesses, is neither here nor there. That's their job, call them!'

'And say what exactly? That I think I was pushed over on purpose?'

'What do you mean, "you think?" You said you were attacked?'

'I was. I mean, at least I *think* it was done on purpose. He was walking close behind me, and when I moved to the side to let him past, he just charged into me. He sent me sprawling to the floor, only when I looked up, he was walking towards the main gates as if nothing had happened. He didn't say anything, and he didn't look back. It was as if he hadn't even seen me.'

'He didn't threaten you? He didn't try to hurt you or take your bag?' Jamie shook his head, staring at Rebecca in disbelief as he tried to piece together her story that had changed completely since she'd called him. This was far from the description of an actual assault she'd claimed had happened over the phone.

'That's what I can't make sense of. If he wanted to hurt me or threaten me, he had the perfect opportunity and if he wanted my bag, it was hanging on the handles of the pushchair...'

'Where was Ella when all this happened?' Jamie said, looking down at the baby monitor that seemed to be permanently fixed to Rebecca's hand.

'She was in her buggy, fast asleep. She's fine. She didn't even stir when I carried her up to her nursery,' Rebecca repeated, before crying harder. 'What if it was just an accident?'

'Rebecca, he pushed you to the floor. He would have had to use considerable force. He knew. You were assaulted and you need to call the police. Let them do what they are paid to do,' Jamie said, exasperated at this being yet another thing for Rebecca to get stressed out and upset about, he picked up the house phone to make the call. Whatever had happened to Rebecca had left her distraught enough for her to be locking herself away in the house, distraught enough to be calling him out of work to come home. And if it was nothing, and somehow Rebecca had

83

got it all wrong, at least having the police look into it would ease Rebecca's obvious fears.

Rebecca had other ideas. Snatching the phone from Jamie's hand, she pleaded, 'No, Jamie, please! I don't want to call the police. That will just make things worse. Please, just leave it!'

'How could it make anything worse?' Jamie said, watching as Rebecca paced the lounge. 'Rebecca, you're not making any sense,' Jamie said truthfully.

'Because what if I'm wrong? What if I've made a mistake? They'll think I'm crazy. I mean, I was walking along in a world of my own… daydreaming…'

Thinking about you cheating on me.

Thinking about your betrayal.

'I'm so tired and stressed out lately, Jamie. I'm not thinking straight. I keep going over it again and again in my head, but what if I've somehow exaggerated everything in my mind? What if this guy just accidentally walked into me? And he didn't realise that I fell? Maybe that's what happened. That's why they didn't stop? I mean, it's possible isn't it?'

Only Rebecca knew it hadn't been an accident. She remembered it. The quick, jerky shove of the man's body, shunting into her just as he passed her. There was no way he wouldn't have known he pushed her. He would have felt it too.

'But you said you were attacked, Rebecca?' Jamie said now, forced patience to his tone now. 'You sounded terrified. What's changed since we got off the phone?'

'Nothing. Everything,' Rebecca replied, aware of how pathetic she sounded. 'I can't even trust my own mind. I'm so tired, Jamie. I hardly slept last night. And I feel so on edge all the time. I just freaked myself out.' There was a part of her that wanted to tell Jamie about the medication she'd been prescribed. About the doctor diagnosing her with post-natal depression. Maybe that was all part of it.

Maybe that's why she felt as if she was starting to lose her mind. Forgetting everything all the time. Feeling so anxious and paranoid. And now this.

Only, she was too scared of Jamie's reaction.

What if he thought she wasn't a fit mother, that she wasn't to be trusted looking after Ella?

She was so desperate to show him she was still the woman he'd fallen in love with and married, but she had everything against her now and she already felt as if she was slowly losing him.

'It's happened a couple of times now,' she said quietly. Unsure whether to tell Jamie or not. Uncertain of how he'd react. 'It happened the other day too, when I took Ella to the café. I thought I was just being paranoid, because whenever I looked, there was no one there. And I know it sounds crazy, but I felt it. It's as if I can sense someone watching me. Following me. And I can't shake the feeling that I'm not safe...'

'Jesus Christ,' Jamie said, running his hands through his hair. 'Why am I only hearing this now, why haven't you told me any of this before? If that's the case, then that's even more reason to call the police!'

'No, Jamie. Wait. I don't want to call them, because what if it's all in my head? What if it's me, and I'm freaking myself out over nothing?

You know, overthinking everything. Feeling paranoid. I keep thinking all kinds of things are going to happen to Ella. I keep worrying that I'm going to mess up.' Worried that he was going to walk out on her, that he'd go back to the office and she wouldn't see him again until tonight, Rebecca knew she had to be honest with him. That when he did finally return home, he'd retreat to the solitude of his office. Rebecca knew she had to be straight with him.

'The doctor has given me these,' she said, reaching into her handbag where she'd been hiding the box of medication.

'Antidepressants?' Jamie said, his voice quieter now. He looked hurt.

'I was going to tell you. I've only just started taking them… a few days ago…' She trailed off.

Opening the box, Jamie eyed the sealed blister packets, and saw that Rebecca was telling the truth. Only a few of the tablets were missing.

'I was embarrassed, Jamie. And I felt like a failure. But the doctor said post-natal depression is more common that most people realise,' Rebecca said, desperately trying to explain, to make him understand why she'd kept the truth from him. 'And it hasn't been that easy to talk to you lately.' She faltered, suddenly nervous to say what was really on her mind. 'You're never home and when you are, you barely talk to me. You seem so distracted. And then today when I saw you with your PA… Jenna. I just thought…'

She tails off then, searching Jamie's eyes for a hint of understanding, only she sees his expression change.

'You thought what?' A strange, twisted sound escapes from his mouth. He's looking at her strangely and Rebecca can't meet his eyes.

'Me and Jenna?' he says incredulously, as if he's finally pieced everything together. 'That's why you don't want me to call the police? You weren't attacked, were you? You made this all up?'

Rebecca paused, biting her lip, knowing that whatever she said next would damn her, regardless.

She didn't want Jamie to call the police.

It was too much of a risk involving them. Because they might start digging around and asking questions about her life before Jamie.

So she simply stood there silently and said nothing. Her silence spoke volumes to Jamie, and he shook his head.

'For fuck's sake, Rebecca! What is this? Just some sick and twisted way of getting my attention, is that it? Why? To punish me for, what? For having lunch with my PA?' Jamie screwed his eyes shut, rubbing his temples with the pads of his hands, as he felt the onslaught of the mother of all headaches coming on. 'I left a client in the middle of a meeting to get back here to check you were okay – a really fucking important client, Rebecca. Business that could potentially bring thousands of pounds worth of new revenue into the company. And I just ran out. I abandoned it, because I was worried about you and Ella. But this isn't about being attacked. Being pushed, or falling, or whatever the fuck you want to pretend is going on here. You think something is going on with me and Jenna. Jesus, Rebecca. Why didn't you just come out and bloody say it? Making up stories? It's playground bullshit.' Grabbing his keys from the sideboard, Jamie took a deep breath, clenching his jaw as he fought to control his temper.

'This needs to stop, Rebecca. All of this. Whatever the fuck is going on inside your head. Either you were attacked today, or someone ran past you in the park and you fell? You'd know the difference because it's a big one! So, which one was it?' Jamie roared, giving her one last chance to redeem herself.

Only Rebecca couldn't. Instead she stood there snivelling, as she tried to stifle her cries. Wanting to confront Jamie about calling Jenna's name out while they'd been having sex, only she was too scared that once she'd said it, Jamie would have no choice but to confess. And there would be no going back after that.

'This all needs to stop, Rebecca. You need to stop acting crazy. If anything, *you're* the one that's going to do that child harm if you keep playing these stupid bloody games,' Jamie said, the anger pouring out of him now, unchecked. 'I'm going back to the office.' He shrugged Rebecca's placatory hand off his arm before storming out of the house.

Rebecca stood watching from the window as Jamie got back into his car and frantically drove off. Convinced now that she'd ruined everything by bringing up her fears about Jenna.

He was probably going back to his office now to tell Jenna everything. Back to his sexy little PA instead of staying here with his pathetic, crazy wife.

Scanning the road once more, she shivered, it was getting dark now. The winter nights drawing in earlier. Making it harder for her to see the entire street clearly. She was convinced that she could still feel someone out there, watching her, even though she couldn't see anyone at all.

Then going to the front door and pulling the latch across, she bolted the door.

Pressing herself up against it, she closed her eyes.

What if Jamie was right? What if this was all her, acting crazy?

But it had felt so real. Despite how scared she'd felt, there was no way she'd let Jamie call the police.

They were the last people she wanted to get involved; people in authority, interfering and snooping around in their lives. Because it would only be a matter of time before they started asking other questions. Questions Rebecca didn't want to have to answer.

Chapter Twelve

It's exhilarating, you know, to take someone to the point of losing their mind. There's an unexpected satisfaction I didn't expect to feel when I first started this.

Making you feel as though you're being watched, but you never really see anyone there.

Thinking you're being followed, only you can't be so sure.

The triumph is very gratifying, but a part of me is so disappointed you're making this easy for me.

It's almost effortless, because you have given me the power to use your reality against you, Rebecca.

Because deep down, no matter how much of an act you like to put on, you are WEAK.

I see you. The person you try so hard to hide from others.

I watch you all the time.

When you're with others, when you're all alone. Especially when you're all alone.

I can see you now. And you have no idea that I'm here. Watching you through the web cam on your laptop as you hide away in the office, searching for some answers.

Only you're searching in all the wrong places, Rebecca.

Trawling the websites for information on post-natal depression, panic attacks, hallucinations. It's almost laughable, how quickly you've succumbed to it all.

Because part of you wants to believe it, doesn't it, Rebecca? Part of you wants to think that you are sick. Because what would the alternative be? Having to face the truth. Having to admit that I'm real. That I am here, watching you.

Can you feel me, Rebecca? I whisper as you lean in closer towards the computer screen. Your eyes staring down the lens at me.

I think you can.

I think you can sense my presence.

I can see the frustration pouring out of you as you narrow your eyes, the beginnings of a deep crevice directly above your nose. As you tuck a loose strand of your greasy hair behind your right ear.

Today, you look older than your twenty-eight years. Devoid of all make-up, your skin is blotchy and peppered with breakouts from the lack of sleep and the stress you've endured recently, no doubt.

You look haggard and worn out and I won't lie, it's not a good look for you, Rebecca. Not a good look at all.

Like an out of shape jumper, familiarity brings comfort, but it's not fit for purpose anymore. Except perhaps for the bin.

You yawn.

Are you tired, Rebecca? Have you been taking your medication like a good girl? All those pills that your doctor prescribed you to stop you from losing your mind?

Your gaze is shifting now. Your eyes, puffy and swollen. The sparkle that used to shine there has long gone.

A noise from somewhere else in the house makes you jump. And I watch you freeze like a rabbit caught in the headlights, startling at every tiny sound you hear.

Are you expecting someone, Rebecca?

I laugh, despite my dark mood.

Slowly, painfully, you're finally piecing it all together.

You're crumbling before my very eyes.

It's such a slow, gradual unravelling.

I wonder how quickly it will take you to work it all out.

Chapter Thirteen

I can hear a voice way off in the distance.

Only I can't see where it's coming from. I can't see anything.

It's so damn dark and I'm trapped, suspended upside down in the seat of the car.

My instincts tell me that I need to get out. Only, as I reach to unclip my seat belt, it won't budge, my body weight restricting the flex. So I push my hands onto the upturned ceiling for leverage and force myself up with every bit of strength I can summon. Easing my weight against the cushion of the chair until I hear the click.

Then I fall. Slamming down into the small battered space beneath me. My hands pierced by shards of broken glass.

Do not look behind you, I instruct myself as I desperately try to get out.

My hand clawing at the handle, but the door is stuck.

Do not dare look behind you.

Twisting my body, I kick at the window next to me with both feet, frantic now.

I'm going to die here. Trapped inside this mangled metal coffin.

And I don't stop kicking until I hear the smash of glass and feel the icy rush of cold air on my skin.

I'm out. The rain pouring down around me, soaking through my clothes as I drag myself along the wet overgrowth to get away.

Reaching a clearing, exhausted, I roll onto my back, staring up at the night's sky. Taking in the blanket of darkness that's speckled with a glistening spray of a thousand stars.

The sight is strangely beautiful and hypnotic, almost.

Because even though every part of me hurts, I can see it, I'm alive. And I just want to lay there for a little while. To close my eyes for a few minutes and give in to the lull of sleep.

STAY AWAKE! a stern voice inside my head commands.

FOCUS!

I need to concentrate, because something's not right.

My eyes strain to follow the trail of breath that billows out from my mouth, like a thin, white mist dancing in the dark night sky, before they settle on the plume of grey smoke.

For a second I don't register where it's coming from, because the air is so dense with smoke all around me, getting deep into my lungs, making me cough and splutter.

I hold my breath. Looking over towards the car, to where the tiny flames lick at the bonnet.

The car is on fire.

I need to move. I need to get as far away from here as possible.

Crawling again, scampering now across the grass in a bid to get away.

It's too late for you… You're already gone.

And I'm crying. Hysterical, because it's all finally over.

But it all went so horribly wrong. I fucked up and I'll never truly be free.

****

'Rebecca!'

That sharp tone of voice pulls her back from her nightmares.

'The cars on fire...' Rebecca screams, incoherent, her body violently shaking and it takes her a few minutes to realise that it's her voice she can hear cutting through the darkness.

'He's dead!' she says before she can stop herself. Her eyes adjust to the blackness of the bedroom and she realises she's no longer in bed. She's standing by the window. The blinds are wide open and her fingers are curled around the window latch, as if she was trying to get out. Disorientated, she has no memory of how she got here.

But Jamie is standing at her side. His hand on her arm. 'It's okay,' he reassures her, but his voice sounds emotionless, robotic almost. Because he's done this before, a thousand times. Tried to talk her down from the terror of her nightmares. 'No one's dead, Rebecca. You were sleepwalking. It's just another nightmare.'

Despite her hysterics, Rebecca catches the contemptuous tilt to his tone when he says the word *another*. Shaking his arm from her shoulders, she pulls away, aware that he's had more than enough of her dramatics lately.

Breathe, Rebecca, she tells herself, trying to slow the erratic pounding of her heart. Lately her nightmares feel as if they are taunting her, coming every night now. As real and lucid as ever.

Breathe!

'Ella? I need to check on Ella,' Rebecca says instinctively, panic flooding through her, as the need to check her daughter's safety consumes her.

'Ella's just fine. She's sound asleep. I checked on her not even half an hour ago. Leave her to sleep. You need to get some sleep too,' Jamie says, squeezing her arm a little too tightly.

She's not sure if he's giving her an order, or simply trying to reassure her, but either way she gives in to the warmth of his body next to her and allows him to guide her back to their bed.

She knows Jamie is right. Ella is fine and Rebecca should let the child sleep. She'd already disturbed Jamie enough tonight as it was. So she does as she's told and slips back underneath the covers, pulling the blankets up around her. She's shivering now, despite the fact that her skin is still clammy with perspiration. Grateful that the hammering inside her chest has gradually subsided.

'They're getting worse, Rebecca,' Jamie says as he slides in next to her, and she hears the sharp intake of his breath. His tone stern. He's lost patience with her.

'You need to go and see someone. You need to get some help. What if you managed to unlock the window? What would have happened then?'

Rebecca nods, the movement concealed by the darkness, but she can't find her words now. Because she knows Jamie is right. She *is* getting worse. Despite the medication the doctor gave her.

Nothing's working.

She feels as if she's completely losing all control. The panic attacks and the nightmares are getting worse. They had been every night since Ella had been born, she's so sleep deprived that she's physically exhausted by the morning.

And she's losing Jamie now too, she can feel it. The huge void of separation that spans out between them.

Even now, as they lay together in the darkness, just inches from each other, the distance might as well be a million miles.

She feels him shuffle angrily onto his side, pounding the pillow with his fist in annoyance before pretending to fall back to sleep.

Only he isn't asleep.

She can sense it. His body language giving him away as he lays still, rigid with resentment. Concentrating just a little too hard on his breathing. It's stilted. But Rebecca knows that if she tries to reach out to him, he'll feign tiredness and push her away again. Like he does most nights she reached out for him.

So instead she lies in silence, staring up at the ceiling and focusing on the thin stream of light coming in from the street outside, making its way through the gap Jamie had left when he'd pulled the curtains shut again. She tries to distract herself by following the twisted, contorted patterns as they span out across the ceiling.

But even that won't shut the thoughts off inside her head.

Jamie's constant rejection of her bringing out the parts of her she didn't want to admit were still there. Making her feel so insecure and jealous all the time. Making her feel so paranoid that she's not good enough.

Parts of her she'd thought she'd dealt with. That had been long buried.

This new perfect life was supposed to fix all of that.

Only, it wasn't perfect at all. Unless you were on the outside and looking in.

Because that was all part of the illusion, wasn't it? The big house, the fancy cars, the perfect little darling daughter.

The perfect couple.

But it's all built on lies.

Rebecca had really thought that she could do this. That if she impersonated someone for long enough, eventually she'd become them.

Only she can't seem to escape the real her.

She's still in there. Inside of her. Hidden between the newly forming cracks, the old Rebecca is waiting to rear her ugly head again.

She's scared.

Because she knows what she's capable of, she knows what she's done in the past in order to survive.

And maybe somehow Jamie senses it too. That deep down, there is something very wrong with her.

He knows he's made a mistake and she'll never be the woman he wanted her to be.

Chapter Fourteen

Gaslighting.

That's what they call it, Rebecca.

The tactic when one person gains control over another by making them question their reality, their sanity.

But then you'd know all about that, wouldn't you?

Creating realities that aren't even real.

You're a fucking expert at it.

Or at least you tried to be. And for a while, you almost had everyone fooled.

The perfect mother, the perfect wife.

Hiding here, inside your oh-so-perfect life.

Only you never fooled me.

I know exactly who you are. And others will too, soon. Because the cracks are starting to show, Rebecca, and you're falling down them. Sinking into the deep, dark abyss, never to be seen again.

Chapter Fifteen

'So, are you going to tell me what's going on? Because you didn't sound yourself on the phone earlier,' Lisa says as she pours out two glasses of wine for herself and Rebecca, now that Rebecca has managed to settle Ella upstairs in her cot for the evening.

Rebecca sounded upset on the phone, so Lisa turned up armed with a bottle of wine and now that she was here, she figured Rebecca could definitely do with a drink.

'I don't even know where to start with it all, Lisa. This is going to sound crazy…' Rebecca says, gearing herself up to explain, glad that Lisa agreed to come over tonight and keep her company while Jamie was at a late-night meeting.

Suspicious that he was really meeting with Jenna, she needed the company and the distraction, because the truth was she still felt shaken up by the events of the other day.

'Something happened the other day, when I met you at the coffee shop…' she starts and watches Lisa move the glass from her lips mid sip, immediately picking up on the seriousness of Rebecca's tone.

'What do you mean "something happened"? Are you okay?'

Rebecca nods. 'I'm fine. I just got a scare. I think I was followed,' Rebecca says knowing that Lisa won't be happy that she kept this from her, but she hadn't wanted to bring that up too, when there had been so much else going on.

And really, what was there to tell?

'And before you say it, the only reason I didn't tell you sooner was because I wasn't really sure. I didn't actually see anyone. It was more of a feeling.' She takes a deep breath and shrugs. 'But then, the other day, I went to see Jamie at his office, to talk, like you suggested. And to cut a very long story short, it didn't go very well. We had a row and I ended up walking home with Ella. I cut through the park and it was raining heavily. And I could hear someone walking close behind me. So close that I actually stopped to let them pass, only they pushed me and sent me flying to the ground.'

'What the actual fuck…?' Lisa started, unable to hide the alarm in her voice at her friend's confession, before falling silent again and allowing Rebecca to continue. 'You were assaulted?'

'Or maybe I fell? Shit, I don't really know. I know that sounds crazy, trust me, I'm well aware. But it all happened so fast. But this man, he just kept walking, as if it hadn't happened, or as if he hadn't seen me. It was bizarre. So maybe he didn't mean to charge past me, maybe he didn't realise I fell?' Rebecca bit her lip, wondering whether to bite back her next words, but she could tell by Lisa's stern expression that she wasn't going to be able to hold anything back. She needed to tell her the truth.

'I've felt it a few times now. That someone's watching me, that they're following me. But every time I look, there's no one there. It's more of a feeling… as mad as that sounds.'

'Becks, I can't believe you kept this from me. I don't care how busy I am, I'm never too busy to not be there for you. This is serious. Someone's following you? They pushed you? What did Jamie say?'

101

'He insisted I call the police.'

'Good! And what did they say?'

Rebecca took a sip of her wine. Her lack of eye contact was not lost on Lisa.

'You did call them, didn't you, Becks?'

Rebecca shook her head.

'Becks, you have to call the police. Even if you're uncertain. You need to report it.'

'And say what, exactly?' Rebecca replied, thinking how Lisa was starting to sound a lot like Jamie. 'That I'm being followed by the invisible man, by a ghost I haven't actually seen?' Rebecca wondered if perhaps confiding in Lisa was making things worse. She could be just as forthright as Jamie, and the last thing Rebecca needed was them joining forces and ganging up on her, insisting that she reported the incident to the police, despite the fact that she didn't want to involve them.

'It's down to them to look into it. You are the victim here; you have nothing to prove. That's their job...' Lisa tailed off, the genuine concern obvious in her tone.

'No. I don't want the police involved. That will just make everything worse.'

'How can it possibly make everything worse? They might be able to help you, Becks. They know how to deal with these things. Surely it would give you a bit of peace of mind, if nothing else. God, it's no wonder you didn't want to be by yourself tonight.'

Lisa continued, choosing her words carefully, 'I don't want to scare you, but what about your ex?' Lisa said, broaching the subject after gesturing to the scars on Rebecca's arms. 'You said the other day he did that to you? That he hurt you? You don't think it could be him, do you?'

Rebecca shakes her head. 'No. It can't be him. He's dead,' she says finally, taking another mouthful of wine, desperately needing something to take the edge off the conversation. 'He died in a car accident.'

'I'm so sorry,' Lisa said, unsure what to say. Rebecca never spoke much about her life before Jamie, but it was clear that whatever she'd been through hadn't been good.

'He wasn't a good person...' Rebecca shrugs.

'Have you spoken to my brother about any of this? About Mark? About being followed?'

Rebecca shook her head. 'I told him about being followed, but not about Mark. I don't like to drag it all back up. That's not my life anymore. I've moved on. And to be honest, I think your brother thinks I'm losing the plot.' Rebecca laughed, though she wasn't joking. 'In fact, I know he does. After I said I didn't want to call the police, he accused me of making everything up. I think he thinks the medication and post-natal depression is messing with my head.'

'I'm sure he doesn't think that at all. He's probably just worried about you and doesn't know how to deal with it all,' Lisa said, her brow creasing, unconvinced.

'What if he is right though, Lisa? What if this *is* all in my head? I mean, I'm not doing it on purpose. I'm not lying about it. But what if I'm seeing and thinking things that aren't really there? I'm finding this all so hard. I thought I'd be good at it, being a mother, because I love Ella so much, more than I ever thought possible. But I just seem to be making a mess of everything. I just keep fucking everything up. Sometimes I feel like I'm falling apart. What if Jamie's right, and I don't even realise that I'm doing it?'

'Oh, please! You're being too hard on yourself! Look at her.' Lisa nodded down to the monitor where Ella was soundly sleeping now, her face still and soft, her breathing slow and steady. 'You're doing a bloody amazing job. You're a good mum. Just look at her. She's perfect.' It was Lisa's turn to take a big gulp of wine then, shocked at her friend's admission.

Being attacked and followed was one of the last things Lisa had thought that Rebecca would want to talk to her about tonight. She thought she was coming over to cheer her friend up. That they'd talk about her lack of sleep, or what a pickle Ella was being. Anything but this.

'Jamie loves you. Why would he suggest you were making it all up?' Lisa said, trying to piece together the disjointed story. It didn't make any sense.

'Because I accused him of having an affair...' Rebecca said, watching Lisa closely, taking in her expression and her body language, as she tried to gauge if Lisa knew. 'He thought I was saying it to get his attention.'

'What?' Narrowing her eyes, Lisa shook her head adamantly, trying to make sense of what she was being told. 'I mean; there's no way Jamie would cheat on you. Trust me, he might be my brother, and Christ, even I know he's not perfect. I mean to start with, he's a man. That's a pretty big handicap right there…' Lisa quipped, trying to lighten the mood. 'But there's no way on this earth he'd cheat. We spent too many years watching our own mother fall apart after our father walked out and left her completely alone. Me and Jamie had to pick up the pieces and trust me, after how grief-stricken and humiliated our mother was, there's no way Jamie would ever do that to his wife.' Lisa spoke with conviction, but Rebecca still wasn't convinced.

'But why would he accuse you of making all this up? That's crazy!'

Rebecca nods her head. 'Which is exactly what your brother thinks I am. He hasn't said it so directly, but I know that he's thinking it. We're having problems…' she admitted, relieved to say it openly to someone, at last. 'I didn't want to say anything at the café, because, well, he's your brother, and I don't want to put you in an awkward situation, but I don't know who else to talk to. I feel so alone, Lisa.'

'Don't be silly, Becks. You know you can always talk to me. I'm here for you both. I love you both.'

'I know. It's just, I don't even know where to start with it all. Things feel so different between us. Since Ella. It's like, lately, I can't quite reach him. He's been working all hours, hardly ever home and when he is, everything I do seems to irritate him. Or he spends all his time alone in his office. And I can't shake the feeling that he's hiding something from me. He's being so secretive. On his phone all the time…' Rebecca skirted around the issue, not wanting to say out loud what she really wanted to say. As if speaking the words out loud would somehow make it all real. 'And the other night, when we slept with each other… he called out his assistant's name.'

Rebecca finally admitted the thing that had been bothering her the most of all.

It *was* real.

She was certain of it.

'Who? Jenna? No way?' Lisa said, instantly dismissing the idea. 'He was probably still thinking about work, you know how he can never switch off.'

'I really hope so. I mean, tonight, he says he's away on business. And I should believe him – he hasn't given me any reason not to, only I can't shake the feeling that he's lying to me. What if he's with someone else, right now? What if he's with her?'

'There's no way! He wouldn't do that to you, Rebecca. He loves you,' Lisa said with conviction. When Jamie had first told her about wanting to marry Rebecca, Lisa had thought he was acting completely out of character. They'd only been dating for three months, but he was besotted with her and Lisa had never seen him so happy. Despite the early alarm bells that screeched inside her head, she was happy to say now that she'd been wrong.

Jamie and Rebecca were perfect for one another, and now they had Ella too.

There was no way Jamie would cheat.

'Honestly, Becks. You have absolutely nothing to worry about. You've just had a baby. And as beautiful and perfect as my darling little niece is things are bound to feel difficult at first. You're both parents now and that changes everything. It's all new dynamics, and that's bound to add pressure to even the strongest of relationships. But you'll get through it, it's just a stage. As much as my brother can be an arse at times, there's no way he'd ever cheat on you.'

'Do you really think so?' Rebecca sniffed, wiping her nose with her sleeve. She felt stupid now and Lisa's words of reassurance were instantly resonating with her.

Things had been so intense lately, but all she really had to go on was her suspicions and a drunken, mumbled name. It was hardly concrete evidence that something was actually going on. Maybe she really was just overthinking things.

'I don't think so, I know so,' Lisa said vehemently. 'Honestly, you have nothing to worry about. You and Jamie are the modern-day cliché; you're made for each other. The rest of us mere mortals would kill to have just a taster of what you two have.' Lisa smiled then as Rebecca visibly relaxed opposite her. 'You're both adjusting, Becks. That's all. These things take time. The only other woman in Jamie's life is that little one upstairs. Trust me.' Lisa nodded towards the baby monitor that Rebecca had placed on the coffee table in the middle of the room.

'You're right. Of course, you are.' Rebecca shrugged. 'God, I feel so embarrassed that I even questioned it. I think I'm just exhausted. Sometimes I wonder how he even puts up with me.'

'He doesn't put up with you, he loves you. And I love you too,' Lisa said, raising her glass of wine and giving Rebecca a big smile. 'Now, drink up! We've got this bottle of wine to get through and didn't you mention something about a Chinese takeaway, because I don't know about you, but I'm starving. Plus, I've been dying to tell you about this hot delivery guy who came into the office this week. OMG, Becks, he is just about the finest looking man I've ever set eyes on.'

Rebecca couldn't help but laugh. Chinking glasses with her friend, she finally felt herself relaxing for the first time in ages.

Lisa was right.

She was overthinking things, creating problems that weren't even there.

Jamie was out working and having Lisa here was just the tonic she needed.

Chapter Sixteen

It's safe to say that the first night I met Jamie, I caught him off guard.

Because he wasn't looking for anything more than a one-night stand. That's the sort of guy he was.

I could tell by the upmarket hotel bar that we were in, a place that he regularly frequented according to the staff, what sort of women he was used to. Women who weren't any real challenge, who gave no chase. Dolled up to the nines, out in their packs, ready to snare someone who had some real money.

I was different to them all, and I think he realised that right from the very start.

Jamie had looked bored, standing awkwardly with a group of colleagues, who I guessed he was only with that night out of obligation. He was out of place, surrounded by mindless drunken gossip. Voices high-pitched and slurred.

It was one of the group's birthdays by the sounds of it, and they were getting louder and rowdier with every drink they downed, only Jamie seemed somewhat reserved.

Nursing his glass of Scotch, he had a look on his face that said he was hoping it would hurry up and kick in and numb him from the monotonously long evening he had ahead of him.

I saw him scan the bar for a better option and he was spoilt for choice. Women seemed to gravitate around him, huddled in their little packs nearby. Their tables cluttered with bottles of wine and half-finished cocktails. With their caked-on make-up and revealing outfits.

Aware of him of course, because a man like Jamie oozed money. Dressed in an expensive designer suit, adorned with a flashy watch.

At six foot two, with blond hair and ice-blue eyes, he wasn't the type of man who was ever short of attention.

But I could tell by the bored expression on his face that no one really piqued his interest, as I sat there at the far end of the hotel bar, by the wall. My book open, pretending to read while discreetly looking over the top of it and taking everything in.

He caught my eye. I quickly looked away, taking the first opportunity I could get at playing hard to get. In the hope of reeling him in, of spiking his intrigue at the woman sitting in a crowded bar on a Friday night, oblivious to the noise and chaos all around her as she sits on her own reading a book.

Hoping that the book gave him the impression that I'm alone and not waiting for anyone.

It worked, because I could feel his eyes on me as I sipped my drink. Looking back, that was the moment I had him. Intrigued, he let his guard down and let his ego take over. Isn't that what all men do?

Whereas women are generally led by our intuition. Isn't that what they say? *Always trust your gut.*

Because your gut doesn't know how to lie. It just feels. And it feels everything. From the tiniest flicker of emotion to the very extreme. I've always lived by that rule.

And right now, my sense of intuition fared me well, because I knew I'd already sucked him in as he slipped away from the table of rowdy drunken staff and made his way toward the bar. Towards me.

As he stood beside me, I pretended not to notice him scanning the book's cover, keeping my eyes down, pretending to be too enthralled in the story, flicking my way through the pages.

'You look as if you're a million miles away,' he says. I look up and smile at him then, even though we are both aware his opening line is weak.

'I'm an unapologetic bookworm,' I say, shrugging my shoulders, before looking around the packed bar, as I've only just noticed how busy the room's become. 'And I've lost my phone, so…'

'You've read it?' I ask, and he thinks I'm warming to him now that we have something in common. I can see straight through him, see how he's pleased with himself by impressing me with his love of books.

'George Orwell's *Nineteen Eighty-Four*. Absolutely. It's one of my all-time favourites. So accurate, yet so bloody depressing,' he says earnestly.

I can tell he's trying to read me and suss me out. His eyes scan my body for hints I'm welcoming the interaction. But of course, I'm not going to make it easy for him just yet.

He's already thinking I'm a contradiction.

Beautiful, but I play it down. Wearing a simple black dress. Flat shoes. My red, curled hair sweeping loosely just below my shoulders. My face natural, fresh, unlike the other women in the bar who all look as if they've tried too hard.

He drinks me in, licking his lips when he's talking. I know he likes what he sees.

'You know they say that seeing someone reading your favourite book is like the book recommending a person.'

I laugh then, despite myself.

'Yeah, well, I spotted this on one of those "books you must read this lifetime" articles. It's not my usual read. Fascinating though and chilling at the same time. Makes me glad I stay away from social media, if I'm honest,' I say, casually, tucking a strand of loose curls behind my ear.

'All that "Big Brother is watching you"?' He nods, I see the way he's taking in what I'm saying in, probably making a mental note that he won't be able to look me up online like he normally does with the women he meets. Women who make it too easy to find out all about them these days, the ones who lay everything out there for the whole world to see. Their thoughts, their beliefs, their favourite song, their favourite food.

There's no mystery anymore.

As he smiles at me, I know I was right all along. I pose a challenge and he's more than keen to pursue me.

'So, what do you think? A literary genius or did he have a vivid premonition of the future?' he says. I smile and realise that he's not interested in the book, but he wants to keep talking and he's trying to keep my interest on him.

'Well, I'd say he was definitely on to something, I mean look around. Everything we do is documented these days.' I nod towards a group of ladies on the table next to us, taking pouty selfies and no doubt uploading them to their various social media accounts, every one of them distracted by their phones. 'Do they look as though they are "living their best lives"? Because that's what they're telling the world right now, as they update their Facebook status and their Instagram whatever's. The irony, hey?'

'You might be right there. Maybe Old Georgie-boy's book was a warning to us all, 'eh? That it only gets worse from here on in.' He smiles, pursing his mouth thoughtfully. 'Though I must say, it's a very deep read for a place like this. I'm surprised you can concentrate on the book with all the noise? I'd have probably sat out in the lounge area. Unless you're meeting someone, of course?'

'It sucked me in, I thought I'd have a drink and flick through a few pages to see what it's all about. I must have zoned out,' I say. 'Easily done, though, isn't it, when you find a book as good as this.'

'Well, good luck with finishing it. They have a band playing here later, apparently. It's one of my employee's fortieth birthday. And if that lot are anything to go by…' He points over to where the group he'd left are now sitting in a large booth at the back of the room. Already drunk and talking over each other. A couple of the women were dancing. 'Let's just hope none of that lot manages to get hold of a mic. Because believe me, it won't be pretty.'

I laugh, fully aware that he's dropping details about his workforce into the conversation in a bid to impress me.

'Can I get you another drink?' he offers, nodding at the barman before I have a chance to reply and taking out his black credit card, flashing it purposely. I pretend not to see.

'I'll have a Scotch please,' I say to the barman. It's his turn to laugh then, as he shakes his head, holding up two fingers to the barman.

'Scotch? Lady after my own heart. That's my tipple too.'

Before he can pass his card to the barman, I instruct him to put the drinks on my tab. 'No, please, it's on me.'

The look on his face tells me he's not used to women buying him drinks. 'I'm Rebecca,' I say, holding out my hand and shaking his.

'Jamie. Jamie Dawson,' he says.

And he's watching me. Wondering if I'll make the link to Dawson Recruitment. The company he owns in the huge building next door to the hotel we're in. But I give nothing away. Not so much as a flinch.

'Well, it's been a pleasure meeting you, Jamie. But I think I'll make my getaway before that band starts up.' Downing my drink, I gather my things together and stand up. Slipping my handbag over my shoulder and picking up my book as if to leave.

'You don't fancy hanging around for another?' he says, trying to keep the disappointment from his voice, only he doesn't quite achieve it. And he looks embarrassed at appearing too eager, too desperate.

I look at his face and realise these were unfamiliar feelings for him.

'Sorry. I've got an early start,' I say, as the barman places my tab down in front of me and I sign for the drinks I just bought.

'Oh, go on. One more for the road,' he insists, unused to not getting his own way. He nods to the barman to pour us both another, but I'm up from my chair and crossing the room, making my way through the main bar doors without so much as a glance back.

Leaving him there, in a room full of people, feeling suddenly alone again. And as he drains the Scotch, I know that he'll see the scrawled writing I left on the receipt.

Room 117. Rebecca X

I know he'll smile and finish his drink before coming to find me.

That was Jamie Dawson's first mistake.

Trust your gut. That was my mantra. Your intuition is always right.

Because if he *had* trusted his instincts, Jamie would have known I was always too good to be true.

Chapter Seventeen

Rebecca's eyes flicker open.

Dazed and still half asleep, she sits up in bed and stares around the darkened room, wondering what woke her, grateful for the narrow stream of light that pours in from the gap underneath the doorway. Complete darkness has always terrified her.

It's ridiculous how at twenty-eight years old she still needs to sleep with some form of light on.

Especially on nights like tonight, when Jamie wasn't home and she woke in the middle of the night, traumatised and disorientated from yet another nightmare.

Only, it wasn't a nightmare that woke her this time. She's not breathless or covered in a film of sweat. Her heart isn't pounding violently inside her chest, as if it's going to smash through her ribcage.

This is different.

This is something else?

Ella?

Rebecca's heart starts to pound as she strains to listen out for Ella's cries, only to be met with a wall of silence.

Turning, she glances at the clock on her bedside cabinet, the florescent green glow of numbers telling her that it's almost one a.m. Ella's not due for her feed for another few hours. And as her eyes move across to the baby monitor screen, she does a double take at the man standing in Ella's nursery.

Jamie?

Has he come home early?

Every sense in her body is on red alert. Paralysed with fear.

Taller than Jamie, and broader. The sinister way he's just standing there, staring down at Ella, makes the adrenaline surge inside of her, heart pumping frantically inside her chest, and for a second she's completely in shock. Her gaze is stuck on the dark grainy image of a man standing by the side of Ella's cot.

Rebecca opens her mouth to scream, but no sound comes out.

You're asleep. You're still dreaming. Get a fucking grip, Rebecca. Get a fucking grip. This is all in your head. She tries to convince herself but the burn of the thick bile that she can taste on her tongue tells her otherwise.

Her first instinct is to run to Ella, to protect her daughter.

But how could she protect her on her own? She needed to get some help.

Reaching for her mobile phone, she presses frantically at the button, cursing herself as the screen stays black. The battery's dead. She meant to charge it earlier, but she was just too tired to get back out of bed and fetch the charger from where she'd left it in the office earlier.

Rebecca can't think straight. Her head is fuzzy, and her legs are tumbling beneath her as she gets out of the bed.

Her only thought is to keep Ella safe. She needed to make some noise and try to scare this intruder off, so stamping loudly across the room, she reached for the main light, making a clattering noise as she grabbed her dressing gown, smashing the wardrobe door closed behind her.

'Jamie. Someone's in the house,' she calls out, cursing the tremor in her voice that gives away her fear. Praying that the man will hear her and think she's not alone.

She hears footsteps.

Retreating? Or is he coming this way?

Cowering behind the bedroom door, Rebecca prays that he is leaving. Her head up against the wooden panel, she listens carefully cursing herself for not bringing the monitor.

There's nothing now. No sound at all. And suddenly she's gripped with fear that he's taken Ella.

MOVE!

Picking up the china figurine from the side of her dressing table, a statue of a woman and child, a gift from Lisa when Ella had been born, she clutches it tightly in her hand, opening the bedroom slowly. She shouts out again.

'I've called the police. They're on their way.'

When she's met with silence, her entire body trembles with fear. She has to get to Ella. No matter what.

She moves, rapidly, ready to take whatever she's faced with.

Ready to fight. Despite her fear, Rebecca is fuelled by something else.

Something far more powerful than she ever realised she possessed. A mother's instinct, to protect their child no matter what. It was like an unspoken superpower she'd gained since giving birth. She knew that if she had to, she'd kill for Ella. She'd fight to the death.

Pushing the nursery door ajar, she peered through the narrow gap until she could see the room fully.

Dark and empty. She stepped inside, rushing to the cot, and almost collapses in a heap on the floor when she sees Ella, her arms stretched out above her head as she blissfully sleeps. She stands shivering for a few minutes more, watching Ella's chest rise and fall, fighting the urge to wake her up, to pull her into her arms and hold her close. To breathe in that familiar sweet smell of hers.

The anxiety in her stomach is quickly replaced with a bubbling warmth of love, then quickly she's overcome again by fear as she rubs at her forehead. The steady throb behind her eyes brings her back to reality.

Did she just imagine seeing someone standing in here? She wonders, as she scans the room. Checking inside the wardrobe before squatting down and looking underneath the cot.

Had she been hallucinating? Rebecca wanted to cry, terrified of what was happening to her, of what she was becoming.

Ever since Ella came along, it was as though every tiny fear inside of her had become magnified. Like a thick fog of uncertainty had descended on her, making her see monsters that aren't really there.

For a second, she's on the outside looking in and she sees how crazy she must appear, standing in her daughter's nursery at this time of the morning, a china ornament clutched tightly in her hand.

She knows she should go back to bed, even though she knows there will be no sleep for her now, that her demons have all come alive inside her head.

But as she makes her way back to her bedroom, she hears another noise.

Chapter Eighteen

She definitely heard it this time.

A loud bang, then a scrape of a chair against the tiled floor. Someone was downstairs, in the kitchen.

Her first instinct is to move, to run... to get Ella and get out of the house to safety, but her feet feel like lead, as if they'd been welded to the floor beneath her.

'Jamie?' she calls out tentatively, her voice tinged with hope as she makes her way down the stairs and towards the kitchen, trying to convince herself that he's come home from his business trip early. That he's too wired for sleep, so he's fixed himself a large Scotch before he goes to bed.

Even through her fear, she can imagine what he'll say when she confronts him. How he'll tell her that she's being stupid. Crazy. Walking around the house in the middle of the night and acting so paranoid.

Only, Jamie doesn't reply, and she feels the fear gripping at her insides.

She knows it now, without uncertainty. She's not alone, someone's here. Taking a deep breath, she reaches out and places her hand on the door handle. Trying to stay rational, as her mind retraces her steps from earlier. How she'd locked all the doors and windows before she went to bed. She'd set all the alarms.

No one could get in here, Rebecca's rational mind tells her. Yet, still her skin is prickled with goosebumps, and she knows she can't just stand here all night. She pushes the kitchen door wide open with much more bravado than she feels, her hand instantly going for the light switch just inside the doorway.

The sudden brightness startling her, she drops the ornament on the kitchen floor, jumping as the china smashes loudly against the tiles, breaking into tiny fragmented pieces.

In the sudden light, she sees that the room is empty. A chair has been pulled out from the table, as if someone had been sitting there but the room is deserted.

In her peripheral vision, she catches a movement at the side of the room, the white fitted blinds dancing rhythmically with the breeze, pushing a cool flurry of air into the room.

The blood inside her veins turns icy cold with fear, as she realises that the patio doors are wide open.

Someone has been here. They were here, in Ella's room.

She wasn't imagining anything.

Scrambling across the kitchen and sifting through the drawer beside the sink, she rooted around for something to protect herself with. Picking up the largest knife, her fingers curl around the handle as she holds it out in front of her, willing herself to edge towards the doorway.

She feels suddenly weightless now, so scared of what might be out there that her body feels as if it's floating. Aware that Ella is alone upstairs without her.

Taking another step towards the open door, she stares out into the darkness. The only noise she can hear is the deafening sound of blood whooshing inside her ears as her eyes try to adjust to the dull stream of light that beams out from the kitchen. Illuminating, ever so slightly, the patio and a few feet of the lawn's edge.

She gasps as her eyes adjust, and she sees him.

The same dark, shadowy figure she'd seen in Ella's nursery. He's real, here's here. Hiding up against the hedgerow under a cloak of shadows.

The crack of a breaking branch pulls Rebecca from her trance. She realises it's the sound of twigs snapping beneath footfall. He's moving. *Is he coming towards her?* She wonders. No! He's not. He's running away?

The knife. She's still holding the knife, she realises, tightening her grip around the handle, fighting to steady her violently shaking arm through. She can't just let him leave. Because whoever he is, he'll be back. And next time Ella might not be safe.

Rebecca finds herself moving on autopilot. It's fight or flight, and following her instincts, she's chosen to fight. Before she knows it, her bare feet are padding across the dewy wet grass, towards the back gate, towards him.

Rebecca is vaguely aware that she's chasing him. It's become like a fucked-up game of cat and mouse. He's teased his prey, but now his target is fighting back.

Only the silhouette is moving too fast, and she can't keep up. He's too fast. Reaching the back gate in just seconds, the wooden door slams violently behind him and in an instant, he's gone.

Rebecca knows there's no way that she can catch him now and screeches as she loses her footing, her ankle giving way beneath her as she stumbles. There's a twist and the pain is so agonising she crumples like a rag doll into a heap on the grass, landing with her hands splayed out in front of her to break her fall.

But she forgets about the knife still clutched tightly in her shaking fist, and the fall causes the sharp, jagged blade to slice through the flesh of her palm.

She lets forth another loud scream as her gaze moves to the back gate.

Because it's opening again, and the dark figure is back, striding towards her.

Only she can't move now, she's helpless. Broken and bleeding on the floor, she can't even get up. Her ankle's too weak for her to stand. So she shouts and screams and prays that someone will hear her. That Lisa might hear her. That someone will come to her aid as she rolls across the grass verge, desperate to get away from the intruder as she army crawls her way back towards the house, her fingers digging into the wet, cold earth, blood seeping down her wrist from the cut.

Despite her fear, she still has the knife in her grasp and knows she will use it if she has to.

And she might have to. Because suddenly he is on her, his hands wrenching her up, dragging her roughly onto her feet.

She hears a voice, the words blurred as she starts to scream, louder this time, wild and ferocious like a wounded animal.

Terrified, her survival instinct kicking in, she lashes out, clawing and biting and hitting out as hard as she can.

Fighting for her life.

For Ella's life.

But the man is too strong for her, his arms wrapping tightly around her, overpowering her as she struggles to wriggle free.

And for a split second he loses his grip.

It's enough. She holds up the knife and plunges it towards his chest.

'Rebecca! *REBECCA!*' Broken out of her trance, she looks down, looks clearly at the man for the first time, her eyes fixed on the blood that's spreading out across his shoulder.

'Jamie?' she screams, the pain in her voice evident. As she sees the twisted expression of pain flashing across his face. 'What have I done? What the hell have I done?'

Chapter Nineteen

'Blood always makes things look a lot worse than it is,' the paramedic said, in an attempt to reassure Rebecca, as she sat nervously on her sofa, tugging at the frayed edges of the bandage which had been wrapped around the jagged cut on her hand.

She could see Jamie out of the corner of her eye.

He was angry with her.

He wasn't voicing it openly, but she could feel it coming off him in waves.

'Here, you're in shock. Let's keep this on for a bit, and keep you warm,' the paramedic said, placing a blanket around Rebecca's shoulders to shield her from not only the cold but also the sight of her torn, blood-soaked nightdress.

'You'll need to get to A&E after you've made your statement,' the paramedic said then, looking at Jamie, aware of the tension in the room as he stood holding his hand over the bandage wrapped around his shoulder. The wound where Rebecca had nicked him with the knife.

She'd gone for his chest.

In her trance-like state, the attack had been frenzied, but luckily Jamie had acted quickly, twisting his body as the knife came towards him.

And now the house was crawling with paramedics and police officers and Rebecca was terrified that they're all here. Snooping around and asking her questions. And it's all her fault.

'It's just a flesh wound, but I'd say you'd need a few stitches. You've been lucky, really. Both of you.'

'Lucky isn't a word I'd use tonight. I'll go later,' Jamie said tightly, staring at the lead officer who came into the room, ready to take their statements now that Rebecca had been seen to.

'But first I'm going to make some tea. Rebecca?'

Rebecca nodded her head, aware how angry he was with her. How exhausted he was from all of this. How exhausted he was of her.

'Tea, Officer Blythe?' Jamie asks.

'No, thank you,' Officer Blythe declines, taking a seat opposite Rebecca as the paramedics pack up their things and leave them alone.

'How are you doing, Rebecca?' Officer Blythe asks, aware that she was still in shock as he took in her ghostly white complexion, the frightened expression on her face still registering the terror of tonight's ordeal. Her hands, resting in her lap, were visibly shaking.

'I just want to know who he is? And what he wants? He was in Ella's nursery. Shit! What if something had happened to her? What if he took her?' The high-pitched screech in the back of Rebecca's throat was more of a plea than a statement.

Officer Blythe nodded. 'You and Ella are safe now, Rebecca,' he reassured her. 'Has anyone else got a key to your property? A cleaner? A family member perhaps?'

'No. No one,' Rebecca said with certainty, before quickly adding, 'only Lisa, my sister-in-law. She lives next door.' Watching as Blythe made a note in his notepad, Rebecca added, 'But she's got nothing to do with this. It was a man I saw tonight. Not Lisa… I gave you his description.'

Again, Officer Blythe nodded his head.

'This is all just procedure, Mrs Dawson. We'll send a couple of officers round and check that Lisa hasn't seen or heard anything tonight. We can also check that she still has her key in her possession too. Just to be on the safe side,' the officer confirmed. 'Rebecca, we're going to do everything in our power to catch him. You have my word on that. I have my officers searching the garden and the rest of the street. There are patrol cars searching the neighbouring roads too. You and Ella are safe now, whoever broke in here can't get to you now,' Officer Blythe said, offering the woman a small reassuring smile as Jamie came back into the room carrying two mugs of tea.

They lived in a wealthy area of Kensington. The detached houses on the street were set back with large gardens and ample driveways.

'Trust me, if he's still out there, Rebecca, we'll find him. Especially once we get a clearer image of whoever he is from your security footage,' Officer Blythe added, nodding at another officer to set up the surveillance footage on the TV in the lounge so they could go through it together.

He hadn't disclosed the investigation's findings so far to the couple, because the truth was that he and his team had nothing to go on as yet. There was no sign of a break in. No footprints or fingerprints anywhere.

The intruder had somehow managed to get away almost without a trace. Whoever it was had covered their tracks expertly, knowing exactly what they were doing.

'And you didn't see anyone in the street when you returned home, Mr Dawson, is that right? There was no sight of anyone leaving your garden just before you entered?' the officer said, directing his question now to Jamie, his tone slightly stilted. He was more than aware of the building tension in the room.

Jamie shook his head.

'No. I didn't see anyone. All I heard was Rebecca's screams. That's why I ran through to the back garden. I thought someone was hurting her. Christ, when I found her on the grass, bleeding and covered in mud, I didn't know what to think. I've never seen her look so scared. It was like she was in a trance...'

'You don't believe me,' Rebecca said, raising her eyes, her voice almost a whisper.

Whatever he said, he didn't believe her.

He thought this was all just another one of her nightmares. That she'd been sleepwalking. That she'd simply imagined this intruder tonight.

That this was all in her head.

'Rebecca. I'm not saying don't believe you. I saw how scared you were, I believe that you thought you saw someone.'

'*Thought* I saw someone, Jamie. In our house. In our daughter's nursery. It was real.'

'Your nightmares always feel real, you've said it yourself enough times. And what about the other day? The man in the park you claimed attacked you? Was he real too?'

'You were attacked, Mrs Dawson? Recently?' Officer Blythe interrupted the couple as he picked up on the undercurrent of their stilted conversation.

'Yes... No... I don't know,' Rebecca admitted. 'I know this sounds crazy, but I'm not sure. I think someone pushed me, but I'm not certain. I mean, it all happened so quickly, and I wasn't really paying attention. Maybe I fell...'

'So, you didn't call it in?' Officer Blythe said, raising his brow questioningly at Rebecca, before scanning back over the notes he'd already made. He was unaware of any previous incidents reported at this address even though he'd asked control for a background on his way there.

'You should have let me call the police,' Jamie spat.

'There wasn't anything to report. I didn't even get a good look at whoever it was, and it all happened so quickly,' Rebecca explained, searching her husband's eyes for some understanding, some compassion at least. But all she could see was Jamie's embarrassment that they were having this argument in front of the officer.

'So, you can't describe this person?' Officer Blythe asked, poising his pen again, hopeful of any additional information or detail about the perpetrator to his statement. 'Can you describe him to me? His build? What he was wearing? Anything at all?'

Rebecca shook her head. 'No. Not really. He was dressed all in black, his hood pulled up around his face. But that's to be expected isn't it? It was raining heavily. He was tall, I guess, and broad. I mean I could be describing half the male population here...'

'And tonight? Can you describe what you saw tonight?'

Rebecca shook her head sadly.

'The image on the baby monitor wasn't clear, it was too grainy,' Rebecca said with a shrug. 'Outside in the garden, it was too dark to make out his face. I could only see his silhouette. He was tall and broad too...' She shuddered, her voice trembling at the recollection. She'd felt the menace coming off the man in waves as he stood there, deadly still under the blanket of darkness at the edge of the garden, watching her.

'You think it might be him. The same man? That he followed me home? He knows where I live?' Rebecca asks Officer Blythe.

'We don't know anything just yet. We just need to get all the information we can to piece everything together and do our best to catch this man,' Officer Blythe said, sensing that Rebecca was holding something back, that she wasn't telling him everything.

'Is there anything else you can tell me, Rebecca? No matter how trivial, or how silly you think it might sound...' Blythe said gently, watching the couple closely as they exchanged a look.

Rebecca spoke first.

'I've been feeling as if I was being watched. When I went out. If I took Ella for a walk in her pushchair, or if I went to the supermarket, I kept getting the feeling that I was being followed. But every time I turned and looked, there was no one there. I tried to convince myself I was imagining it, but then I started feeling that someone was watching me inside the house too.'

'Someone inside your home? Can you elaborate on that? Were there signs of a break in?' Officer Blythe waited patiently for Rebecca to continue.

They still hadn't been able to discover a point of entry for the intruder which was troubling him greatly. Even more so with what he was hearing now. It was starting to become very apparent that tonight may have been a targeted attack.

'I know how it sounds weird. I mean, nobody can get in here, can they? It's just this horrible feeling…'

'I can't do this,' Jamie said suddenly, his voice coming out louder than he anticipated. 'I can't just sit here while we waste this police officer's time.' Jamie shook his head at Rebecca, before directing his attention back towards Officer Blythe. 'Rebecca's been having a hard time lately. Since Ella. They don't tell you any of that, do they? The doctors and midwives at the hospital, when you're getting ready to go home with a new baby. About the shitstorm that could be waiting for you. Rebecca has been struggling. She's not been well.'

Officer Blythe nodded his head, keeping his judgement to himself as he waited for Jamie to explain.

'She was diagnosed with post-natal depression. She hid it from me at first, the fact that the doctor prescribed her with some medication, antidepressants,' Jamie said, his tone tinged with sadness. 'I didn't realise how bad she was until now.'

'Jamie! You saw me. You saw the state I was in. How scared I was. How can you think I just made it all up?' Rebecca said, fighting back her tears once again.

'Because that's all I saw, Rebecca. You. There was no one else out there. You were hallucinating. And I know you believe what you saw was real, but it wasn't...'

'Mr and Mrs Dawson.' Sensing the rising tension between the couple, Officer Blythe held his hand up to silence them both and restore some normality. 'If it's okay with you both, I'd like to have a look at this CCTV tape?'

As the room fell silent, Officer Blythe, Jamie, and Rebecca all stared ahead, eyes fixed to the TV screen as another officer picked up the remote control and pressed play.

All of them thinking the same —this security footage was their only real lead. Everything was hanging on what they were about to watch.

Soon they'd have all the answers they needed.

Rebecca was convinced she'd seen someone out there tonight, but the doubts were creeping in.

What if she'd imagined it after all and the tapes proved she'd made the whole thing up?

What if she really was going crazy?

Chapter Twenty

Lurching forward in her seat to get a better look at the television screen, Rebecca cringes as she recognises the figure running across the screen.

It's her.

Looking vulnerable and exposed, dressed only in her nightdress and dressing gown, as she runs across the lawn. Her back to the camera, the knife gripped tightly in her hand.

It had been stupid of her to try to confront the intruder by herself, alone in the dead of night, while Ella lay helplessly in her cot. She knew that now.

Only she hadn't been able to hold back the need to protect herself and her child from whoever it was that had been lurking out there.

Waiting now, she's holding her breath and her heart is pounding again inside her chest as she braces herself to see him.

She'll prove to Jamie that he's wrong. That she didn't imagine any of this.

It was real.

She narrows her eyes, seeking out his silhouette among the dark, grainy footage, but the seconds turn into minutes and there's no other movement on the screen.

There's no one there.

No one in the room speaks. No one says a word.

Until Rebecca has no choice but to break the silence herself.

'I don't understand why we can't see him? He should be there? Over by the bushes?' Shaking her head in confusion, she points to the corner of the screen, to where the man should be standing. 'Maybe he's a little further back than the camera reached…'

But she can see the fence and the hedgerow that had been behind him, so it didn't make any sense. If he was there, the camera would have captured his image.

'He was there. Right there.' Rebecca gets up from her chair and taps at the screen, irritated that the footage keeps cutting out, the recording jumping every few seconds, sending a series of thick, jagged black lines across the screen. 'What's wrong with the picture? Why does it keep doing that?'

She knows what Jamie and the officer must be thinking.

That she was lying all along.

That this was all inside her head.

'It's the signal. It does it all the time. The company said they would send an engineer over to have a look at it…' Jamie sighed. 'But it's only the picture *quality*, Rebecca. It doesn't affect the actual recording. We would have seen him by now, surely, if he was there. Grainy or not.'

'Go back,' Rebecca insists to the other police officer. 'Rewind it. It's skipped too far ahead.'

Seeing Officer Blythe nod his head in permission, the officer rewinds the tape and plays it again.

But not before Rebecca sees his dubious expression, the doubt lingering in his eyes.

He's just humouring her.

He doesn't believe her now either.

Furious, Rebecca turned back to the screen, flinching as she sees herself awkwardly stumble forward, her arms stretched out in front of her, before landing in a heap on the damp, dewy grass. She sees the knife slicing through her skin of her hand.

'I don't understand. He was right there. *Right there!*' Speaking with such conviction, Rebecca jabs her finger angrily against the glass as another thick black line scrawls across the screen. 'What's wrong with this bloody thing?'

About to stop the recording, Rebecca holds her breath as she watched the figure come in through the back gate.

It's Jamie.

And then she sees herself just as Jamie had. Unable to recognise that it's Jamie, she fights him wildly. Raising the knife and striking out.

Jamie is right. It's as if she's not even present, it's as if she's in a dream like state.

But she couldn't have been sleepwalking, could she?

'I saw him. He was real?' Rebecca says quietly, clearly doubting herself, as she dragged her gaze away from the TV screen and stared intently at Officer Blythe. Willing him to talk. To say something. Hoping that he would have the answers.

Only it was Jamie who spoke.

'Just stop, will you, Rebecca! Please!' Standing up. His voice shaking with emotion, mirroring the angst on his face. 'This isn't real. None of this is real. The attack the other day. This intruder tonight.' Locking his jaw tightly, Jamie's brow furrowed, just as it always did when he was angry. Which always set Rebecca immediately on edge. 'When are you going to admit it? You are not well!'

Pausing, Jamie took a deep breath to calm himself. Aware who was present, he tried to regain control of his temper. 'No one can get in here. No one is watching you! This has got to stop, Rebecca, because next time someone's going to get really hurt.'

Rebecca saw it then. The look that Jamie exchanged with the officer. Like an unspoken secret code had passed between them.

She knew Blythe agreed with Jamie. That they didn't believe her.

Instead of proving her innocence and helping them identify the intruder, the security footage was only proving to serve against her.

They'd only played it to her to prove their point.

They thought she was a danger to herself. To Ella.

She couldn't breathe, her chest constricted as the pressure inside of her rapidly spread out through her entire body.

Hot and dizzy suddenly, she recognised the onset of another panic attack.

Breathe!

'Mrs Dawson? Are you all right? Shall we call the paramedics back?' Officer Blythe says, now also on his feet as he rushes to Rebecca's aid.

Rebecca shakes her head, doubled over, concentrating on taking slow deep breaths, doing her best to fight it. *Not now,* she tells herself. Not right now, when they already think she's going mad.

Calm once more, she stands.

'What if someone's tampered with the tapes?' she asks, her eyes pleading with the officer now to believe her, desperate to make him realise that she was telling the truth. 'It's the only feasible explanation. It would explain why there are lines on the screen and why the recording keeps jolting about?'

'We can take the tapes in and have them analysed, Mrs Dawson—'

'Jesus, Rebecca, please!' Jamie interrupts Blythe, shaking his head now, unable to hide his frustration. 'We can't all keep pandering to these crazy notions of yours. There wasn't anyone there. When are you going to accept that?'

Rebecca stared at the two men.

'Someone was here, in our house, Jamie. In our daughter's nursery. Why would I lie about that?'

Right now, her only concern was Ella. She was the only person that mattered.

'You know what, this whole conversation is pointless. I'm going to check on my daughter.'

'You don't need to keep checking on her, Rebecca. She's fine, she's sleeping.' Jamie nodded to the baby monitor in the centre of the coffee table as usual. He laid a conciliatory hand on her arm to try to calm her down, but his small movement only seemed to ignite her temper further.

'Don't tell me what I can and can't do with my own child. Someone's got to keep her safe, because you don't seem to be taking any of this seriously.'

Yanking Jamie's hand from her arm, Rebecca couldn't get out of the room quickly enough.

Scared that what Jamie and Officer Blythe were saying was true.

What if she had been hallucinating?

What if she really was losing her mind?

Chapter Twenty-One

Taking a slow deep breath, she grips the wooden railings of Ella's cot in a bid to steady her trembling hands.

Rebecca knows she needs to stay calm.

Jamie was right. Ella was still fast asleep and the last thing she wants right now is Ella to wake and pick up on her own troubled mood, no matter how much she wanted to hold her close right now. Adding a crying baby to the already fraught atmosphere wouldn't be fair to any of them.

The irony wasn't lost on her though, as she stared down at Ella's tiny hands, relaxed at her side, her chest rhythmically rising and falling with each slow, laboured breath.

Tonight, of all nights, was the first since she'd been born that Ella had slept through her night feed.

Rebecca was thankful for that, relieved that Ella was completely unaware of the drama that had unfolded around her tonight.

And she knew she needed to calm down before Ella awoke. That she needed to use the time wisely to get her head straight.

Because all that mattered right now was Ella.

It still shocked her how much love she felt for her daughter. How this one tiny person could invoke such strong feelings within her.

It was probably the first time since she was a little girl, that Rebecca had felt anything like it.

This real, genuine love had floored her.

She could still remember the icy terror that had swept through her as she'd eyed the blurred blue letters on the pregnancy test she'd done less than a year ago. How she hadn't trusted the word that presented itself to her. *PREGNANT.*

Not until she'd gone out and bought another four tests, which had all confirmed the first test was true. She *was* pregnant. That word had sent her head into a complete spin. Just the thought of having a child growing inside of her, a life, had both terrified her and excited her at the same time.

And she'd been petrified from that moment on that it would all be so cruelly snatched from her.

Because she didn't deserve to be a mother. To have her own child. Not after what she'd done.

So, she'd kept the pregnancy as her own little secret, just for a couple of days. So she could work out what she was going to do. Pretending that her morning sickness, sudden exhaustion, and the fact that she was turning down alcohol all down to a mild stomach bug.

Only Jamie had been suspicious, and she'd been careless and not hidden the tests deep enough in the kitchen bin.

She'd told Jamie that she'd been trying to let the news sink in, that she'd been getting her head around the fact that she was going to have a baby, before she told him. Part of that had been true.

But there was something else stopping her; she knew that the minute she told Jamie, it would all be real. There would be no going back. She'd have no choice but to go through with the pregnancy then.

Having a child of her own terrified her.

She wasn't capable of looking after it, she wasn't capable of giving it everything it would need.

And her fears about Jamie had been right. From the second that he found out Jamie had been ecstatic. Wanting to know every detail of her pregnancy. All about her cravings, and the chronic morning sickness she endured, and the first time she felt Ella move inside her.

He had been excited enough for them both.

And quickly Rebecca had felt as if the baby wasn't just hers anymore, knowing that she would be forced to share all those precious moments that she'd wanted to quietly savour and relish while she got used to the fact that her world was about to completely change.

She worried that Jamie would see her deepest insecurities, that she wouldn't be a very good mother.

But as soon as Ella was born it felt like Rebecca had never been without her. From the second the midwife had laid Ella in her arms and Rebecca had drunk in Ella's red, squishy face. Her tiny pink mouth wide open as she squealed loudly, her tiny plump hand gripping at her mother's finger, letting her know in every sense of the word that now she was here, everything would forever change.

And she *had* changed everything.

Ella had changed Rebecca.

She'd ignited something deep within her that wanted to protect Ella with every ounce of her being. No matter what.

Calmer now, Rebecca tiptoed over to the nursery doorway, lingering at the top of the stairs as she listened to the muffled voices in the hallway.

They were whispering about her.

Their voices were too low to make out any words, but Rebecca could imagine what Jamie was telling the officers. How he thought she was unstable. How she was acting crazy. The night terrors and panic attacks, and now this. Now she was seeing things that weren't really there. She'd stabbed him with a knife.

But she *had* seen someone tonight. She was sure of it, though even she could see how unbelievable that might appear now.

How could there be no trace of him on the tapes?

Rebecca could hear another voice then, a woman's.

Then more hushed whispers.

Wondering if it was another officer with an update on the intruder, thinking that perhaps they'd found him, Rebecca moved quickly, hurrying back down the stairs, stopping in her tracks when she saw Lisa looking up at her.

'Becks! Are you okay? I heard the police sirens. Then an officer came to my door. I came over as soon as I heard,' Lisa said, rushing to her sister-in-law's side and throwing her arms around her as Rebecca came down the last couple of steps.

'I'm fine. Ella's fine. Did you hear anything? Did you see anything?' Rebecca asked, grateful for Lisa's concern.

Lisa will believe her. She's sure of it.

'Sorry, no. An officer told me what happened. I checked and I still have your key. They had a look around the place and searched the back garden. But they didn't find anyone,' Lisa said, pulling away from

Rebecca to scan her face, worried. 'You poor thing, Becks. You must have been petrified…'

Rebecca started to speak, but eyed Jamie standing with his car keys in his hand, holding her coat.

'Where are you going?' she asked, her eyes darting from Jamie to the police officer.

'Lisa's going to keep an eye on Ella for us. We're going to go to the hospital,' Jamie said, his gaze not meeting hers.

'So, you can have your stitches?'

Jamie doesn't answer, and she guesses he's still angry with her, so Rebecca dutifully takes her coat, wrapping it around her shoulders. 'Why didn't you let the paramedics take you when they offered?'

'She hasn't woken for her feed yet. She might sleep through, but if she does wake, her milk's made up in the fridge,' Jamie continued, dismissing Rebecca's question as he continues reciting a list of instructions to Lisa.

'When she wakes, you just need to warm the bottle through, and she'll need changing too…'

'Don't worry. We'll be fine. I know I've been slacking the past week or so, but I had lots of practise when you first got home from the hospital. I think I've got it covered,' Lisa said, holding her hands up to show that she had everything under control. 'Take however long you need. I'm sure you'll feel better after you've seen a doctor, Becks.' Lisa steps forwards and gives Rebecca a kiss on the cheek.

Only Rebecca steps back and shakes her head.

'No, it's not me that's seeing the doctor. It's Jamie.' Wondering why Lisa is directing her concern towards her. It's Jamie who has the bandage wrapped around his shoulder.

'I'm fine.' She holds up her bandaged hand before catching the look on Lisa's face that tells Rebecca there's something deeper going on.

And when she looks to Jamie for reassurance, there's none. He still won't meet her eye.

'What do I need to see a doctor for? I don't need a doctor?' Defensive now, as she was met with silence. 'Can someone tell me what hell is going on?'

'Please don't make this any harder than it already is, Rebecca. I think we should get you checked out, that's all. Just to be on the safe side.'

'Checked out? For what?'

Jamie shook his head.

'You're not right. Surely you can see that. Please, think of Ella.'

Rebecca almost laughed.

'I *am* thinking of Ella. She's all I ever think about. I'm staying here. In my home. With my daughter. I don't need to see a doctor. The police need to do their job and find this man, because he's still out there.' She raised her voice now, incensed by how the situation was playing out. How suddenly all the suspicion and concern was aimed towards her.

'For Christ's sake, Rebecca. Will you stop being so damn difficult! I'm trying to help you here.'

'If you want to help me, then you'd listen to what I'm telling you. You'd believe me.'

'We have listened to you. And we all saw the tape. There was no one else out in that garden with you. There was nobody in the house.' Jamie looked genuinely sad, his eyes filling up as if he was about to cry, though he quickly regained his composure. 'You're not well, Rebecca.'

Rebecca looked at Lisa and then to the officer, hoping that someone would speak up for her, only they both continued to stand in silence, which only confirmed that they agreed with Jamie.

They were all against her.

'Can't you look at the tapes properly? Someone must have tampered with them. Please, I know how it looks. But I saw him. He was real!' Begging now, unashamedly, Rebecca pleaded with Officer Blythe because he was her only hope.

'Maybe a visit to hospital wouldn't be such a bad idea, Rebecca. You've had a nasty shock tonight,' he said gently, trying to talk Rebecca into going of her own free will.

The conversation was stopped by a rap at the door and Officer Blythe excused himself to open it.

Rebecca eyed the two officers out on the path, as they all spoke quietly among themselves.

She could only pick up on a few sentences.

'There was no sign of any of the doors and windows being forced for him to gain entry. There's nothing that we've found that is likely to provide any traces of any DNA. No clothing left behind. No cigarette ends. No footprints in the mud outside.'

Then there were hushed whispers again, before the second officer glanced in Rebecca's direction.

They were talking about her. Officer Blythe was telling them that Rebecca was going to hospital. They thought this was all her. That tonight had been in her head.

She laughed then, the sound loud and maniacal, exploding from her mouth.

'This is some kind of a joke. Can't you see what's happening here? Someone is doing this on purpose. They are deliberately making you think I'm going mad. That's what this is. So that they get away with it,' Rebecca screeched, pushing past the three officers, and ignoring Jamie's instructions to come back into the house.

That she was making a spectacle of herself.

'If you people aren't going to take my claims seriously, if you aren't prepared to help me protect my daughter, then I bloody will.' She sped out into the middle of the road, her coat sliding off her shoulders as she ran.

Rebecca knew she should feel cold, but all she felt was the rage surging inside her as she stood there with her blood stained nightdress exposed to the neighbours that had come out of their homes to see what all the commotion was about.

She didn't care what she looked like. Let them look. Let them stare.

'I know you're out here,' she screamed. 'And I'm not afraid of you!'

'Come on, Rebecca. You must be freezing, let's get you back inside, yeah?'

She could feel Officer Blythe at her side then, trying to gently coax her back into the house.

'Like you give a shit about me? I'm telling you the truth, why won't you help me?'

Now she could feel Jamie beside her as well.

'Come on, Rebecca, please. This is just madness. Everyone's looking at you.' Jamie placed a hand firmly on her arm as he tried to lead her back into the house, away from the crowd.

Madness.

The word ringing repeatedly then in her ears. Unsettling something inside her.

Was this madness? The sane part of her brain told her that it was. But her anger got the better of her.

'Let them fucking look. Because someone needs to do something. *HE'S STILL OUT THERE!*' she bellowed into the darkness. 'I'm not scared of you, you know. You're a coward. Hiding from us all. Running away! Come on, show yourself, you bastard!'

'Rebecca!' Jamie said, his voice stern as he held his wife's arms down at her side, gently trying to walk her back inside.

But Rebecca knew what he was doing. He just wanted to shut her up. He didn't want her to make a scene and have all the neighbours talking about them.

'Get your fucking hands off me.' Striking out with her fist as she yelled, Rebecca twisted her body to escape, so that she could at least make a run for the stairs, her only thoughts being that she now needed to get to Ella, to get to her daughter. This was all just one big conspiracy so that they could get her away from Ella. Because they didn't think she was a fit and capable mother. They thought she'd become a risk.

Only Jamie is too strong.

'Get off me!' she screams again, having lost all control now. The thick anger bubbled away in the pit of her stomach as she shrieked loudly, fighting with everything she had to break free of Jamie's grip.

'Rebecca, you need to calm down...' Officer Blythe says softly, trying to intervene, but Rebecca doesn't hear him. She doesn't hear anything.

She lashes out one more time at Jamie, but misses, her fist connecting with the police officer's face. The crack of cartilage silences them all for a few seconds, then Rebecca is suddenly surrounded by all three police officers as they restrain her.

'Rebecca Dawson, I'm detaining you under section 136 of the Mental Health Act,' Officer Blythe says reading Rebecca her rights, almost apologetically.

He has no other choice.

The woman had already accidentally cut herself and her husband, and now she'd struck an officer in front of a street full of onlookers. It's clear that Rebecca Dawson is out of control, so Officer Blythe has to detain her for her own safety.

'Please, I didn't mean to do that. I'm sorry. I just wanted you to listen to me...' Rebecca is crying as two officers lock her arms down by her sides, before leading her towards what looks like a patrol car.

'You can't arrest me, I haven't done anything wrong?'

'We're not arresting you, Rebecca. We're going to get you some help. Our main priority right now is to make sure that you're okay,' one of the officers said, as he led Rebecca towards the waiting ambulance.

The officer must have made them wait outside. Already anticipating that this might happen. They were determined to get her to hospital no matter what, that was clear to her now.

'You are going to be properly assessed and given the adequate care, should you need it.'

Rebecca noted how the officer's words were spoken so slowly and precisely, as if he thought she might not be able to comprehend what was going on around her.

But he was right. Part of her couldn't understand what was happening. This was all madness.

'Jamie, tell them. Please. Tell them this is all wrong,' she said, pleading with Jamie to say something, do something. Only he didn't say a word.

Because this was what he wanted, wasn't it? Rebecca realised now. This was all his idea.

Doing as she was told, Rebecca kept her head bowed as the officer guided her into the back of the ambulance, ignoring the female paramedic inside who tried to give her some words of reassurance.

'It's okay, Rebecca, you're in safe hands,' she said softly, but the woman's soothing words only had the opposite effect.

Slumping back against the seat, Rebecca closed her eyes and kicked her legs out against the stretcher in front of her in pure frustration, before staring back at her house, at Lisa standing in her doorway.

Her only real friend, and yet Lisa hadn't even stuck up for her once.

She'd just stood back just like everyone else and let these people take her away.

And as the ambulance doors started to close, Rebecca stared over at Jamie one last time as he got in Officer Blyth's car, to follow them, she assumed.

Only this time, he did look at her and his blank expression caught her off guard.

Because there was a coldness in his eyes now. Looking into the eyes of her husband, Rebecca saw a complete stranger staring back at her.

And that was the moment that she knew it was over.

Jamie had already detached himself from her.

It had taken him long enough, she figured. But he'd finally seen what she'd been hiding from him for all this time.

That she wasn't what she pretended she was.

Underneath that cool, hard exterior, she was damaged goods. Only now Jamie knew it too – and he'd thrown her away.

Chapter Twenty-Two

Segregation.

That's the key to real power. Do you know that, Rebecca? You must do?

Of course, you do.

Because you're a clever woman. Or at least I used to think you were.

It's strangely compelling, the task of singling someone out and making them feel as if they are completely on their own.

You'd know all about that, Rebecca, wouldn't you?

Only it's you who's alone this time.

You and your crazy, fabricated stories.

Who's going to believe anything you say anymore?

Nobody, Rebecca, that's who.

Divide and conquer.

Fuck, I love that term.

I know I'm not completely there yet. There's still so much work to be done. But I'm getting there. Even though it's exhausting sometimes, all this crawling around in the unoccupied space left inside your head. Wiggling and slithering my way underneath your skin as I cause you to crumble under your own self-doubt.

Because even you're doubting yourself now, aren't you, Rebecca?

I've done such a good job in covering my tracks.

Some might say I've learned from the best. You've become my obsession, Rebecca, my dear.

I'm ravenous now and looking forward to the final feast.

Chapter Twenty-Three

'What is this place?' Rebecca stared over to where Jamie stood behind the two paramedics who were helping her out of the ambulance. She could see Officer Blythe standing next to him. 'This isn't the hospital?'

Her eyes came to rest on the old Victorian building, the illuminated sign stating 'University Hospital.' The building was in the middle of a huge lawn flanked with rows of trees, the long winding driveway leading them away from the busy main roads of London. The perimeter of the building lined with a low brick wall and high wrought iron fencing. The place looked more like a prison, eerie at this time of the night, with the dim security lights shining down from the building casting out weird, obscure shadows all around them.

She'd suspected it had been a trick at first. Convincing herself that Jamie and Officer Blythe had been lying to her all along, and that they weren't detaining her for her own good at all. That they were really talking her to the police station. Arresting her for breach of the peace, or assaulting Officer Blythe.

Her eyes scanned the words etched on the plaque over the main doors as they walked her towards the building.

'What's Suite 136?' she asked.

Jamie still wouldn't look her in the eye. Instead, he simply stood there, awkwardly, waiting for someone else to answer her question, his eyes fixed on the ground. Anything to avert his eyes from her stare.

'Suite 136 is a psychiatric unit. You are being detained under the Mental Health Act. We believe that you are experiencing a mental health crisis and for your own safety, we feel that it would be in your best interests to be assessed,' one of the paramedics explained softly, her words startling Rebecca for a few seconds.

'You've brought me to a mental hospital?" Rebecca's voice was high-pitched, and full of panic.

She didn't know whether to laugh or cry.

'You've made a mistake. I don't belong here! This is crazy…' Even as she said the words she knew it was no good. They wouldn't listen to her. Not now they'd brought her here. But she had to at least try to get them to see sense, to make them see they were wrong.

Whatever the CCTV footage had shown, Rebecca was sure she had seen the intruder.

'Seriously, Jamie? You think this is right?' Rebecca pleaded, feeling a wave of panic ripple through her as the gravity of the situation hit her. Her eyes turned to the double doors as they opened and yellow light flooded the pathway from inside, illuminating the silhouette of a woman in a cream dress as she held the door open for them.

'Please, Jamie, you know I'm telling the truth. Please, tell them. You came back… You saw me tonight. You saw the state I was in. You know it was real. You know me,' Rebecca said, recalling what she'd overheard Jamie say to Officer Blythe. That his business meeting the next morning had been cancelled, so he'd come back early.

Just in time by all accounts.

'That's just it, Rebecca,' Jamie said. 'All I saw was the state you were in. I didn't see anyone else. Just you. And the tapes confirmed it too. There wasn't anyone there.'

Jamie's words stung. Forcing back her tears, Rebecca shook her head.

'He *was* real. Jesus Christ! Why won't you listen? What about Ella, all the time I'm here, she's not safe!'

She closed her eyes in despair, aware that right now she was playing into their hands, proving them all right. Acting every bit as crazy and irrational as they were making her out to be.

She took a deep breath, then, looking at the officer, she tried again, trying to keep her voice calm and measured.

'Please? This is wrong. I'm not crazy...' Pleading with him to believe her, but Officer Blythe simply held his hands up, as if to say that it wasn't up to him anymore. Making Rebecca feel as if she was losing all hope. He had been her only ally and even he was turning against her.

'Rebecca Dawson?' The lady smiled, appeared friendly, but Rebecca could detect a curtness to her tone. 'My name is Davina. How about you come inside, Rebecca, and we can talk properly? It's ever so cold out here and you look like you could do with a hot cup of tea.'

Rebecca paused, scared to go with the woman because then she'd be admitting defeat. She'd be condoning the police and the paramedics bringing her here.

'They've made a mistake...' she said again, helplessly.

The nurse simply nodded.

Pacifying her.

That's what they were all doing; tiptoeing around her, because they all believed she was unwell.

They were all in this together.

And she was on her own.

Opening her mouth to speak, Rebecca faltered, no longer having the energy to protest her innocence.

What was the point? No one was listening to her.

Rebecca sucked down a mouthful of cool night air, trying to replace the oxygen in her lungs.

'It's freezing out here. Come on, let's get you inside and all warmed up, shall we? The tea's not bad here, as it goes. Might even be able to find a couple of biscuits too. How does that sound?'

Exhausted, Rebecca quietly complied with a nod. What else could she do? In the back of her mind she wonders whether she could get through to the nurse instead, if she could just contain her frustration and her temper.

If that's what it took to get everyone to finally listen to her, then that's what she'd do.

Fixing her gaze on her slippers as she steps across the pavement, Rebecca is suddenly conscious of what a sight she must look. She's grateful for the coat that's back around her shoulders, though she has no recollection of anyone placing it back on her. She tugs the material tightly around her in a bid to shield herself from the icy cold night, and also to hide her soiled nightdress, trying to conceal the streaks of mud and the grass stains from where she'd fallen earlier.

And all the smears of blood. Most of it is Jamie's.

Turning and looking back at Jamie, who is walking just behind her now with Officer Blythe. Rebecca felt her fury subsiding, allowing room for guilt. She'd never meant to lash out and hurt him tonight, that had been an accident. She'd been scared. In time, hopefully he would realise that.

'Here we are, Rebecca.' The nurse smiled, guiding Rebecca into the warmth of the reception area, before quickly popping behind the desk and saying something to one of the other nurses there that Rebecca couldn't quite hear. Their quiet voices only made her more paranoid about what they must be saying about her.

She only caught a few words as the two women checked the computer system and exchanged a few comments about which room was available for her.

Then speaking over her, as if she wasn't even there, the nurse asked Jamie for their home address.

Rebecca bit her lip, pretending that she didn't care, that she was too preoccupied with taking in her new surroundings. She allowed her eyes to sweep the reception area, taking everything in, all the while telling herself over and over to stay calm. Part of her still unable to comprehend that she was here. Inside a psychiatric unit.

A place for crazy people.

Not for people like her.

It was as if she'd stepped into some weird, distorted universe tonight. The world and everyone around her had gone mad. Not her.

And this place felt strange, as if it was trying too hard to disguise itself from what it actually was, the walls painted with muted shades of greys and lilacs instead of the usual cold, hospital white, broken up with abstract artwork. Bold streaks of purple and turquoise.

But it still smelt like a hospital. Clinical and sterile.

She eyed the small seating area to the right of her, seeing a coffee table with a stack of magazines splayed out and a water dispenser, before letting her gaze wander farther down the corridor, to a nurse writing on a chart that was pinned to one of the doors.

The place was so quiet, she thought, as everyone around her spoke softly.

Rebecca had imagined that these sorts of places would be rife with chaos and noise. That there would be people everywhere and no order.

But here even the staff seemed to talk in whispers.

Rebecca zoned back into the tail end of the conversation between Jamie and the nurse, caught the last hushed sentence.

'Arrangements have been set in place. A private suite. She'll be assessed first thing in the morning.'

The nurse's words finally broke through her dazed spell.

'First thing in the morning? You mean I have to stay here overnight?' Rebecca interrupted, more confused than ever. 'I thought I was just going to talk to someone?'

'We'd really like you stay overnight, Rebecca. It's almost 4 a.m., it's very late now but we have a psychiatrist available first thing in the morning to offer you an assessment and then we can go from there,' the nurse intervened, plastering on a fake smile again, her words coming out through tight lips.

'I can't stay here. What about Ella? What about my daughter? You can't just keep me here against my will?'

Blinking back her tears, Rebecca felt herself losing her grip on sanity. She'd been foolish to believe that the nurse would listen to her, that maybe they'd believe her.

She was just the same as Jamie and the officers. Blinkered to the truth.

She wasn't going to hear Rebecca out.

She didn't want to help her at all, she just wanted to admit her without a fuss. All her niceties had just been a ploy to get Rebecca to comply and Rebecca had stupidly fallen for it.

'Rebecca, you have been detained for your own safety. Technically, we're allowed by law to keep you here for twenty-four hours. But we aim to get you seen by our psychiatrist as soon as he's available, which is first thing tomorrow morning. Your initial assessment will let us know the necessary arrangements for any treatment or care that you require.'

Rebecca laughed then, incredulously.

'I don't need any treatment or care. I keep telling you all. There's nothing wrong with me.'

'If there's been a mistake and you don't need to be here, then please trust me, the psychiatrist will ensure the correct protocol is taken. But now that you have been detained and admitted you do need to have your assessment with him in the morning. This is all standard procedure, Rebecca. Until then, all I can do is make you as comfortable here as possible.' The nurse spoke softly, trying to ease Rebecca's concerns.

'And what if the psychiatrist thinks I need further care? Then what?' Her heart was hammering inside her chest at the thought.

Because the odds were against her now, weren't they?

No one else believed her, not even her own husband. What if the psychologist didn't either?

'*If* the assessment shows you need further care then you will be transferred to a different, more semi-permanent unit.'

An involuntary groan leaves Rebecca's lips as she moves her gaze to Jamie, desperate now for him to help her.

'Please, Jamie. You know, don't you? You know that I shouldn't be here. Please, think of Ella?'

Yet Jamie just stands there quietly, his demeanour awkward.

While she sees the concerned look on his face, she sees something else staring back at her too.

Embarrassment. At his mess of a wife.

Finally, he speaks, his voice so quiet that Rebecca can barely hear him.

'I am thinking of Ella, for fuck's sake, Rebecca. This is who I'm doing this for. Ella.'

She looks at him clearly, almost for the first time. She sees the bags under his eyes, the deep frown lines etched across his forehead.

He looked completely broken and exhausted.

Exhausted by her.

He wasn't going to help her.

Eyeing the main door she'd just been led through, her only escape route, Rebecca noticed the electronic locking mechanism and the door release on the wall that required an access code.

Was this the true reality of where they'd taken her? The 'normal' people see the perfectly presented outside façade, while the 'crazy' people get locked away behind secure keypads.

It would be almost impossible to make her escape.

She was trapped.

Her heartbeat quickened as she scoured the room for another way out, another doorway, an open window. Only she knew there wouldn't be a clear exit. This was a secure unit. For people with mental health problems. They weren't going to let her out of here until she'd seen the doctor.

'Let's walk you down to your suite, Rebecca. It's a bit more private there,' the nurse said, sensing Rebecca's obvious distress and the tension building between her and Jamie. 'I know you've had a really difficult time tonight, but we're here to help you. You'll feel better after you've had some rest. You are safe here.'

'But what about Ella? Is she safe? With some fucking nutcase running around out there and breaking into houses in the middle of the night. And you lot.' Rebecca nodded towards Officer Blythe who was standing back now and letting the staff at the unit do their job. 'This is how you deal with criminals, is it? You let them roam free and lock up the victims instead. Because he's still out there!'

Rebecca raised her voice, aware that the nurse was trying to guide her down the corridor and into her room, but Rebecca had no intention of staying here the night.

These people were not going to lock her up. They couldn't just keep her here against her will.

'I can't stay here. Why won't any of you listen to me?' she screamed now, so loudly the words burned at her throat. 'While you're all treating me like some crazy mental patient, he's still out there and that means Ella isn't safe.'

Finally, Jamie meets her eye, his cool grey eyes fixed on her.

'She is safe now.'

Rebecca winces.

He means from her. It's the final blow.

Blinking back her tears, she swallows down the lump in her throat, hoping to relieve the tightness that's leaving her breathless.

She's on her own, it's her against all of them.

Lunging backwards, she makes a run for the door. Only the nurse has already anticipated Rebecca's move and she's on her, instantly calling out for back up from another member of staff.

'Rebecca! Calm down!' Jamie shouts. 'Is she okay?'

This is for their own protection,' she hears Davina say as she's pinned down to the floor. Winded on impact, Rebecca's face is pressed against the cold ceramic tiles as she's surrounded by strangers all holding her arms and legs down.

'*She's not coherent,*' another voice says as she screams and kicks out. Clawing at any skin or clothing she comes into contact with, fighting for her survival.

Someone's straddling her back, her head twisted awkwardly to the side, and she can't breathe, the weight on top of her ribcage feeling like it's crushing her.

The flesh of her arm is pinched tightly between someone's fingertips before she feels the sharp searing pain of a needle plunged deeply into one of her veins. Her head lolls involuntarily to the side as the liquid from the syringe rapidly enters her blood stream.

The wave of numbness that washes over her entire body is icy cold and immobilising, leaving her body as weak and limp as her depleting spirit.

All she can do is watch now and her eyes are on Jamie, who has his back to her, walking away from her. His silhouette shrinking smaller and smaller as he moves farther into the distance.

She feels a single tear escape her right eye at the realisation that not once did he look back at her.

Not once did he turn back to see if she was okay.

It was as if he couldn't get away from her and this place quickly enough.

And she can't fight it anymore.

Rebecca gives in to the thick blanket of darkness that descends upon her.

In fact, she welcomes it.

Chapter Twenty-Four

Light floods the room.

The sudden brightness makes Rebecca squint as she lies there for a few seconds, before finally opening her eyes and staring up at the ceiling.

It takes her a few seconds to gather her bearings. To remember that she's not at home.

She's not alone. There's an unfamiliar noise in the room.

Footsteps.

Then the gravelly sound of someone clearing their throat before they speak.

'Good morning, Rebecca. Did you sleep okay?'

Rebecca turns her head, eyeing the nurse stood at the end of her bed, smiling down at her.

She winces as she recalls the chaos of last night, as fragmented images flash inside her head.

It comes back to her all at once. She's in a psychiatric unit. Jamie left her here.

Part of her still can't believe that he'd do that to her.

That he'd simply just walk away.

'I'm Nurse Rabe, but you can call me Marlene. How are you feeling this morning?'

Rebecca stares at the nurse. She's younger than her, and there's a warmth to her eyes that seems genuine.

But then this is what staff at this sort of place does, isn't it? Rebecca reminds herself. They lull you into a false sense of security. They make you believe they want to help you when really all they want to do is keep you here. Away from your own child.

Just like the nurse from last night, who admitted her. Davina. With her sharp features and her equally sharp, condescending tone.

'Rebecca?'

'I feel a bit better this morning. I think,' Rebecca lies, her head still fuzzy as she sits up in the bed, realising that the nurse is staring at her. That's she's waiting for an answer. 'I slept, so I guess that's something.'

Rebecca glanced at the clock on the wall, shocked to see that it was almost 9 a.m. She must have slept right through. Her first restful bit of sleep since Ella. The irony being that as much as she needed her sleep, she didn't want it to be like this.

A combination of complete physical and mental exhaustion, along with whatever was in that syringe.

She watches as Marlene crosses the room, fussing with the breakfast tray that she lays out on the coffee table, before she swings her legs around to get out of the bed, wincing at the pain in her side. She remembers how she was pressed to the ground when the nurses restrained her.

Another memory then, of Jamie walking away.

Ella.

She needs to get home. Soon.

'Rebecca?'

The nurse is still talking, she realises and she tries to concentrate on her words, trying to pretend that the room isn't spinning slightly off its axis, that her skin isn't prickled with fear underneath the layer of newly formed perspiration, that her hands aren't shaking.

'I said that's good to hear! That you slept. I always feel better after a few hours sleep.'

Marlene is chatting away as she arranges the food on the tray for her. 'I've got you some breakfast here. Most important meal of the day, they say. Funny old saying, because if you ask me *all* my meals are important!' Patting her non-existent stomach, Marlene winks, willing Rebecca to smile, but she can't although she can't help but think that if they'd met under any other circumstances, Rebecca would probably really like this girl. She seemed kind, funny.

But she was a nurse, Rebecca reminded herself. She was one of *them*.

Rebecca looks down at the floor. Her head is groggy, and she can feel a headache pulsating behind her eyes. She rubs her forehead, before glancing back at the soft, fluffy pillows behind her, fighting the resistance to lay back down and close her eyes. To give in to the lull of sleep. To just close her eyes and make all of this go away.

'You not hungry?' Marlene asked. 'Maybe just have a little bit of toast, or some fruit, yeah? There's some orange juice here too. And I can get you some tea or coffee?'

Rebecca wonders if this is all part of her assessment too? That Marlene is secretly taking notes. Monitoring her behaviour and reporting back to the psychiatrist.

She moves from the bed, picking up a slice of toast. Tearing at the crisp, dried corner of the crust with her teeth. She picks up the glass of orange juice and forces herself to swallow it down.

All she can think about is Ella.

Is Jamie with her now? Is he watching her continuously like she would?

Is she missing her too?

Because Jamie doesn't know Ella's routine, he doesn't know how Rebecca always sings her to sleep with 'You Are My Sunshine' softly recited in her ear, as Ella nuzzles against her chest after a feed. Or how Ella likes to sleep with her comfort blankie draped over the right side of her face, covering her eye and cheek.

And part of Jamie's incompetence is her fault, she can admit that.

At least to herself.

Because she's pushed him out. She's been so wrapped up with Ella that she's driven a wedge between Jamie and his daughter. Because deep down, Rebecca didn't want to share her.

She wanted to keep Ella all to herself.

She'd never thought she would be good enough to be a mum but having Ella had changed her completely. She tried so hard to do right by her daughter, but that desperation to get everything perfect had turned into overprotectiveness.

'Your husband packed you some belongings. Some clean clothes and toiletries,' Marlene says brightly, interrupting Rebecca's train of thought.

Rebecca forces herself to gulp down the last mouthful of toast, coughing violently as it lodges against the tight ball of emotion sitting inside her throat. She spots the familiar designer bag down on the floor near the dresser and bending down, she unzips it, selects a few of the items of clothing from the top. She holds up the oversized cream sweater Jamie must have pulled out from the bottom of the wardrobe; it's been so long since she wore it. And her blue skinny jeans, dirty, retrieved from the bedroom floor, and a pair of tatty old plimsolls that she no longer wore.

The expression on her face must have said that he couldn't have picked a worse selection of clothing, because Marlene laughed, rolling her eyes.

'Most men haven't got a clue, have they, when they're left to their own devices. Too used to having everything done for them,' the nurse quipped, trying to make light of Jamie's abysmal attempt of helping her.

'At least it's warm.' Rebecca shrugs, not wanting to appear ungrateful as she holds the thick woollen jumper up to her face and breathes in the familiar scent of home from the fabric.

Feeling the warm wool against her skin, it's only then that she realises she's shivering, her arms prickled with a spray of goosebumps. She feels so cold that it's hard to imagine ever really warming up. Maybe the jumper isn't such a bad choice after all.

Besides, anything is better than this hospital nightgown they must have given her to change into. Though she has no memory of changing into it. They must have changed her clothing when she was out cold.

She scans the room, wondering for a second where the clothes are she arrived in. Her coat, and nightdress. Torn and streaked with mud and bloody smears.

Marlene reads her thoughts.

'Your husband took home all of your dirty clothes too.'

Rebecca nodded.

So he came back? He must have.

He must have gone home to fetch some clean belongings.

He didn't just leave her here once. He'd done it twice.

'You've got an appointment with the psychiatrist this morning. So as soon as you're ready, I'll take you down,' Marlene says, the smile still fixed on her face as she starts busying herself again, pulling back the curtains and tidying up the breakfast tray.

'I'll get washed and dressed,' Rebecca says, glad to retreat to the sanctuary of the en suite bathroom. She's eager to get her appointment over and done with so that she can get out of this place.

Pulling the nightgown over her head she can't get ready quickly enough.

Soon this will all be over, she tells herself.

Once she's seen the psychiatrist, once she's explained exactly what's been going on, they'll understand. They'll let her go home.

To Ella.

And Ella will be missing her. Nowhere near as much as Rebecca's missing her though. The pain of being away from her baby catches her off guard then, so acutely she has to steady herself against the edge of the sink so her legs don't give way.

Rebecca washes her face, splashing cold water onto her skin, before gazing at the sallow, tired reflection staring back at her in the mirror.

She looks like a complete stranger. Her eyes, dark and puffy.

Her hair, unbrushed and wild. Her face devoid of any make-up. Jamie didn't pack any, she has no mask to hide behind.

She wonders how she became this woman.

How she got here.

But deep down, she knows.

Of course, she does. She knows exactly what got her here.

It was always the same. No matter how fast or far she tried to run from her past, it always caught up with her.

Only this morning isn't the time or the place for her to reminisce.

She needs to make herself look presentable. To try to look at least half human.

Scraping her hair back into a ponytail on the top of her head, she almost laughs at the whole concept of beauty sleep. Because last night she'd slept well, better than she had in a long time, yet judging by the state she looked today, the benefits of it had been completely wasted on her.

Outside the bathroom, she can hear Marlene flitting around making the bed and fluffing up the pillows. Killing time as she waits for her, but Rebecca has no intention of keeping her waiting any longer.

Pulling at the door handle, she strolls back into the bedroom feeling somewhat more 'Rebecca' now that she's washed and dressed.

It's time.

She's ready to go and see the doctor.

She's ready to get home to her baby.

Chapter Twenty-Five

We lived in fear as children.

Because they threatened us all the time, telling us we'd be taken away if we told anyone the truth. And as dark and unpredictable as our house could be, somehow the risk of being taken away always felt that much scarier than if we were forced to stay.

Because we knew what would happen if *they* took us.

We'd heard all the stories a thousand times.

About the kind of people who would harm us. All the things they'd do to us.

We could never let that happen.

So, we did everything we could to hide the truth from anyone on the outside world.

Spending hours helping our mother and father to hide all our secrets. Cleaning the house immaculately anytime we knew we were expecting a visitor: a social worker, a teacher, our landlord. We worked tirelessly for hours before we started school, my sister and I. Down on our hands and knees scrubbing the floors or carrying the empty bottles of alcohol out to hide them in the shed. And my mother was good at hiding things. Often concealing smashed mirrors in the house with a random throw and some cheap fairy lights they'd used one year at Christmas, to try make the destruction look as if it was some kind of decorative feature.

Only there were some things we couldn't hide.

Like the stained, threadbare carpet. Or the thick black mould that spanned its way up most of the walls.

But being poor wasn't punishable.

As long as we appeared like a normal family, as long as we kept our secret hidden. What could anyone in authority really do?

I remember once how we were nearly caught out.

Our mother had said they'd done it on purpose, turning up unannounced. She said they must know.

She'd still managed to put on a stellar performance. Pretending to be an attentive, loving mother to us. Putting on a playful, fake voice that we'd never heard before.

She'd put on a good show.

Yet, she'd been on edge, and she was careless that day, not quite quick enough to hide the ripe, blackened bruise that peeped out from the bottom of her sleeve as she reached for a cup to make the social worker some tea.

We all saw it; how the woman's expression had quickly changed. How that look of suspicion had lingered, concern gleaming out like a beacon from her eyes.

And there was a sudden change in questioning, from her earlier enquires about how me and my sister were doing at school. If we had any interests outside of the house, or any friends, as she asked my mother if everything was all right. If she needed help.

I remember how we stayed so silent, sitting on the bottom step in the hallway, watching the scene play out through the crack in the kitchen door. Like rabbits caught in the headlights, huddled close together, wide eyed, and full of trepidation, both thinking the same thoughts.

This was it. This is when they'll find out about us. This is when we'd get taken away.

But my mother was ready. Quickly composed with her ready-made excuses, extinguishing any suspicions the woman might have.

She was so clumsy, so accident prone. She'd fallen.

Her words were followed by that godawful cackle.

And some days, that's what I hated her for the most.

For laughing.

For never giving us away.

For not so much as hinting at the truth.

Because of that we suffered greatly, all of us.

Yeah, she was always such a great actress, my mother.

The best.

And for a long time, she had all of us fooled.

Chapter Twenty-Six

'Rebecca Dawson. I'm Doctor Westly.' The man behind the desk stands up, introducing himself as Rebecca lingers awkwardly just inside the doorway.

Stepping towards her, he holds out his hand for her to shake, which she does, nervously as she glances warily around his office, her eyes resting on the pile of paperwork that sits next to his notebook.

Full of notes about her, no doubt. She wonders what they say.

He holds out his hand to emphasise the welcoming gesture, ushering her into the small room, as Marlene leaves, closing the door behind her. 'Please, get comfortable, take a seat.'

Rebecca crosses the room and sits down on the empty chair opposite the doctor. She's feeling nervous now and she's not sure why. This was supposed to be the moment she'd been waiting for. When she gets to explain everything that's been happening, the moment she clears her name, so that the doctor will allow her to go home.

Home to Ella.

Instead she feels vulnerable and awkward, as if she's about to be placed underneath a microscope. Because she knows that everything – her freedom and ability to get back home to her baby girl – depends on what is said between these four walls.

'How are you feeling this morning, Rebecca? I understand that you had a very disturbing evening last night. Shall we talk about that?'

His expression and body language are neutral, Rebecca notes. Just like the rest of the staff here, he's hard to read. He gives nothing away.

'I'm feeling...' She starts to speak, but her mouth feels suddenly dry, and there's a lump in her throat. It's silly, she knows, but before she's even managed a whole sentence, she already feels judged, as if the odds are already stacked up against her.

She'd just spent the past twenty minutes reciting to herself what she was going to say to this doctor to make him realise she shouldn't be here, but now she is here, in front of him, she's lost for words.

'I don't really know how I'm feeling, to be honest. I guess, I'm a bit overwhelmed...' she says finally, breaking off mid-sentence.

Breathe. Keep eye contact. ACT NORMAL, she tells herself.

Whatever the fuck 'normal' is anymore. Rebecca's not even sure.

'I know that you probably hear this all the time, but there has been a genuine mistake. I shouldn't be here.' She keeps her voice slow and steady, choosing each word carefully before she speaks, despite the surge of panic that ripples through her, knowing that everything is hanging on this one conversation. As she speaks, she tries hard to keep her voice neutral, fully aware that the doctor would have already heard accounts of last night from the police and from Jamie. That his mind might have already been made up about her.

And what if he doesn't believe that she's telling the truth? What then?

'It's normal to feel overwhelmed. Our priority is to make sure that you're well, Rebecca. What you went through last night, and indeed, the past few weeks, must have been a terrifying experience for you. So, why don't you talk me through what's been happening?' He nods, encouraging her to continue talking as he sits there poised, ready with his notepad and pen.

Rebecca doesn't really know where to start. Scared to tell him the truth. Scared to admit how she's been feeling so overwhelmed. But what if the doctor just thought she was mad, that she was a danger to Ella?

What then?

She thinks about lying. Concealing her real feelings, so that she appears strong and capable instead.

But he'd only see through all that, surely?

So she opens up, giving him a detailed account of everything she can remember about last night and about the last few weeks leading up to it. She tells him about all the other things that have been bothering and tormenting her. About the constant feeling of paranoia, that someone is following her, watching her.

She's not sure how long she's been talking, but when she finally stops, she feels exhausted. As if the words have just spewed from her mouth.

'Have they found him yet? The police?' she asks the doctor.

The doctor shakes his head.

'As soon as we have any news, I'll be sure to let you know.'

He waits.

The silence in the room is thick between them and Rebecca senses that the psychiatrist already doubts her claims. His face – deep set with furrowing lines that cover his forehead – unmoving.

He doesn't need to speak as Rebecca can see it in his eyes.

And that's what happens, isn't it?

When the people around you are convinced that you're going mad, others start to question it too.

'Do you remember picking up the knife last night, Rebecca?'

'Yes. I was scared. I used it to protect myself,' she says vaguely, remembering going to the drawer in the kitchen and looking for a weapon. 'I was alone with Ella. I was scared.'

The doctor nods, still quiet, encouraging her to continue.

'But you don't recall seeing your husband? Not until after you'd attacked him?'

Rebecca shakes her head and takes a deep breath. Knowing full well he was trying to imply that she suffered some kind of psychosis which caused her to see her husband as someone else.

She needed to explain.

'It was dark,' she starts, then pauses, looking down to the frayed bandage on her hand. 'I know that's not an excuse, but I was so scared. So terrified that the intruder had come back, that maybe for a few minutes I wasn't thinking straight.'

'Just for a few minutes?' the doctor replies, an underlying tone to his question.

Rebecca closes her eyes, recalling the splashes of blood all down her nightdress.

Jamie's blood.

'Shall we talk about the security tapes, Rebecca? Why do you think it is that the intruder can't be seen on any of the footage?'

His question lingers in the air between them and she knows that he's testing her now. He's trying to catch her out, just like they all are, because he doesn't believe her story.

'I think someone tampered with the tapes, because he would have been on there. It's impossible for him not to be on there...' she says with certainty. Convinced of this.

'Impossible...' The doctor repeats her words. 'Yet, there's no trace of him?' he reiterates. 'Your husband has informed us that you've been suffering from a lot of stress lately, Rebecca. Severe anxiety and panic attacks. Do you want to tell me about that?'

'I've not really been feeling myself lately. I've been a bit down, I guess. A *lot* down, actually. I've been seeing my GP about it and she diagnosed me with postnatal depression. She gave me some antidepressants. She said that it's very common in new mothers,' Rebecca says. Wondering if he's already aware of this. He would have read her notes.

'And is the medication helping, do you think?' The doctor gives her an understanding nod and encourages her to continue.

'I'm not sure?' she says honestly, before shaking her head. 'I've been having trouble sleeping, and if I finally do manage to drift off for a while, I have horrible nightmares.'

'And do you remember what the nightmares are about?'

She nods, because she knows that if she lies, he'll know. That's his job, isn't it? To read people.

She takes a deep breath, and swallows, her throat dry. 'I'm inside a car. It crashes.' She doesn't want to divulge any more than that, but the doctor just sits there patiently, waiting for her to elaborate.

And so she does.

'I'm driving. And it feels as if I'm being chased or I'm desperate to get away from someone? It's fast. So fast that I'm almost flying. And without warning, I hit something. I'm not sure what it is? A large jagged rock? Or the remnants of an old tree stump?'

She pauses for a moment, trying so hard to concentrate on what it is she hit. Because it feels important. When she wakes up, her conscious mind never holds onto the details of the dream long enough for her to see, and all she's left with is a vague niggling, suggesting it's something significant.

'Then what happens, Rebecca? In your dream…'

'The car veers off the road. I lose control. Suddenly, it's darker. I think at first that the sun has gone down and it's turned to night, but then I realise that I'm in the thick of trees, surrounded by dense woodland. The car starts spinning. And I hear an awful noise. Deafening, like the screeching of metal. Glass smashing. Then everything stops. Dead still. And that's it. That's when I wake up.'

'And you don't remember anything else?'

Rebecca keeps her gaze resting on the doctor, praying that he doesn't see her lies.

'No. Nothing.' Her words come out too quick. Too abrupt even to her own ears, so Rebecca quickly continues. 'It's the same dream every time. And when I wake up, I'm not in my bed. I'm heading for the nearest door or window. As if I'm trying to escape.'

'Do you think that maybe the dream is perhaps symbolism, Rebecca?'

She frowns. Unsure what he means.

'You're inside a car, spinning out of control. The feelings you describe of not being able to escape. Of trying to get away. That everything around you is just too much. You said you sometimes feel overwhelmed?'

'I guess...' Rebecca starts tentatively. 'I mean, I don't really analyse them for a meaning. They are just bad dreams.' She shrugs. 'You think I'm crazy, don't you? That last night was all just a dream. That I was sleepwalking?'

'Nobody thinks you're *crazy*, Rebecca. But yes, a possible explanation to what's going on right now, could be that you're experiencing trauma which is surfacing again in the form of night terrors,' the doctor concludes, placing down his notebook and pen, before shifting slightly towards her on his chair. 'Night terrors can be your mind's way of making sense of a past wound. Essentially, they are panic attacks that you're experiencing in your sleep. And if you're not fully awake when you experience them, they can feel very real and often terrifying. In effect, they cause us to act out by sleepwalking and talking about what our subconscious mind is fearing the most. For instance, running away and trying to escape from the room. Because you're running away from something that you've buried in your subconscious mind.'

'But it felt real!' Rebecca cried out, aware that the conversation wasn't going the way she'd intended, that the doctor was making her talk about things she didn't want to talk about.

Her head was spinning, hands clammy with perspiration, yet she needed to stay calm.

'What concerns me, Rebecca, is that you believe it's real, because you were hallucinating. I want to talk to you about something called "Postpartum Psychosis". Or PPP as it's sometimes referred to. Has anyone ever mentioned that term to you before? Your GP perhaps?'

'My GP told me they've had trouble locating my medical records. They can only find records from since I had Ella,' Rebecca said, shaking her head. And pretending that she has no idea why her life pre-Ella is nothing more than a blank space.

The term Postpartum Psychosis was unfamiliar to her. 'Is that the same as Postnatal Depression?'

'Yes, it's very unfortunate that we've yet to locate them, but we're confident they will turn up,' Doctor Westly says, pursing his mouth. 'Postpartum Psychosis is something a little less common than Postnatal Depression. It's a mental illness that can affect new mothers. It only affects about one or two in every thousand women soon after childbirth. So, it's pretty rare, but it can be very dangerous if it's not diagnosed and treated as early as possible.' The doctor is speaking slowly now, allowing all this new information to sink in.

'I don't have that...' Rebecca tries to speak, to argue that the doctor is wrong, only the words that almost leave her mouth are lodged at the back of her throat.

She can barely breathe.

I'm not crazy, am I? This wasn't all me?

'Having a mental illness is nothing that you need to be ashamed of, Rebecca,' the doctor interrupts her. 'Think of it this way, just as a diseased heart struggles to keep up with the blood that pumps through it, or a broken leg struggles to bear the weight of the rest of the body, a brain can struggle to maintain function too. It can misguide us unintentionally, coughing up frequent delusions and hallucinations. A bit like when you mentioned those nightmares. It can make them seem real.'

The room starts to spin.

She's losing this conversation. He's diagnosing her. He thinks she's sick.

Rebecca tries to zone back in. To concentrate on what he's saying to her.

'Postpartum Psychosis can cause a litany of symptoms, from a constant state of heightened anxiety, to a deep, profound feeling of sadness. It can cause hallucinations and delusions in some patients, making people believe they can see and hear things that aren't really there. Often it can make patients lose touch with reality for a while. For days at a time, sometimes even weeks. There are other symptoms too, Rebecca, that are very similar to what you've spoken to me about today. The insomnia that you've been suffering. The paranoia. That feeling you described of being watched and followed. Of being unable to trust the people around you. It's all part of it, Rebecca. Childbirth can trigger an old wound or memory…'

She closes her eyes. The room is spinning out of control now.

183

Her rib cage constricts so tightly that her breathing becomes laboured and wheezy as she recognises the familiar start of another panic attack, only this one is all consuming.

The walls are starting to close in on her.

'This is good news, Rebecca. Because once we've worked out your diagnosis, we can run some tests and start a treatment plan for you, with the correct care, and perhaps some mood stabilisers and an anti-psychotic. Some counselling too. We can have you back to your normal self again in just a few weeks.'

Weeks?

Rebecca feels as if she's floating outside of her body.

She needs air, and gets up on her feet, stumbling towards the door, but loses her footing.

The doctor is there then, at her side, helping her stay upright as he calls out for assistance from one of the nurses.

Marlene is back. Guiding her into a chair she talks softly, gently coaxing her out of my panic attack. It takes a few minutes, but gradually the air returns to her lungs, the dizziness and blackness subside.

'I think we should take a break for a couple of hours, Rebecca. We can chat again this afternoon, after you've had some rest,' the doctor suggests.

She nods her head, numbly, as the doctor instructs Marlene to take her back to her room, and for once, she doesn't fight it. She does as she's told.

Because she knows she's losing this battle.

The doctor believes she's ill only she refuses to accept it.

Because that would make her more like her mother than she'd ever care to admit.

Chapter Twenty-Seven

I'm back there again. Crawling through the thick wet grass to try to escape the inferno, but something grabs hold of my leg, pulling me back towards the wreckage. Towards the smouldering heat.

The car is on fire. I'm trapped.

Those blood-curdling screams.

The dream is different this time, though, because suddenly I'm back at home, surrounded by the paramedics and the police.

But there's no sign of Jamie. He's left me.

Offering to make me some sweet hot tea, for the shock, he'd said. Even when I'd insisted that I didn't want it, that I felt too sick to drink it. My stomach in tight knots of angst. He's left me anyway as the paramedics bandaged up my hand and the police started taking my statement.

I've lost track of how long he's been gone for.

Long enough to disappear into the office and access to the security system?

I wake, my heart pounding. It takes me a few moments to realise I'm safe. Only the terror has taken hold of me and I can't breathe.

Pushing myself up into a seated position on the bed, the panic consumes my being as I frantically gasp for air.

My eyes home in on the small stream of light that flows in from the gap in the blinds.

Focus. You're safe. You're home.

Only I'm not at home.

I'm at the hospital.

I vaguely recall the nurse giving me something to help me sleep? A sedative?

Trapping me inside my nightmares this time.

But this time I can recollect every tiny vivid detail and more.

I'm thinking about the tapes and why there was no sign of the intruder.

That someone must have tampered with them. That Jamie was unaccounted for, for long enough to have done this.

It can't have been Jamie.

But my body won't listen to my reasoning. My lungs are empty and screaming for air.

I double over. The crushing sensation so tight and constricting that it feels as if my rib cage is caving in on me, squeezing out my very last breath, my heart pounding so fast that I fear it might explode. Like there's no chance of it ever slowing down, unless it's to stop completely.

Oh my God, my heart is going to stop!

And there's no one here. No one to help me.

Shivering, I clutch at my left arm flinching as a pain shoots from my armpit to my bicep and the sharp pain is excruciating.

I'm having a heart attack.

I must be, I can feel it. All the signs are there. The tightness in my chest, the shortness of breath. My fingers numb and tingling.

I need to get help, but I can't stand up. I can't get out of bed. My legs have gone to jelly and the pain in my chest and arm is consuming me entirely.

I can't move.

But I can't stay here.

MOVE.

I roll onto my side and lower my body onto the floor, the coarse carpet beneath me softening the impact of my fall.

I can't just die here, in this hospital room.

Not here on the floor, splayed out on the carpet next to a ball of yesterday's clothes and my dirty underwear.

Ella.

She's my only thought as I reach for the panic button.

Frantically, my hand sweeps the bedside cabinet.

Wheezing, coughing as everything falls down, landing with a thud in a heap beside me.

A reading book that I was allowed to select from the hospital's library, a plastic beaker of icy cold water. My wedding ring.

I can't remember taking it off. But I must have.

Because I'm so angry with Jamie. For bringing me here. For leaving me here.

And still I can't find the panic button. *Where the fuck is the panic button?*

My heart is hammering away. And my fingers are tingling and numb. I'm running out of time.

Crawling across the carpet, I drag my fingers through it as if to get some leverage, edging myself towards the door.

I reach up for the handle.

But it's locked.

They've locked me in, and the room is spinning.

I'm crying now as I slump down against the door, trying to reassure myself.

BREATHE, REBECCA. BREATHE.

So, I do. I breathe, slowly and controlled. In through my nose and out through my mouth.

Breathe, Rebecca. Breathe.

This is a panic attack. You're going to be okay.

It's working. My heart slows and I lean back against the wall and close my eyes.

The door behind me moves, a forceful judder that sends me scurrying across the room.

I scamper across the carpet and sit on the edge of the bed, the covers pulled up around me.

BREATHE. ACT NORMAL. THEY ARE WATCHING YOUR EVERY MOVEMENT.

'Rebecca? Are you okay? I heard some noise?' Marlene is back. Standing in the doorway, her hand hitting the light switch, before casting her eyes around the room and seeing me.

I squint at the brightness of the lights, rubbing my eyes to hide any tears and to add to the pretence that I've just woken up.

'I must have knocked the bedside cabinet in my sleep,' I say.

The actress in me is playing it down so as not to draw any more attention to myself as I nods to the mess on the floor and try to ignore the hammering in my heart.

It's enough... the nurse believes me.

After helping me pick everything up, the nurse leaves the room, turning the light off before she goes and plunging my room back into darkness.

I laid in bed, my head whirling as I try to piece everything together, because it wasn't the nightmares that woke me up this time.

It was something else. A realisation.

Thoughts that have been niggling from the darkest recesses of my mind have surfaced.

Did Jamie tamper with the tapes?

Because he's the only other person who was in the house.

And why had he come home early? Right then... when I'd been in the garden.

He said that his meeting the next day had been cancelled. But, why didn't he do what he normally did and stay at the hotel, regardless? It was all booked and paid for.

Why would he come home in the middle of the night, passing up a rare night of uninterrupted sleep?

Right then?

There's something else too.

The clothes he picked out for me?

Jamie was always so well turned out and meticulous, and he wanted everything in his life to be a reflection of him. He couldn't have picked a worse selection to dress me in. A ratty old jumper, and a pair of dirty worn jeans.

Unless he'd done it intentionally?

So that I look the part he wants to convince them all I'm playing.

I think about all our arguments lately. About the way he was with Jenna.

I lean over the side of bed just in time to throw up the contents of my stomach, the acidic residue bitter in my mouth.

Jamie has been doing all this to me. And I know deep in the pit of my stomach it's true.

But why?

Because he regrets marrying me? Because he's fallen for Jenna? He wants to take Ella away from me?

Or has he found out? Does he know the truth?

That I'm not the woman I'm pretending to be.

I have secrets.

And if Jamie is trying to set me up, trying to force me out of his life for good, out of Ella's life for good, then I needs to play him at his own game.

I need to be smarter, stronger, and cleverer than him.

And I need to get the fuck out of here.

Chapter Twenty-Eight

'It's all lies,' Rebecca says, staring the doctor dead in the eye while making a conscious note to stop fiddling with the frayed edges of her bandage.

Sitting up straighter, drawing her shoulders back, she maintains eye contact the entire time, knowing she needs to stay focused and in control.

'I need to be honest with you.' She pauses, gearing herself up for her confession. 'I'm actually really embarrassed... Because... I made it all up. There was no intruder. Nobody has been following me. No one's been watching me. That's why you can't see anyone on the tape. And that's why Jamie doesn't believe me. It's why he thinks I'm going crazy. Because he can see through my stories.'

'So you're now saying you've made all this up?' the doctor asks, clearly not convinced at her sudden admission.

Rebecca holds up her hands, showing complete surrender.

'I'm really sorry,' she says, letting him know that she's coming clean, that she's laying everything out on the table for him. 'I can't do this anymore. I can't play these games.'

The doctor shuffles awkwardly in his seat, purposely not interrupting so that she can explain herself properly.

'My husband has been having an affair,' Rebecca declares, staring down at the floor. Her face is ashen, awash with shame as if the words are harder to voice than she anticipated, fighting back tears, struggling with the conflicting emotions inside of her.

The shame and guilt of being exposed as a liar.

The raw pain of admitting that she's being cheated on by the man she loves. Despite herself, Rebecca laughs. The noise unexpected, catching them both by surprise. The doctor raises a brow and she shakes her head in wonderment before attempting to explain.

'Do you know, that sentence has been eating away inside of me for months. You're the first person I've said it to out loud to. You are the first person I've told. *My husband has been having an affair,*' she says it again. As if wanting to feel the words roll off her tongue once more.

Only her expression crumbles.

'It's funny how cold and final it sounds when you say it out loud. It's just one sentence. A few words. People have affairs all the time, don't they? But this... it's my life...' She trails off, wanting the doctor to understand her torment. The pain and angst she'd been made to feel. 'Jamie said he loved me. We have a child. And it's completely broken me inside.'

Still, the doctor doesn't speak, just nods, allowing her to continue, which Rebecca takes as a good sign.

He's listening finally.

'It started when I was pregnant with Ella. Such a cliché, isn't it? A pregnant, fat, exhausted wife at home. I don't know why I ever thought Jamie would be different? I believed him, you know. When he told me that he'd never hurt me. I trusted him.'

If the doctor is surprised by any of her frankness, he doesn't show it. His expression is of no judgement.

And Rebecca expects that these four walls have seen and heard it all, and much worse, a million times over.

'He tried to hide it from me at first. But it's obvious, isn't it. You get to know the signs. All the secret phone calls. How he started hiding his phone, making a point of never leaving it absently lying around. And then he started going on lots of "business trips" overnight. Heading straight for the shower when he got home. Christ, he must have thought I was stupid not to know what he was doing. Washing away all the telltale scents of whatever woman he'd been screwing behind my back. But I could still smell them. Their cheap lingering perfume or a smudge of make-up on his clothes.'

Rebecca was crying openly now, tears streaming down her face as she spoke.

She eyes the doctor. Poised with his pen on his notebook as he listens.

'I always wanted a family all of my own. I never really had that.' Rebecca gives the doctor a small smile. Coy, almost embarrassed that she's laying herself completely bare. 'Do you know the only thing worse than the man you love cheating on you? Than the father of your child humiliating you like that?' She shakes her head again, laughing again. The pain inside her so raw and so revealing. 'It's what it turns you into. What that rejection, that ultimate betrayal makes you become. It dissolves you as a person. It makes you completely pathetic. That's what it did to me. It left me crippled with anxiety and jealousy and the feeling of not being good enough for Jamie. Of not being worthy of him. Worthy of him. That cheating, lying bastard.' She shakes her head. 'And the moment you know the truth, that's when you know you should walk away, isn't it? *Have a bit of dignity for yourself! Have some self-respect! If they do it once, they'll do it again.* That's what everyone says, isn't it? Only I didn't walk away, I couldn't. I stayed. For all the wrong reasons, maybe. For Ella's sake. For mine, for a million different reasons.'

She looks at the doctor then, questioningly, wanting to know what he's thinking about her behind that blank expression he wears.

Wondering if he's silently judging her for being so weak.

'I mean it's only sex, isn't it? When you really think about it. A physical, primal act. A few moments of selfless pleasure. And he was still coming home to me at the end of the night. Or at least he was at first, at the end of my pregnancy. So, I guess it was just easier to turn a blind eye. I thought we could just pretend everything was normal. And that eventually he'd come back to me.'

Rebecca shrugs again, her cheeks burning with humiliation at her frank admission, how vulnerable and exposed she sounded.

How pathetic she'd allowed herself to become.

Because this was pathetic, wasn't it? Letting a man treat her this way.

Allowing Jamie to drag her so low.

'I thought that once Ella was actually here, the affairs would stop. Only Ella came, and Jamie didn't stop, if anything he got worse. Going off on his "important business trips" and leaving me alone to deal with Ella. The truth is, I was struggling. And Jamie was becoming more and more distant. We barely talk anymore. Not really. And I was scared I was going to lose him completely. That he'd leave us both. I was desperate...'

She wipes away the single lone tear that trickles down her cheek.

'So, I made it all up. I lied and said that someone was following me. That someone pushed me in the park. That someone broke into our home. It's pathetic isn't it? I know. I'm pathetic.' Rebecca looks down at her hands. She's shaking. 'But for a while it worked. He seemed genuinely worried about me. Concerned. But then he started to lose patience. He saw through my stories, he found threads that didn't add up. He started calling me out. At first, I think he thought I was crazy. That I actually believe my own lies.

'You think I'm pathetic, don't you?' Her loud, involuntary, sobs fill the room.

'I don't think you're pathetic at all, Rebecca,' the doctor says finally. 'You're only human and you've clearly been through a lot. A new baby. Your hormones. Jamie's alleged infidelity.'

He believes her. The doctor actually believes her.

'But last night, you had a knife. You hurt yourself and you injured your husband?'

Rebecca nodded.

'That was a genuine accident,' she explained. 'I was in the house alone again, and I just convinced myself I'd heard noises. You know, the usual house noises, like creaking floorboards. I guess I just worked myself up. All these stories I'd been telling Jamie about someone watching me, well, the truth is... I must have started to spook myself out. Because I was convinced someone was trying to break into the house. I mean, I really thought I heard something. And I only picked up the knife as protection. I had no intention of actually using it. And there was no one out there. I didn't see anyone. Not until Jamie came running through the gates. He startled me. And that's when I lashed out. I wasn't expecting him home and I was just trying to protect myself. It was dark. And as soon as I realised what I'd done I'd gone too far. So I had to continue the lie. Only Jamie got in the way, and then he called the police. Everything just escalated from there.'

Rebecca shook her head, angry with herself.

'That's why there's nothing on the security tapes. Jamie only had them installed to keep me quiet. I think by that point he'd had enough of all my stories. And I think part of him just wanted to prove a point. To physically show me that there was no one there. That this was all in my head. The irony that they would be used against me to make me look as if I was going insane...'

Rebecca was crying then. Softly.

'I was only ever thinking of Ella. Of her having a mother and father, together. A proper family. I never had that. I just wanted Jamie to love me. To give a shit about me. To show me that he cared. But it backfired on me. What you said earlier... about the dreams. Of me being in the car and it spinning out of control. You were right. My life is a mess and I don't know how to make any of it stop. But I'm not crazy. I'm desperate and stupid, and Christ, pathetic. But I'm not crazy.'

The doctor nodded his head in agreement.

'Opening up and being honest about what's going on is the first step, Rebecca. I think you should be honest with your husband. You both have issues that need to be discussed.'

The doctor picked up his pad and scribbled some notes there, then placing his hands on his lap, he looked at Rebecca intently.

'Okay, here's what I'm going to suggest. I don't think you need to be admitted, but I would like to treat you as an out-patient, Rebecca. We have an excellent crisis team and a community mental health team that can offer you some support. We can organise some counselling for you and Jamie so you can talk through your issues in a calm, controlled environment. And I also think you'd benefit from some personal therapy too. We can delve into how you're feeling and perhaps review the antidepressants you've been subscribed for the post-natal depression. Because despite your claims that this is all about Jamie cheating, I do think that you're dealing with severe post-natal depression and you do need some form of proper after-care.'

The room was quiet for a few moments as the doctor turned and made some notes on the computer.

'So you are going to let me go home?' Rebecca asked, her words coming out in almost a whisper, as if she was too apprehensive of the answer.

'Yes. I don't think it would be in your best interests to be treated as an inpatient.' He paused. 'Perhaps there are things that could have been dealt with a lot differently than you did, but you've been under an enormous amount of pressure and sometimes that pressure can make us act in very irrational ways, you've been trying to survive the only way you know how. But we can help you now. If you let us?'

Rebecca nodded.

'I'm going to do a review of the medication that you're currently taking, and I'll write to your GP and see if we can set up the first session of counselling for you. There's no reason to keep you here any longer. We can look into getting you discharged shortly.'

'I'm so sorry for wasting your time. I know I shouldn't have let it get this far, but it really did just all spiral out of control,' Rebecca says gratefully, as the doctor presses a button on the desk and Marlene comes back into the room.

Rebecca stands up and shakes the doctor's hand, before letting Marlene lead her back down the corridor towards her room so that they can start the discharge procedure.

Soon she'll be home with Ella.

A small part of her is a little shocked at how easy it was to put on such a stellar performance.

The real her is still in there somewhere, buried deep inside her.

And if Jamie Dawson is behind all this, it will be his undoing.

Chapter Twenty-Nine

'Are you sure you're okay, Becks? You've barely said two words since I picked you up,' Lisa says, watching Rebecca's hands tremble as she turns the key in the door.

She'd been silent for the entire journey home. Lisa understood. Rebecca was annoyed Jamie hadn't answered the phone when the nurses had called him to pick her up. Lisa had had to go instead.

Lisa hadn't known what to expect when she got there. Even now, she had no idea what was going on. All she knew for sure was what the nurses had been willing to tell her, that Rebecca was being discharged and treated as an out-patient.

Rebecca hadn't spoken to her. The whole way home she'd seemed so angry. Angry with Lisa too, she guessed. Which Lisa had been expecting. For not sticking up for her, for not being able to do anything about Rebecca being sectioned.

Lisa had been dreading what state she'd find Rebecca in.

'I'm fine. I'm just exhausted. And I need to see Ella,' Rebecca says, eagerly pushing the door open. But the minute she's inside the house she senses that something's not right.

The house feels cold and echoey. There's an eeriness that tells her that there's no one home. 'Jamie?' she calls out, but she already knows she won't get an answer as she scans the coat pegs in the hallway and sees that his is gone. The space on the shoe rack that hold his boots is empty.

This is why he didn't come and collect her.

'Why isn't he here? Why wasn't he waiting by the phone to hear when I'd be coming home?' Her voice shakes with raw emotion. She's been so desperate to get home, to see her daughter. Jamie would know that too. How eager she'd be to reunite with Ella. How it physically pained her to be away from the child. It had felt as if a part of her was missing. 'Is this his way of punishing me? For what? For not being well? Where's he taken her?'

She'd had a feeling something like this would happen when the nurses Lisa was coming instead. Rebecca had dutifully nodded. Not giving them any kind of reaction.

Focusing instead on the full assessment that the doctor insisted she complete before they discharged her and listening carefully to her instructions about taking her new medication instead.

'Jamie?' she called again, climbing the stairs, in the vain hope that maybe he just hadn't heard her. She ran from room to room, with Lisa following closely behind her trying to calm her down. 'Maybe he just took Ella out for some fresh air. He might just need a bit of space? You've both had a manic couple of days.'

'Space? He had that last night when he walked out and left me all alone in a fucking mental hospital. He can't do this, Lisa. He can't just take Ella from me,' Rebecca screeched, trying her hardest to stay rational and in control even if the last few days had thrown her whole life off balance. Her whole world seemed upside down. And the only thing she knew with absolute certainty was that she missed Ella so much it was like a physical pain. 'He's got no right. He's got no bloody right!'

'Rebecca, I really think you should try to calm down. Wherever he is, I'm sure he'll be back soon and when he does come back, the last thing you want is to be in a state. You need to keep calm. Think of Ella.'

'Oh, please, Lisa! Ella is all I ever think about,' Rebecca said, angry at her sister-in-law for making such a flippant comment after everything she'd been through. She'd thought about nothing else *but* Ella.

Her daughter was her entire life and Lisa knew that.

'This is your brother's way of punishing me. He's done this on purpose. He's taken Ella away from me.'

Flinging open the wardrobe in her bedroom, Rebecca's worst fears were confirmed as she noted the empty space where some of Jamie's clothes usually hung. She raised her eyes towards Lisa then, as if she'd just proved her point.

'I bet he's taken Ella's stuff too.'

Running into the nursery, Rebecca pulls open the drawers in the dresser, her hand sweeping the small pile of baby grows Jamie left behind.

She runs down the stairs her head spinning as she wrenches the hallway cupboard open, eyeing the empty space that normally occupies the pushchair and travel cot.

'He's taken her,' Rebecca said, turning to see Lisa standing awkwardly on the bottom step. 'The bastard's taken her. He is doing this to punish me, isn't he? He's doing this to hurt me.'

'Why on earth would Jamie want to hurt you, to punish you, Rebecca? He's worried about you. We are all worried about you,' Lisa said, doing her best to calm Rebecca down, but realising it was proving an impossible task.

Rebecca was on the edge, hands trembling, and her voice shook with raw emotion every time she spoke. She was hysterical and Lisa wondered if the hospital had got her diagnosis wrong.

'You can't see it. No one else can see it. This was all *his* plan. *He's* behind all this. He wants to make it look like I'm going mad. He's been setting me up.'

'Why would he do that?' Lisa said, watching as Rebecca slipped into the office and booted up the computer, before picking up the phone from the desk and dialling a number.

'He's worried sick about you,' Lisa said now, tactfully, aware that Rebecca wasn't making much sense. 'Maybe he just wanted to give you some time to yourself. You've been through so much the past few days. Maybe he thinks that a break from Ella would do you good?'

'I don't need a fucking break from Ella. She's my daughter. I want to see her!' Biting down on her lip, Rebecca suppresses her scream as she listens to the dial tone, before the call goes straight through to voicemail, just as she expected it to.

Rebecca leaves a message.

'Jamie, where are you? This isn't fair...' She's sobbing now, her words barely coherent. 'You can't just take her from me? I haven't done anything wrong.'

Holding the phone to her cheek, she knows it's useless. That her pleas will fall on deaf ears.

'He won't answer.' She hangs up the phone and flings it down on the desk in anger, before frantically searching through Jamie's desk, pulling all the drawers open and searching through the piles of paperwork, looking for some sort of clue as to where he might have gone.

'Do you know where he is, Lisa? Please if you do, you have to tell me.'

'No, Becks. Of course I don't.'

'How did he seem last night, when he came back from the hospital? Did he seem angry? Did he say anything at all?' Rebecca asked, searching Lisa's face for clues.

Lisa had told her in the car on the way home how well behaved Ella had been when she'd looked after her last night. Wanting to put Rebecca's mind at ease, she'd told her how she hadn't woken up until the early hours of the morning and how Lisa had fed and changed her just as Jamie had walked back through the door.

She'd said it was weird how no one could reach Jamie, but she'd played it down.

Not wanting to stress Rebecca out any further than she already was.

'He was fine,' Lisa said resolutely. 'Worried, exhausted.' She shrugged. 'You know my brother... he doesn't give much away.'

Rebecca scoffed, bitterly.

'He said you were in safe hands, that the doctors were looking after you, and then he poured himself a large Scotch. He was sitting on the couch staring into space for a while, and in the end, he told me to go home. He said that he was going to try get some sleep.'

'And that's the last you saw of him?'

Lisa nodded her head.

'The next thing I heard was the nurse on the phone asking if I would come and collect you, I tried his phone to see what was going on, but he didn't answer.'

Making her way towards Rebecca, she crouches down beside her and wraps her arm around her. 'Rebecca, please. You need to stay calm. We will sort this. Jamie will be home before you know it. Everything will be okay. I'm sure there's a reasonable explanation. Jamie would never just purposely keep Ella from you without a good reason. He knows how much you worry about her,' Lisa says, trying to appease her sister-in-law, though she's angry at Jamie now too.

He's playing a dangerous game keeping Ella from her mother and seeing the distress on Rebecca's face is almost too much to bear.

'Maybe he's gone into work? Do you think he'd have taken Ella with him?' Rebecca says, without waiting for an answer as she picks up the phone and dials Maggie's number.

But Maggie tells her she hasn't seen Jamie this morning, that he's called to clear his diary for the next couple of days, saying Rebecca wasn't well. Maggie wishes her a speedy recovery.

Rebecca thanks her before hanging up. A surge of panic ripples through her, as she wonders if he's with Jenna.

Surely he wouldn't do that to her though, would he? He wouldn't take Ella to stay with his mistress?

'Maybe I should call the police?' she says, feeling her anxiety building.

She has to do something. She can't just sit around and wait for him to come home.

'The police won't do anything, Rebecca,' Lisa said, trying to reason with her friend. 'I know you're upset, but Jamie *is* Ella's father. Technically he hasn't done anything wrong. And you've just been discharged from a psychiatric unit. Maybe you should just wait for him to come home?'

Her words hit the mark.

Rebecca pauses, her fingers hovering over the phone's keypad. 'You're right.' Rebecca says resignedly, placing the phone back down on the dock. Jamie *hasn't* committed an offence. He's taken his daughter somewhere. A child he had as much right to as her.

And Officer Blythe wasn't exactly her biggest fan. He probably wouldn't blame Jamie for taking some time out.

Poor man, being married to a woman so broken like her.

She takes a deep breath, swallowing down her hurt and anxiety. Aware that Lisa is still staring at her, concern etched all over her face as she hovers just inside the office doorway.

Rebecca knows exactly what she's thinking. She's wondering If she's really okay. If the doctors haven't made a mistake letting her out again.

Looking at her sister-in-law's face, Rebecca knows she needs to keep her head together and takes a deep breath.

'You know what, you're right. Jamie probably just needs some time, he'll be back. I think the past few days have just caught up with me. I'm not myself. Maybe a lie down will help. I'm exhausted. I've barely slept,' Rebecca says, rubbing her forehead, trying to iron out the increasing throb behind her eyes.

'Are you sure you're okay?' Lisa asks, still not convinced. Watching as Rebecca wipes the beads of sweat that have formed on her top lip. As she sits back in the chair and unclenches her fists.

'Yeah, I'm sorry. I'm overreacting. I just wanted to see Ella, that's all. But you're right. Jamie isn't going to keep Ella from me on purpose. He wouldn't do that.'

She sees Lisa visibly relax, before asking, 'Shall I make us some tea before I go?' But Rebecca shakes her head.

'I think I'm going to go straight up. I'll feel better after I've had a nap,' she says, with more conviction that she thought she could muster.

'Okay, babe. You do that. It's almost three o'clock now, so how about I call you in a few hours? Maybe I can grab us a takeaway for dinner tonight, yeah? When Jamie's home?'

Rebecca agrees, leaning into Lisa by the front door and hugging her goodbye.

'Thank you so much for today. For coming to the hospital to collect me. And for minding Ella last night. I know things have been mad around here lately. But I'm going to get back on top of everything. I'm going to make everything right. You don't need to worry about me. I'm going to be just fine. We're all going to be fine.'

'I know you are, darling. You just get some rest,' Lisa says, pulling away. Rebecca sees a flash of something in her eyes, as if she wants to say something else, only she changes her mind at the last second and instead blows Rebecca a kiss, closing the door behind her as she leaves.

Rebecca waits. Leaning against the front door as if to steady herself.

Her legs are trembling and the pain in her head is tearing through her skull now, as a million thoughts whirl around inside her brain.

The banging has returned, and she feels sick and dizzy all at once. She recognises the onslaught of another panic attack, only she was doing her damnedest to rein it in. To hide her angst from Lisa so that she didn't have cause to be concerned.

But now she's gone, Rebecca is burning with rage.

He's done this on purpose. He's done this to hurt her.

She can't even see straight now, the pain behind her eyes so severe.

That familiar tightening inside her chest.

She needs her bed. She needs to close her eyes and pretend for a few hours that none of this has happened.

She needs it all to go away, just for a little while, so she can gather her strength and work out what she is going to do next.

Because something's not right and she won't be the victim in all of this.

Not again.

Not after last time.

When Jamie finally comes home, she needs to be ready for him.

Chapter Thirty

Let's bring it back, Rebecca.

Right back to where it all started.

How did I get here? To this dark, abysmal place.

How did I sink this low?

You.

You brought me to my knees.

You did this to me.

I was blinded by you, Rebecca. By the act you put on. By your charm and your beauty.

But do you know what, Rebecca? I see through all your pretence.

Your beauty has faded to nothing these days.

And you're pitiful.

I know this, because I can finally see you for all that you are.

It's tiring, watching you. The sight of you, wallowing in your own self-pity, jumping at the sight of your own shadow most days.

You're a fucking mess, and for a while that bought me great satisfaction.

To know that you're suffering greatly.

Because you deserve to suffer.

And I will make sure you do, because I know all your secrets, Rebecca.

And I'm going to use them to break you.

Despite the act and the bravado you once might have possessed, you're weak now.

Rebecca Dawson, a loving wife, the doting mother. Don't make me laugh.

It's all lies, isn't it?

And having Ella... becoming a mother... it's made you vulnerable, hasn't it?

That's when the cracks started appearing.

It pleases me immensely, how something so tiny and fragile has made you so unexposed and weak.

But you don't deserve her.

Not after what you did.

Not after what I know.

I'm still waiting for you to start piecing it all together. All the fractured pieces of this fucked-up puzzle. For you to finally work it out, Rebecca.

Though you're taking your own sweet time. Squirming with paranoia, not sure who to trust, overcome by the fear that at any given moment she will be taken from you.

It fucking hurts, doesn't it? The want and need for your child to be safe, it's eating you up inside.

All your fear laced with guilt. Because you, of all people, know how quickly things can be snatched away from you.

You don't deserve any of it, do you? This life? This house? This child?

I hope the anxiety in the pit of your stomach crawls up inside your throat and chokes you.

Part of me feels a bit disappointed, if I'm honest. I was so ready to go into battle with you and fight the raging war that roars inside of me. Only there's barely anything left of the old Rebecca these days.

You're nothing more than a shadow, a ghost, festering inside your home. Once your sanctuary, now your prison.

You're such a weak opponent that the novelty of tormenting you is starting to wear off now.

All this fucking with you and messing with your head. It's not enough for me anymore.

I want you to suffer so much more than this.

I want you to feel real pain.

I'm done with playing these games, Rebecca.

It's time.

Chapter Thirty-One

Rebecca's eyelids flicker open, and immediately she feels unsettled. It takes her a few moments to work out where she is as she sits up in her bed and automatically listens out for Ella, but then she remembers that Ella isn't here.

Or has Jamie come home?

Because she can hear another noise, the sound of gushing water coming from the shower in the en suite bathroom.

She stares toward the closed bathroom door.

'Jamie?' He must have come home while she was sleeping, but he mustn't be able to hear her over the running water.

Rebecca is disorientated from sleep, can still taste the vile, acrid sharpness of Scotch that she'd drunk earlier this afternoon to take the edge off her exhaustion and help her sleep. Just the smell of it made her want to gag, but she needed something to take the edge off her exhaustion and help her sleep. Not wanting to risk taking sleeping tablets in case Jamie came home with Ella.

And she *had* slept. Glancing over towards the clock on her bedside cabinet, Rebecca saw that it was already six p.m.

She was surprised that she'd managed to sleep at all.

Her head was still pounding. A loud hammering radiating inside her skull.

Shaking her head, she tried to expel the fogginess that lingered there, still not completely coherent. She must have underestimated the strength of the medication they'd given her at the hospital, because it was probably still working its way through her system too.

Hoisting herself up from the bed, she makes her way unsteadily to the bedroom's en suite to confront Jamie. Only, when she pushes the door open, he's not there.

The shower is running full pelt, the water blasting loudly off the walls and echoing around the bathroom. The spray of water is ferocious as it hits the tiles and pours down the glass shower screen. Gallons of water, swirling aimlessly down the drain.

Reaching for the taps, she winces as a shock of icy cold water sprays her body and face, soaking her in the process. Shivering, she wonders how long it's been running for, as she shuts it off.

Did she turn it on?

She doesn't remember if she did or not.

Her head is fuzzy. And even now she can feel a wave of dizziness descending over her as she holds onto the wall for support, steadying herself.

And then she notices the smell. Wrinkling her nose, the scent is bitter like charcoal or a wood-burning stove.

Something was burning.

Like a bonfire? Only the smell seemed closer, as if it was coming from inside the house?

Running from the bathroom, her stomach flipped with trepidation.

The smell *was* inside the house. A fire?

Shit.

Her suspicions are immediately confirmed as she sees the thin wisps of smoke trailing in from beneath the gap in the bedroom door.

She panics, yanking at the door, recoiling as a thick, dense wall of smoke blankets around her. Coughing and spluttering as she makes her way down the hallway, Rebecca is panicking now. She needs to get out.

The smoke is everywhere. She can barely see. It's filling the house and filling her lungs.

And as she reaches the top of the stairway, she can hear another noise. Something strange and unexpected.

Classical music is playing somewhere way off in the background. The melody is unfamiliar to her, though every chord that swims through the air sets her senses on edge. The noise is eerie and unnerving. She follows the sound, moving as fast as she can down the stairs, wondering what the hell is going on. She hasn't got time to think. To call anyone. She needs to get out of the house.

As she makes her way down the stairs, the smoke is thicker now, a black wall of fumes in front of her, blocking her way. She shields her eyes and face.

Keep low. Smoke rises.

She squats down on the floor, the smoke too much to bear, she can barely breathe. She reaches out a shaking hand, patting her way along the carpet with a sense of fear and urgency, desperate to locate the bottom step without falling and breaking her neck.

Guiding her way toward the front door.

Her hand reaching up to the keys, only to find they are gone.

She'll have to make her way to the patio doors in the kitchen instead.

Crouching again, her hand is clamped firmly over her mouth and nose to reduce the smoke intake.

But already she's breathed in the toxic fumes.

Her head is spinning.

Her throat dry, burning now, which in turns makes her eyes stream with tears, restricting what's left of her already blurred and strained vision, but she's determined to keep going. Intent on battling her way through the black, hazy stream of smoke that leads her into the kitchen.

She still can't see a fire.

But there's a lot more smoke in the room. It's thicker here, stronger and blacker.

Pouring out from the oven which glows a dim yellow, barely visible.

She left the oven on?

Rebecca shakes her head, unable to recall what she'd started cooking as she runs and shuts the power off. Then, yanking open the oven door, she recoils as a thick plume of smoke pours out, engulfing her.

The fumes are so strong now she almost passes out, but, grabbing at the cloth next to the oven, she reaches inside, the heat of the oven tray radiating through the cotton rag, searing her hand.

She slams the tray down into the sink and turns on the cold tap.

The pan hisses violently and she eyes the thick, solid black mass smouldering there.

The charred remains of a roast chicken?

A whole roast chicken?

And that fucking music, blasting out from the stereo on the kitchen windowsill. It's all she can hear now as her hands are searching for the keys to unlock the patio doors.

She needs to breathe. Coughing fiercely, her chest raspy, her lungs are screaming for air. She needs to get out.

The keys? Where are the fucking keys?

She cries out now, almost defeated as she grasps at the empty lock. They're gone.

There's no sign of them.

Why aren't they here? Did she move them?

She can't remember.

She can't remember anything.

And she can't think straight.

If she doesn't get out of the house, fast, the smoke will overpower her. She's going to pass out.

Hoisting herself up onto the window ledge, she slams the stereo down onto the floor, pushing it out of her way, as she pushes the window open as wide as it can go. Welcoming the ice-cold blast of air that hits her, she gulps at it greedily.

The smoke is everywhere now.

In her hair, in her skin.

She throws herself down onto the grass beneath her, sprawled out on the ground for a few minutes, heaving and spluttering until she finally catches her breath.

And despite throwing the stereo across the kitchen, she can still hear that creepy fucking music playing as she lies there and stares up at the blackening winter sky.

She turns on her side then and throws up the contents of her stomach. Retching as the hot bile burns the inside of her mouth, she's sobbing now too.

Did she do this? Rebecca tries to picture what she'd been doing before she'd gone to lie down earlier.

She'd had a drink. Maybe two drinks after Lisa had left.

But she didn't make any food, she's certain of it. And why would she cook a whole roast chicken, just for herself?

And the running shower? And that godawful music that had been blaring so loudly.

She hadn't done any of those, either.

Which only meant that someone had been in the house.

Had Jamie come home while she was asleep?

Was he still playing games with her?

Was this another of his sticks to hit her with? To make his point that she wasn't well? That the hospital shouldn't have discharged her, because she wasn't capable of looking after herself?

Why? So he could keep Ella from her.

Because that's what would happen, wouldn't it? If the house caught fire, and the fire service was called, and they all thought it was her fault.

Staring at Lisa's house, she checks that her sister-in-law isn't watching from a window before quickly dragging herself up from the floor.

She can't afford to be seen.

Fuck Jamie and his pathetic games, she thinks as she composes herself, making her way back into the house so she can start cleaning all the mess up.

Whatever crazy game he's playing, she's not going to let him win.

She's got to stay one step ahead of him – because no matter what, she needs to get Ella back.

Chapter Thirty-Two

Things could have been so different for you, Rebecca. Do you know that?

Course you don't.

The irony, seeing as you think you're so damn clever.

But then you always have been a smart-arse. Too fucking conniving for your own good I used to think.

But you're not clever enough to outsmart me.

I know exactly who you are, and I know what you did.

I know all your secrets, Rebecca.

All those lies you tried to keep buried.

Only, secrets don't stay down for long… they have a way of rearing their ugly head and catching up with you… eventually.

You think you're safe here, don't you?

Hiding in plain sight, in this picture-perfect little life.

Cowering away inside your home. A sanctuary of sorts, which in time has slowly become your prison.

Only you're not safe here, Rebecca. And you're starting to feel it aren't you? How the walls are starting to close in on you, how the bricks are starting to crumble, soon they'll start crashing down all around you.

And the funniest thing about all of this is that you're completely oblivious to the fact that you're going to lose.

Yet still you're doing your absolute best to cling on to the tiny scrap of hope you have left, that your world isn't about to be blown wide apart.

It makes me almost feel sorry for you, Rebecca. Do you know that? When I look at you these days, and I see what you've become.

How you wormed your way into this lifestyle, trying so hard to take it for yourself.

Under the illusion that you're still in control. That you call the shots.

But this is all just part of my game.

And I have big plans for you, Rebecca. I really do.

Chapter Thirty-Three

'You need to tell Becks that you're here at least. She'll be worried sick,' Lisa says as she places Ella down on her changing mat so that she can change the child's nappy. 'You didn't see the state she was in, Jamie. I mean, she's stronger than she looks, but everyone has their limit.'

'What's that supposed to mean?'

'It means I'm worried about her. What if she does something stupid? She looked completely broken when she realised you and Ella were gone.'

Lisa had spent most of the day trying to talk some sense into her brother, to no avail. He was being standoffish, refusing to talk to Rebecca, and Lisa was starting to lose her patience with him. He could be so pig-headed at times and nothing Lisa said would make him change his mind.

'You need to talk to her. You should go home.' She was now regretting going along with Jamie's request to lie to Rebecca, annoyed with herself for allowing him to persuade her to cover for him. She got it, he needed space. And he'd promised her that he'd only be here for a couple of days. Just until he worked out what he was going to do.

She couldn't refuse him; he was her brother after all.

Her loyalties should lie with him.

Only as much as she loved Jamie, this all just felt so wrong.

'I stood in front of her and lied to her face for you, Jamie. That's not fair, that wasn't part of the deal. I said you could stay here, but I didn't expect to have to lie and hide that fact from Rebecca.' Lisa was riddled with guilt for not telling her sister-in-law the truth about where Jamie was really staying and annoyed that her brother couldn't see how awkward that had made her feel.

She'd seen the state that Rebecca was in. She knew how much she'd be hurting, having Ella kept away from her.

'Look, just let me deal with this my way. Okay?'

Lisa shrugged, still unable to get the words that Rebecca had used earlier out of her head. She'd said that Jamie was punishing her. That he'd taken Ella away from her on purpose.

And Lisa was starting to question if perhaps that was Jamie's intention all along. Because Rebecca was suffering greatly right now, and Jamie would be well aware of that. She was starting to wonder what the real reason was for him wanting to hide out here. He seemed so angry with Rebecca. As if she'd done something intentionally wrong.

'Look, I don't know what's going on here. But Rebecca has only just got back from the hospital, you should be at home with her, but instead you're here. It doesn't make sense?' Lisa said honestly. 'You know that I will always help you, Jamie. But I really feel like I'm stuck in the middle here. Rebecca is my friend, and I don't want to hurt her any more than she's already hurting. And she *is* hurting, Jamie. Surely you guys can fix this? Can't you just talk to each other? Sort out whatever it is that's going on between you?'

'Oh, suddenly you're an expert in marriage guidance, are you? Remind me again, how long have you been single for now?' Jamie said, his tone full of sarcasm. His guard instantly up.

'Oh, piss off, Jamie. You know I'm only trying to help,' Lisa retorted. It was obvious Rebecca was struggling and needed help right now, yet Jamie was behaving like he didn't have a compassionate bone in his body when it came to his wife.

'I know it's a crazy concept and all that, but I just think you'll resolve everything a lot quicker if you actually speak to each other.' Then, serious again, she adds, 'and it can't be good for Ella either, being away from her mummy. She'll be missing her, Jamie. It's not fair on her either. And whatever you think about Rebecca, whatever's going on between you, she's a good mother, Jamie. She does her best by Ella. You know she does.' Scooping up her tiny niece into her arms to ease Ella's soft cries, Lisa kissed her gently on the forehead. Ella was fractious. Despite being so tiny and too young and oblivious to know what was happening around her, she could feel something wasn't right.

'It's okay, darling, there's a good girl. Auntie Lee-Lee's here, darling.'

'It's not as simple as just going home and talking. Talking isn't going to fix this,' Jamie said, losing his patience and shaking his head. 'I'm not really sure anything will. You don't understand.'

'Well that's one thing we agree on.' Lisa shot a look to her brother that told him she wasn't going to be so easily pacified. 'Jesus, Jamie, Rebecca isn't well. She's struggling. It's hardly a crime. I don't understand what's going on? So why don't you enlighten me?'

'They discharged her from the hospital, but what if Rebecca lied to the psychiatrist?' Jamie said, hanging his head down into his hands and running his fingers through his hair, as if contemplating his own question. 'What if she fooled them into thinking that she's okay when really she's not?'

Lisa laughed, unable to keep up with her brother's irrational trail of thought. 'Are you for real? Why would she do that? How would she trick them? That makes no sense. She was assessed by a team of mental health workers and a qualified psychiatrist. They'd see past any pretence. They'd know if she was sick or not. And she's not, Jamie. At least not in the way you thought. She's got post-natal depression. The hospital discharged her. They are going to treat her as an out-patient. She needs your support, not this. Christ, Jamie. I'm sorry but if anyone's talking crazy right now, it's you!'

Lisa was fuming.

Placing Ella down in her travel cot she busied herself tucking the child's blanket in all around her and placed her dummy in her mouth. Anything to busy herself for a few minutes, so that she didn't lose it completely with her brother. He should be doing all of this.

Jamie took Ella purposely away from Rebecca. He should be stepping up in terms of looking after his daughter.

Ella seemed to relax now, and Lisa smiled as the baby finally gave in to sleep and closed her eyes.

Arguing wasn't going to help them either, she reminded herself. Her brother was tired and stressed. She got that. He'd been through an ordeal these past few days too.

'I'm making coffee, do you want one?' It was a peace offering of sorts and Jamie nodded his head.

'Seriously, Jamie, why would she lie to the doctors? If she really was sick, don't you think that maybe she'd want to get better?' Lisa said, crossing the room and switching the kettle on, keeping her voice soft, aware of Ella sleeping peacefully.

She sees Jamie falter at her question, a flicker of doubt flashing in his eyes, confirming her suspicions that he was holding something back.

'What is it you're not telling me?'

Jamie paused. Taking too long to gather himself and speak. Giving himself away. Then, raising his eyes, he figured he had nothing to lose.

'I think that Rebecca manipulated the psychiatrist. I think she's been manipulating us all. It's what she does.'

'Okay...' Lisa said doubtfully, rolling her eyes now at her brother's latest crazy notion but she was interested to hear this theory of his. At the very least it might shed some light on why he's acting the way he is, hiding from his wife, taking their baby daughter away from her. Lisa stares blankly at him, waiting for him to elaborate, only he's struggling to put whatever he's thinking into words and Lisa has to coax it out of him.

'Jamie! What is going on?'

There was another thing niggling at her now too.

Jamie had been acting distracted since he got here. Sneaking off to make private phone calls out of Lisa's earshot and constantly staring at his laptop or his phone.

As if he was waiting for someone to call.

Lisa knew for a fact that he hadn't spoken to Rebecca yet. So, who was he talking to?

'Do you still love her, Jamie?'

'Jesus Christ!' Jamie said, his temper getting the better of him. 'Seriously, Lisa, do yourself a favour and stop with all the marriage counselling. You don't know what you're dealing with.'

'I know more than you think,' Lisa said, biting her lip, but unable to hold back. 'She thought you were having an affair. I told her that you wouldn't do that, that there's no way you'd cheat on her. But you have been, haven't you?' Lisa shook her head, unable to keep the disgust from her tone as the realisation hit her. 'Is this what this is all about? Is this the reason that you're not going home? Now that Rebecca is struggling, you're using it as your "get out of jail free card"?'

'You saw what it did to our mother when dad cheated on her. You know what he put her through. What he put us all through. Do you really want that for Ella too?'

Lisa feels physically sick. As much as her brother could be a pain in the arse sometimes, she'd never had him down as a cheater. Not after what they'd been through themselves as children. They'd experienced the devastation first-hand when their own father had left their mother after a whole string of affairs. Jamie had lived the heartache of it with her. He'd lived it himself. And now here he was doing it to Rebecca, so soon after their first child was born.

'Why would you jeopardise everything, Jamie, why?'

'Jeopardise everything? And what is it exactly that I have, Lisa? A wife that won't tell me jack shit about her life before we met. A woman who, since we've had Ella, has changed into someone completely unrecognisable. Will you listen to yourself, Lisa!' Jamie shouted, getting to his feet, agitated as his phone started ringing. 'Her saying that I'm cheating on her is just another story she's made up. For Christ's sake, Lisa, she thinks she's got a stalker for crying out loud. She thinks someone was in our house. In Ella's room. But there was absolutely no sign of them on the security cameras. The police saw it. We all saw it. She doesn't know what the fuck she's saying or doing lately. You do realise that, don't you? So do me a favour, dear sister, and don't get sucked into her bullshit too.'

Eyeing the caller ID that flashed up, he took a deep breath. 'Look, I need to take this. It's important. Can you keep an eye on Ella for a few minutes?'

'Sure,' Lisa said, tightly, still stunned by Jamie's overreaction and the venom in his tone when he spoke about Rebecca. Taken aback, she'd never seen or heard him like this before. A few minutes space was exactly what they needed right now. Though in all honesty, it made no difference to her if Jamie was in the room or not; she'd been taking care of Ella all morning while her brother was too busy with his head buried in his laptop and skulking upstairs every five minutes to make his secret phone calls. His whole demeanour was off.

He'd told her earlier that he was busy with 'work stuff' today, but now Lisa wasn't so convinced, though he was defiantly preoccupied by something.

Or someone.

Waiting until she could hear Jamie retreating into the upstairs bathroom, shutting the door behind him so that she couldn't eavesdrop, she carefully made her way over to the sofa.

Jamie was hiding something. Two could play at that game.

Eyeing the laptop that he'd left open on the chair; she quickly pressed her finger on the mouse in an attempt to stop the screensaver locking her out.

It worked.

She listened out for any noise from upstairs, but there was none. Not a movement.

She probably had a few minutes before Jamie would be back down and she was determined to find out what the hell was going on.

Pulling the laptop around to face her, she narrowed her eyes as she scanned the open window on the screen.

Instantly she recognised the image of her brother's lounge. The grainy black and white imagery of the long curtains that lined the window. The sofa just over by the main back wall. It was an aerial view of Jamie and Rebecca's entire lounge? Although there were no signs of anyone. No signs of Rebecca. The sofa was empty and the television screen blank, switched off.

Lisa held her breath.

What was her brother up to? Was he watching the house? Watching Rebecca?

Clicking on a second window, Lisa was now looking at Jamie's office, where Rebecca was. Lisa winced at the sight of her sister-in-law, she looked distraught, frantically ransacking the place as she rooted around inside the desk's drawers and filing cabinets. Discarding a mountain of paperwork, sweeping the pile from the desk with the back of her hand in frustration.

Lisa felt guilty for her part in her friend's angst. They shouldn't be doing this to her. They shouldn't be keeping Ella from her.

Rebecca would be lost without her.

She wouldn't know what to do with herself. And she'd be beyond mad at Jamie.

She must be searching for clues on where they might be.

About to move the laptop back, Lisa hears a ping as a new notification pops up on the screen. An email from Jamie's PA, Jenna, the message header reads *XXX*

And the email address isn't Jamie's usual one?

He's got a secret email account? What was he hiding?

Unable to help her curiosity, Lisa opens the email, her hand shaking. Reading through the entire thread of the flirtatious messages, it was clear that Rebecca's suspicions were warranted.

Jamie *was* having an affair. And judging by the conversation they were having, that was where he'd spent last night.

He hadn't been at a hotel on a business trip like he claimed, he'd been at Jenna's place.

Or at least, he'd spent the first part of it there.

Jenna's messages today were saying how it was such a shame that he'd been called away when they'd just started to have fun. She was being flirty and trying to make light of it. But she'd mentioned that Rebecca had called Jamie away. And that she hoped Ella was feeling better?

Lisa frowned.

Jamie had told the police and Rebecca that his business meeting was cancelled. That he'd come home early and found Rebecca screaming in the garden.

It had been a major coincidence that he'd turned up when he had, and Lisa had been grateful that he'd arrived when Rebecca seemed to need him the most.

But this email implied otherwise.

Jamie had left Jenna's house in the middle of the night.

He'd made his excuses to leave, just as Rebecca was claiming to have seen someone inside the house. Someone watching her from the garden.

What the hell was going on here?

Had Jamie been watching her then too?

About to close the window down, and confront Jamie, Lisa bit her lip as she eyed another email, the weird encrypted email address instantly grabbing her attention because of the strange lettering. She clicked it, listening out for the bathroom door upstairs, but there was still no sign of Jamie.

At first glance, it looked like a list. Just a load of jumbled dates and places that went back for weeks. There were a few key words in there for detail, but Lisa had no idea what she was looking at.

Tuesday 12 April – Park. 14.50 p.m.

Wednesday 13 April – Supermarket. 10.37 a.m.

Thursday 14 April – Coffee shop on Kensington High Street. 12 p.m. Lisa Dawson.

Seeing her own name on the list, Lisa almost did a double take.

What was this?

It was an activity log, she realised. A timeline of somebody's movements.

Rebecca's movements?

Tuesday had been the day they'd met for coffee.

Jamie was having Rebecca followed?

Was that who he was on the phone to right now?

Closing her eyes tightly so she could shut all other thoughts out, she wracked her brain to try to make sense of what was going on here. All Lisa could think about was how Jamie had been so adamant about Rebecca going to the hospital under the Mental Health Act. In fact, it had been him who had encouraged it, under the guise of being worried about her safety.

About Ella's safety. Jamie was convinced that Rebecca wasn't of sound mind. He'd told his sister as much. That Rebecca was constantly acting paranoid and feeling like she was being watched and followed.

That's what Jamie had said. Rebecca had told her too.

Only now Lisa realised that Rebecca had every right to feel that way, because it was true. She *was* being watched and followed.

By Jamie. By her husband.

He'd put her under a microscope and used it against her when she'd reached out for help.

But why?

Lisa thinks back to what Rebecca had said earlier. That she thought this was all Jamie's way of punishing her.

Punishing her for what?

She checked the travel cot to make sure Ella was sleeping peacefully. Lisa didn't know what the hell was going on, but she was going to put an end to this madness right now.

It was time to confront Jamie.

Making her way upstairs, Lisa knocked loudly on the bathroom door, no longer caring if she was interrupting his so-called important phone call. She wanted answers and she wanted them now.

'Jamie?' Lisa called out, rapping louder on the door with her knuckles, only to be met with silence. She grabbed at the handle impatiently and pushed the door open.

'Jamie?' she called out, again, her eyes darting around the empty bathroom. Puzzled, she made her way along the hallway and checked the two bedrooms in case he'd gone there to take his call instead.

Only he wasn't anywhere to be found upstairs, and when she went back downstairs, there was no sign of him.

Ella was still sleeping peacefully in her cot.

But Jamie had gone.

Chapter Thirty-Four

Staring around the office, Rebecca had no idea where to start.

Jamie's good at hiding all his lies and secrets from her. More than good, he's a pro, with months of practice behind him. He'd like to think he was, anyway. No matter how careful and concise he thought he was being at covering his tracks, some habits never die.

And Rebecca had been here before with Mark. She knew what signs to look for.

Which is why she made it her business to know everything about Jamie. He's smart. But she's always had to be smarter.

All those hotel bookings for those 'business trips' when he'd spend a night or two away from home. The receipts he thought he'd hidden deep inside his jacket pockets. For someone who prided themselves as being so successful and clever, Jamie really wasn't as clever as he liked to think he was.

But this time he'd been really thorough. Rebecca hadn't been able to find a single trace of where he'd gone. Bending down, her hands tear through the contents of the bin, but again she finds nothing. Which angers her because she knows the answer, the clues to where he might have gone, must be here somewhere.

Yet there are no signs of any receipts or paperwork. No booking print outs. No half-scribbled notes on the notepad next to the phone.

Sitting back up, she stares at the computer, her mind whirling as she switches it on and waits impatiently for the screen to fire up, a tiny part of her suddenly apprehensive about what she might find on here.

There's a deep feeling of dread in the pit of her stomach, but still she knows she must look. So she taps at the letters on the keyboard.

ELLA2019

Such an obvious choice of password for a man with so much to hide, and for a second, Jamie's predictability almost disappoints her.

Though she can't deny it's served her well in the past.

She's in. The screen lights up and Rebecca scrolls aimlessly though his emails and messages, unsure of what she's looking for. Hoping to see some form of hotel booking made in the last twenty-four hours.

An Airbnb perhaps.

An email from a colleague? Though she doubted Jamie would stay with any of his colleagues. He was too private for that.

There's nothing. Pausing, Rebecca's finger hovers over the mouse, immediately suspecting that maybe he's deleted some.

Because there're emails here that have been opened today, so she knows he's been online.

Of course he has.

Work doesn't stop for anything in Jamie's world. His whole life is work. Why would today be any different?

She clicks on the 'Trash' folder, biting down on her lip as she waits to see what deleted files have been moved there. Only that folder has been emptied.

He's hiding something from her.

There's something he doesn't want her to see, she's sure of it.

Tapping on her hand on the desk, anxious now that she might have missed something, she stares at the screen.

Then it comes to her. Jamie's search history. Though she's not holding much hope of finding anything there either, because he's clearly too astute to leave any kind of trail. Only he must have forgot to clear his history, because everything he's looked at the past few days is here.

Everything is there, listed in chronological order for her to see. The dates and times of every site Jamie has visited. She's searching for a name of a hotel, or an Airbnb, but when she's looked at a few down the list, she stops, her gaze fixed on a webpage that floors her for a few seconds.

It can't be?

Rebecca blinks hard, convinced that her eyes are deceiving her, but when she refocuses, she knows it's true, knows that Jamie's seen this.

That he knows the truth about her.

She clicks the link with trembling hands. Her eyes scanning the newspaper headline.

Two dead in fatal crash.

Physically flinching at the words, her heart beats faster, violently, drumming loudly inside her chest as her blood runs ice-cold inside her veins.

She's holding her breath, as if she is suddenly too scared to breathe.

Too scared to move.

Jamie knows!

Is that what this is all really about?

Rebecca wants to throw up. Her stomach churning.

Unable to look away from the harrowing image of the blackened, burnt-out car. She tries to block out all memories of that fateful day, pushing it back to the deepest, darkest recesses of her mind again, but it's ingrained in her.

Two bodies. Two dead.

Two.

And she thinks of her then, for the first time since that horrific evening. The darkest, most painful memory she has, the one she's spent her life running away from.

Little Jessica. Dead in the back of the car. A raw, vicious pain tears through Rebecca at the memory, a stricken sob escapes her mouth.

It's too much for her to bear and the room begins to spin, suffocating her, the walls gaining speed and closing in. The pounding in her chest is replaced by a tinny ringing inside her ears, her eyesight blurred with a haze of a million tiny white flecks.

It looks like the starry sky she'd laid down and looked up at on that fateful night.

That's Rebecca's very last thought before she sinks down from the chair, hitting the floor with a thud.

Chapter Thirty-Five

Oh, Rebecca! You're not as smart as you like to think you are.

Trawling through the office. Tapping at the computer keyboard, frantically searching for clues.

But you're not as clever as you once were, nor as strong.

Not since Ella.

Becoming a mother has made you vulnerable. And that's good, for me at least, because it means you've let your guard down, Rebecca.

You're losing it.

The old you wouldn't have taken so long to work it all out.

The old you wouldn't have missed the clues in front of you.

But you have. And as you stare back at me through the lens of the webcam, you're still unaware that I'm at the other end. Watching you.

Oh, if only you knew.

I see your eyes scrolling down to the list of web addresses. I see the panic flash behind them when you click the link.

You're trying to work it all out, but you still don't really have a clue.

I've taken my time fucking with you. Savouring every second of your gradual demise.

You thought you were safe here. In your own home. Lulled into a false sense of security, not knowing that I'm all around you.

You pick up your phone, unaware that it's yet another constant gateway I can tap into. I watch you there too, Rebecca.

I watch you all the time. That's the beauty of technology, you see. You think it gives you freedom, but really it's placed you in a cage.

An animal to be observed.

I see you now, as you check your phone for messages or a missed call. Again.

You have none. I've already checked.

And you're panicking now. I can see the fear written all across your face.

That's what happens when you go digging, Rebecca. You find stuff you don't want to see.

You try to stand, but it's all too much for you. Now you know your sordid secret is out.

I'm almost sad that I won't get to watch you carrying out your routine tonight. I won't be able to smirk as you repeatedly check all the windows and doors, pulling at the handles and wriggling the locks. Dragging the curtains across and blinds down as if you're trying to keep the dark night outside from seeping in.

As if you're trying to keep me out.

You won't carry me with you as you make the way to your bedroom and place me down on your bedside cabinet as you stand oblivious to me watching. Undressing, naked, your clothes slipping to the floor, before you slide into bed and pull the covers up around you.

I watch you now, as your eyes roll in your head and your legs give way, smiling as I watch you slam, unconscious, onto the floor.

There's one thing you haven't accounted for, my sweet Rebecca.

You can't keep somebody out when they're already inside.

Chapter Thirty-Six

I'm back there again. Inside the car. With you.

I recall the shock as you lash out and hit me. Hard.

And oh, the pain. As the ball of your chunky fist connects with my eye socket and the white hot, blinding agony of the blow explodes inside my skull.

I bite down on my lip, determined not to let out the strangled yelp that despite my stubbornness still manages to escape my throat, involuntarily, as my head flings back and smacks against the cool firm leather headrest behind me.

We veer off the road then, temporarily immobilised as my foot slips from the accelerator and I slump back in the driver's seat, my grip on the steering wheel loosening.

We mount the grass verge at the side the road and the car starts to twist and spin. Skidding out of control as we glide across the grassy bank, before I pull the car back onto the narrow dirt track.

'Fuck!' I scream. Snapping out of my daze, my reflexes take over, fuelled by adrenaline and my sudden need to survive.

But all I can hear is your voice ringing loudly out in my ears. Echoing round and round inside my brain.

And all I can feel is the pain.

My head is throbbing.

And I'm not sure what is hurting me the most? Your thunderous bellowing or the sharp sting of the blow which has blurred my vision.

Blinking hard, I shake my head. I look ahead, and wonder when the night sky opened up and started to chuck out sheets of treacherous, ferocious rain?

The rain is even heavier now, obscuring my vision even more.

The windscreen wipers can't keep up, sliding hypnotically across the glass, the momentum creating a loud monotonous swooshing noise.

Not loud enough to drown out the sound of your voice though.

And we're hurtling now.

It doesn't help that the light from the main road has gone now that we've made our way onto a deserted country lane. The last of the daylight has rapidly dwindled into nothing as we pelt faster. Under the blanket of darkness, as if we're flying.

'Slow down, you crazy fucking bitch!'

Your voice is thick and heavy, shouting again.

And for a second I glance at you, watching as your entire body violently shakes with rage. Spittle sprays from your lips, peppering the dashboard with droplets of your saliva with every word you scream.

You look capable of murder.

Capable of murdering me.

One fist raised, clenched tightly, your short, jagged nails digging into your skin.

But you don't strike out again. You don't get a chance.

Because the car slams into something solid on the ground.

A rock? A tree stump?

I'm not sure what, because I was busy looking at you.

Busy waiting for another blow that didn't come.

For a few seconds, I wasn't paying attention and suddenly we're soaring through the sky, a second or so of weightlessness as the car twists uncontrollably in mid-air.

And I hear the wailing coming from the back seat.

It's all I can hear.

Loud and deafening; the most frightening noise I've ever heard.

****

Opening her eyes, Rebecca stares ahead, focusing on the blank television screen.

The stench of smoke from the fire earlier still lingers.

It was just a dream. Only a dream, she tells herself as she tries to ground herself, her eyes moving down towards the coffee table, scattered with magazines and an empty coffee cup.

She's in the lounge. Laying on the sofa.

She's safe. She's home.

Only something's not right.

She has no recollection of how she got here. No recollection of falling asleep.

She tries to sit up, but winces as a dull thudding radiates inside her skull. Her head feels sore, as if she's been struck…

She fainted. She remembers now.

Jamie's gone. He's taken Ella. And she'd been in Jamie's office. Reading the articles on his computer.

The articles about her. About the crash.

Jamie knows.

241

She must have hit her head on the floor when she passed out.

She attempts to touch the bump she knows will be there, but her movement is restricted. She can't move her hands. Her skin tugs against the sharp plastic cable ties that are bound tightly around her wrists.

'What the fuck...' The words come out as a whisper as a wild panic spreads through her at the realisation someone has tied her up. Struggling to sit up, she realises that her legs have been tied with rope.

A clanging noise coming from the kitchen tells her she's not alone.

'Jamie?' she calls out, listening intently to the sound of running water from the kitchen tap, the shuffling of footsteps. Though she notes there is no sound of Ella. That alone feels her with the sense of dread.

'Jamie, I saw the articles on your computer. I know what you must be thinking. But please, I can explain everything. It's not what you think...'

Jamie must have come home and found her in his office. He would have seen what she was looking at on the computer screen.

That he'd found out all her secrets. He knew what she'd done. That's why he was acting so cold towards her and distancing himself, because now he'd found out who she really was.

'I wanted to tell you the truth, really I did. But I couldn't tell anyone... not even you...' She tugged at the cable ties, pulling her wrists apart with all the strength she could muster, but it was no use.

She wondered if Jamie had called the police?

That must be why he tied her up, so that he could keep her restrained until they got here.

Rebecca knew he could ruin her now. He had all the evidence, didn't he? Of who she was, of what she'd done. He'd pieced it all together.

It wouldn't take much for the police to join the dots and prove that it had been her that day, driving the car.

'You can't even imagine what I went through back then. How scared I was. How much I needed to get away,' Rebecca said, raising her voice, pleading with him now. 'He hit me. He always hit me. And that night, I don't know what happened. I just had enough. I had to get away.'

The kitchen was silent now. The footsteps had stopped, and the water turned off.

He was listening. That was something at least.

'Because there was always something that I'd said or done to annoy him. Something that angered him. It was dark that night and I was tired. Tired of that life. Tired of him. But I promise, Jamie, I didn't mean for what happened to happen. It was an accident... I swear to God. I was scared, and I was driving too fast.'

Rebecca was sobbing now, aware that begging was all she had left. If the police came for her, she'd lose everything. They'd take her away from Ella, this time for good.

It was a hit and run.

Murder.

And she'd spent the last couple of years trying to hide the truth.

'I'd finally plucked up the courage to leave him. Only he found out, and he got in the car and refused to get back out. And he was shouting and screaming at me, and I didn't know what to do, so I just drove. And he hit me. And I knew that when we got home, there would be much worse to come. There was always worse to come. So, I just kept driving. And he kept shouting. And then we hit something; I don't even know what, a tree stump? A grass verge? But the next thing the car was ploughing through the air. And that noise. God, that screeching …'

She shut her eyes then, as if trying somehow to shut the pain out, trying to forget the screeching that had come from the back of the car.

From *her*. The one person in all this she couldn't bring herself to think about.

'I didn't mean for anyone to die. I didn't mean to kill anyone. Especially not her.' Rebecca stops, unable to halt the tears cascading down her face, unable to even say her name.

Jessica. Her beautiful little Jessica. Dead, because of her.

She imagined Jamie standing over the sink and staring out into the garden like he did so often when they rowed, so angry with her that he couldn't face her. That long moody silence while he tried to gather his thoughts.

'When I realised they were dead, I panicked. I was in shock. I didn't stop to think, I just wanted to get as far away from them as possible. To pretend it didn't happen. And for a while I did.'

She pauses, aware that her secrets had been seeping out for months, despite how hard she's tried to keep them concealed. The night terrors, the paranoia. The way she was always so paranoid and neurotic with Ella.

Because her whole life with him had been a lie, and Jamie knew it now.

'I started out again, on my own. A new identity, a new life. And I know I lied. But I swear, Jamie, on Ella's life. We were real. You and me. Ella. US. All of this was real.'

Rebecca breathed deeply then, part of her relieved that the truth was finally out, because her secrets were what had been silently killing her, slowly sending her mad.

The pretence was over now, if nothing else.

Maybe now Jamie knew the truth, they could really work on bridging the gap that had slowly spanned out between them.

She had to make this right.

She had to make Jamie listen.

'That night in the hotel bar, meeting you. That was my second chance. YOU were my second chance. And I know I lied about a lot of things, Jamie. But I never lied about us. I never lied about me and you.'

She was sobbing uncontrollably having realised there would be no going back now.

All she could do was pray that she hadn't ruined everything.

Because since she'd met him it had been lie after lie after lie.

Their marriage was never real, no matter how much she claimed it had been.

It couldn't be, because Rebecca Dawson didn't exist.

Jamie didn't even know her real name.

She's lied so much, to everyone, she didn't even know what was real anymore.

Apart from Ella.

Ella was the only thing in all this that was real, and she was the one and only reason that Rebecca had to make Jamie listen to her.

She can't let Jamie call the police.

She can't go to prison for this.

'Please, Jamie. You have to believe me. You and Ella are everything to me. This family, it's all I ever wanted.'

And it's the truth, mostly.

All she's ever really wanted was a normal family.

Ella deserved that too.

Unconditional love from two parents who loved her. From the second Ella was placed in her arms she'd sworn that she would never have to endure a childhood like Rebecca had been forced to endure.

Her daughter would never witness the violence and the abuse she once had.

'We can still make this work, Jamie. Now that you know, I'll be better. I'll get better, because I won't be hiding anything anymore.'

And she means it too. If Jamie just gives her one more chance, she'll try even harder to be the perfect wife to him.

She'd forgive him all of his affairs, turn a blind eye to his every indiscretion. She'll make this work.

Her final words are met with the sound of a glass smashing as it's slammed too hard onto the kitchen side. The tap running again.

He was done listening to her.

Then she heard his footsteps coming towards her, into the lounge. Finally, she manages to push herself into an upright position on the sofa, ready to beg and plead Jamie's forgiveness.

She turns her head to him and falters.

It's not Jamie stood in the doorway.

'You?'

The word escapes her like a small strangled moan as she recoils, slumping back limply on the sofa, staring at the figure, convinced her eyes are deceiving her. Struggling against the bonds that bind her hands and feet tightly together.

Desperate to escape.

Because *he* can't be here.

He can't be real.

He's dead.

She killed him in the car crash.

'What's the matter, Alex?' he says, his voice familiar and mocking, thick malice in his tone. 'You look like you've seen a ghost.'

Chapter Thirty-Seven

It's fucking crazy how much some people will put out there on the Internet about themselves for all to see.

Boasting about what car they drive, or what kind of house they live in. How much money they make. Where they're eating, or walking, or holidaying.

The world's gone mad. People don't think about their safety anymore.

They don't realise people can find out anything online these days.

Trust me, if they knew who was watching, they wouldn't be so eager to share every mundane, boring detail of their lives.

Because they are watching you.

Ratters or Rats. That's who they are.

And you'd be forgiven for thinking they're named after the dirty, stinking infested rodents, because there are similarities.

These rats sneak up on you and catch you unaware.

They're riddled with disease and malice.

Only these rats hold so much more power over you as they crawl in and out of the darkest, deepest wormholes of the Dark Web. Lurking just behind the webcams on your computer screen. Hacking deep into your computer. Bypassing your malware software and infecting your machines. Delving deep into your whole life. All your secrets. All the things you don't want anyone else to see.

The things you don't disclose online.

They get to see all of that as they watch you, day and night.

It's a dark world out there. But then you know that only too well, don't you?

You thought you were safe here.

You're not.

It's all around you. Everywhere you go, in everything you do.

The concept is so destitute, so twisted that most people can't even contemplate that these things, these people exist.

But they do, and there's a whole community of them out there.

Ratters.

Though they prefer the term 'Operators'. Of course they do. Because the power goes to their head, and they actually believe that they own you.

And in a way, they do. Because once they manage to get inside, there's no escaping from them. No one can catch them, no one can stop them.

It's near on impossible, because they leave no trace as they add you to their list of their ever-growing army of Girl Slaves.

That's what they call you.

And there are thousands of you out there. Thousands of unsuspecting, oblivious women, just like you. Staring back into their webcams, completely unaware that someone is watching them.

ALL THE TIME.

You are enslaved to a secret world that you're not even aware exists and they collect you like pawns. For pleasure or for money. Usually both.

Accessing your digital life in its entirety.

They steal your credentials and gain access to all your financial information.

Your online banking. Your credit cards. Your passwords.

They can hack into your social media accounts and fuck with your contact list. They can access your diary and find out where you are at all hours of the day.

They have access to your microphone and your camera.

And it's the camera they're seeking out the most.

Because they want to see you.

Day and night. Around the clock.

When you're sleeping. When you're eating. When you fuck.

They watch you all the time and they film you, documenting your every movement.

When you go for a shower, or when you're sitting alone in the toilet. The iPhone in your hand. The Kindle next to your bed. The laptop on your bedroom floor, left open.

All those intimate moments when you think you're all alone, and that no one's watching.

That's when they watch you the most.

It's like some fucked-up, crazy obsession.

A contest of who can get the most sordid, graphic captured moments.

They see you. They hear you. They're with you ALL THE TIME.

You are never, ever alone, always accompanied by a shadowy figure with one hand hovering over the mouse to record you, and one clammy hand down their stinking pants.

They film you having sex, and when you're sprawled out all in your bed, all alone, screenshotting your body throughout the acts you perform on yourself and zooming in. For their pleasure or for your pain.

Zooming in on your face. Your body. Your tits. You're laid bare, completely unaware that in your most intimate, private moments, you're putting on a show just for them. So they can ridicule you with it later, or wank over you.

Sharing your videos and images with the rest of their sick, fucked-up network of perverted stalkers.

They post clips of you in private forums.

They keep files on you.

You're labelled. The ugly ones. The hot ones. The ones who masturbate. The ones who pick their nose.

For the Ratters, it's all about having that control.

They are more powerful than you can ever imagine.

They can literally break you, destroy you, they can bring you to your knees.

And after that it's all just a waiting game until they get bored with you and want to move on to their next pursuit.

And that's when the fun really begins.

That's when they can start really fucking with you.

Let the real games commence.

They'll threaten you then, blackmail you into paying up, to make them and all those intimate videos they've collected disappear. The ones of you masturbating when you thought you were all alone in your bed. Your legs spread wide open, as your fingers plunge deep inside of you. Or the other videos of your partner going down on you, or you on all fours sucking his cock.

They know where to send them. Where it will you hit you the hardest, because they have your entire list of contacts from your phone and your laptop.

They've read your emails and seen your messages. They know all the people who really matter the most.

Your important business contacts, every member of your family.

Your parents. Your kids. Your exes.

For the money.

For the power.

For the knowledge that they are the ones in control and there's nothing you can do about it.

251

And they have other means of torment and suffering. So much more than mere mortals can contemplate.

Just when you thought it couldn't get any worse, it does. Once you've run your course and given them everything they want.

Once they are bored with you, they sell you on to the highest bidder.

To some sick fuck on the Dark Web. So that someone else can carry on where they left off and torment you. Only you're the real prize then.

Because the next sick fuck has bought the golden ticket. They get everything.

Your photos. Your intimate videos. Your address.

It's a high price to pay for all that.

And fuck, you were expensive, Rebecca. I know first-hand.

But you were worth every single penny.

And now it's your turn to pay.

Chapter Thirty-Eight

'Mark?' The word slips from Rebecca's mouth, almost like a low groan of pain escaping from somewhere deep down inside of her.

And there's a flash of confusion that shines from her eyes, her expression a picture of horror.

She's scared. Genuinely scared.

He registers the shock on her face and it pleases him immensely, enjoying the real fear that lingers there, her thoughts almost transparent, as if he can see the clogs twisting and turning inside her head. So much so he can't help but laugh as he enters the room and stands right in front of her. So she can see him properly. So she can get a good look at what she did to him.

'I probably look a bit different to when you last saw me, huh, Alex? Hanging from a burning car wasn't my best look,' Mark quips. 'Oh sorry! Should I say *Rebecca*? Because that's who you're pretending to be these days, isn't it? Suits you. It sounds weak and pathetic.'

He smiles, but there's no humour to his words, and she remembers the low throaty chuckle from all those years ago. The sound makes the hairs on her arms stand on end.

'I've aged. That's what you're thinking, isn't it? More so than I should have in just a few short years. Shit, death does that to a person.' He laughs again. 'Do I look as if I've just been dug up?!'

His face contorts into a twisted smirk, making him look almost unrecognisable from the man he'd once been. His skin is gaunt and sallow and puckered with deep jagged ridges, blistered and scarred from the burns he'd suffered.

The burns she'd caused.

'You don't look so hot yourself,' he says with a shrug, used to the constant stares and questioning looks. People whispering about him, too scared to ask him what had happened to his face.

'You did this,' he spat, grabbing Alex's face and forcing her to look now.

'You have no right to look away. Look at me. Look at what you did to me. Little Miss Fucking Perfect. Living like Lady of the Fucking Manor in this fancy life that doesn't belong to you.' Releasing his grip, he grins as she cowers at his touch. 'You've got fat, Alex. You've let yourself go. From the kid, no doubt. Is it any wonder your husband's fucking everything that moves? She's nice though, this latest one of his. Younger. Prettier. Tighter. I can see the appeal.' He's enjoying letting her know that he knows everything about her new life, that he knows all of her secrets, his well-aimed words stinging her, just as intended.

She flinches.

He laughs. She's always been so incredibly insecure.

She can't pretend that trait away.

Running his hand across her face, he grabs her chin tightly in his hand as he forces her to look at him once more. To really see him and all the damage she did.

There's nothing she can hide from him now.

And because of that, he's more than capable of tormenting her, and hitting her where it hurts the most. The look on his face tells her that this is only the warmup.

Rebecca feels sick with fear as she wonders what he's planning on doing to her.

'You look surprised to see me, Alex? As if I'm the last person on earth you ever expected to see again. Of course, you are! Because you left me for dead. Remember? When you crawled from the mangled wreckage of the car. You left us both for dead.'

The fear in her eyes is genuine, because she knows what he must be capable of, if he's gone to these lengths to find her.

And she knows that she deserves to be punished for what she did.

Because she's punished herself every day since too.

Her eyes flicker towards the front door and she wonders if she can break free from her restraints somehow and outrun him. If she can just get the door open before he reaches her.

Probably not.

She looks up at the security camera that faces the front door.

She might be able make it to where the camera covers, someone might see her. Jamie might be watching.

'I thought I'd never be able to find you,' he says now, matter of factly. 'Two years of searching, and here we both are. Finally reunited. It's funny, because for a while, I thought I'd lost you forever. But then I realised I was searching for a woman who no longer exists. Because you'd have to change your name. You'd have to pretend to be someone you're not. You'd have to go into hiding. Like the coward you are. I'd ask you how you've been, but...' Sarcastic now, he lifts his arms into the air, opening his chest wide and spinning around, his huge frame making him look clunky and awkward as he scans the room, taking in all the plush, expensive surroundings.

'Nothing changes, huh? You always had a knack of being able to land right on your feet, didn't you, Alex. Always looking out for number one.' He stares at her, aware that he's caught her completely off guard. That for once there's no bravado. She's not acting. She's not quick enough nor capable of hiding how scared she is right now. Her apprehension radiates from out of her.

Mark purses his lips together, his face twisted with hate, no longer trying to contain his loathing of her.

'It's all so perfect—' he pauses before adding, '—ly orchestrated. Isn't it, Alex? Your life here. But then you always did know how to spin a fucking lie. And looks aren't everything they seem. You taught me that too.'

He was trying to swallow down the rage that was building inside him as he took in the expensive interior. All so beautifully decorated and immaculate.

The bitch and her perfect fucking life.

How dare she live here like this?

He stands up, composing himself for a few moments as he runs his hand along the long oak dresser that fills the wall beside the sofa. The same sofa that Alex is lying on, hands and feet bound tightly.

He shakes his head, as if to clear it. He didn't think it would be like this, now that he'd found her, now that he was here.

That familiar feeling of the walls closing in on him. Of everything feeling so dark, so abysmal.

He thought he'd feel better somehow.

But he felt much, much worse.

Focus. Do what you came here to do.

Coming back to the present, he slid his fingers over the numerous framed photographs displayed on the dresser. Photos of Rebecca and Jamie, laughing, looking deeply in love. Of Ella when she was born.

He pauses, grasping the photograph of Ella tightly in his hand. The thick solid silver frame. A newborn baby, wrapped in a soft cotton blanket just hours after her birth. Her face still red, and her eyes screwed shut.

His eyes linger on the tiny infant for a few moments, before he turns his attention back to her.

'I knew you'd have to start again, from scratch, as someone new. That you'd go into hiding. Anything so you didn't get caught for what you did.'

He laughs then. This time for real. His eyes crinkling at the corners. 'Typical, eh? You never were any good at just blending into the background, were you, Alex? And I was right. Here you are, living a life of fucking luxury,' he sneered, his eyes slowly sweeping over her body, before meeting her eyes again.

'It took time to find you, longer than I'd hoped, but let's face it, I had all the time in the world, Alex. Didn't I? Nothing better to do. Not now. The only thing that kept me going was knowing that you were out there somewhere. That you thought you'd managed to get away with it.

That's what fuelled my search for you. The police might have given up looking for you, but I didn't.'

Walking over to the window, he stares out onto the private Kensington Road, taking it all in.

Alex's new fake life.

The small handful of houses on the expensive private road, all lined with pristine front lawns and expensive cars on the driveways.

So perfect and picturesque.

Alex hadn't suffered, not nearly enough.

It made him want to throw up, knowing that she'd almost managed to escape her punishment completely. That she'd almost managed to get away with her sins.

Almost. But he was here now, and he was going to put that right.

'I never lost faith, Alex. I knew that you'd slip up eventually. No matter how hard you tried to hide, I knew that I'd eventually find some crumbs. Unintentionally. Of course. Left by other people, perhaps. But there all the same. Little clues that led me to you.'

He takes a deep breath then. His words loaded.

'You were good, I'll give you that. Careful not to leave any trace of your new life online. But there's always someone else who will, Alex. Someone unsuspecting. Someone who doesn't realise the inevitable fallout for you.'

He pauses, watching her reaction as he relishes in the details of how he finally found her.

'And in the end, that's all it took. One click of the mouse and there you were. I have to say, I almost missed you. Staring back at me from that row of frumpy women, all proudly standing in line, displaying their new babies at some generic antenatal group. It was the kid that threw me the most! I really hadn't been expecting that. Fuck, I admit, that one hit me hard.' He shakes his head, incredulously. 'But there you were, different name, different look. A baby in your arms. Sweet little Ella. Completely different. But just the same.'

Rebecca doesn't speak.

She doesn't dare, acutely aware of the danger she's in. Now she knows the lengths he must have gone to find her. Now she can see and hear the venom that seeps from his every pore.

'And you love her so dearly, don't you?' he says, his soothing words mocking her. 'Your precious little Ella but you don't deserve her, do you?' His voice is almost a whisper as he leans down, close now. She twists her face around from his to avoid his sour breath as it fills her nose and makes her feel sick.

'In some ways, she's made you almost human.' His laughter is full of malice. 'I see it, when I'm watching you with her. How she's opened up that ice-cold heart of yours. It's funny how kids can do that, huh? How they make you vulnerable and weak. How you live in fear that someday something awful might happen to them. That someone might hurt them. That they might take them from you.'

He understood that more than anyone.

'This place looks different in the daylight.'

He watches her intently as she registers what he's saying. This wasn't the first time he'd been here, to her home.

She hadn't been imagining it. It had been real. He *had* been here, in her home. In Ella's nursery.

'Bigger off camera too.'

A small noise escapes from the back of Rebecca's throat as she registers what she's being told.

He has been watching her. All this time. It was him.

'I don't... I can't...' Rebecca tries to speak, to make sense of what's happening, only she can't find any words. Her breath is trapped inside her lungs and all she can do is shake her head, the dull throbbing returning instantly, every nerve on edge.

Her hands and feet are tied.

She has no way of escape. No way of letting anyone know that she's in trouble.

The cameras? She stares up to the one that's placed in the corner of the lounge, but Mark follows her stare.

'You really think I'd get this far and forget something so obvious as to fix the security tapes? If anyone's watching, all they'll see is an empty room. I'm playing them an old recording.' He laughs. 'Oh, I'm a lot smarter than you give me credit for, Alex. A lot smarter. Like last night; it wasn't difficult you know, to tap into the security footage and delete any evidence of me being here. To loop earlier footage and change the timings on the camera. To make it look like you were crazy. And you really did do a stellar performance, Alex. Running around the garden in your nightdress with a knife in your hand! Oh, you played the role perfectly. It couldn't have gone any better!'

He comes closer. His voice is quieter. His words sincere.

'See, I want them to think you're losing it, Alex. I want them to think that you've lost your mind. That will make my plan so much easier. Because, that's what all this is about, Alex. Me, watching you, making you feel as if you were going crazy. Fucking with your perfect little life. But it wasn't enough for me. It will never be enough for me. I was going to take Ella, you know. That's what I came here to do. And I came so close, standing there, looking down at her in her crib. All I had to do was reach down and take her. It would have been so easy. Your child for my child. Only I couldn't…'

He shakes his head, full of regret. Having a child around him now would be too painful.

'I wanted you to suffer as much as I suffered. I wanted to take from you the only thing you've ever given a shit about. But it still didn't feel enough. And there was a chance that someone would find her eventually, or they'd find me. And that you'd get her back then. You'd win again.'

He smirks then.

'So, I had a change of plan. Last night, I decided that another innocent life wasn't going to pay for your sins. You were. Because it eats away at you, you know. All that rage, all that hate. It dissolves away every part of your insides, until all that's left is a hollow, empty shell.'

And he is merely just a shell now, he knows it. His body is so thin that the pointy bones jut out from beneath his clothing. His features sharp and chiselled, making him appear gaunt, the black, sunken eyes making his face look almost skull like.

261

'Why should I be the only one to pay the price for what you did? Why should I be the only one to lose everything? Why should you get away scot-free?' Screaming at her. He gets up again, taking the photo frame of Ella and placing it on the table in front of her, so she could see the stakes of exactly what she was about to lose.

'You get it now, don't you? How having a child can change you. How you love them fiercely. How you'll do anything to protect them.'

Reaching out, he grabs her chin, yanking her head upwards, forcing her to look him dead in the eye.

'Only, what if protecting them isn't an option, Alex? What if they're taken from you in the worst possible way? What if all that's left was a black hole of nothingness? What would you do then?'

Chapter Thirty-Nine

Clenching her fists tightly, Rebecca yanks at her wrists, grimacing as she tries to release her hands from the tight cable ties but they just won't budge. They were rigid, digging into the bandaged wound from last night and sending shooting pains radiating up through her arm.

She's stuck here, she knows, inside her own house with this lunatic.

And a small part of her is glad that Jamie and Ella aren't here. That they are somewhere else. Safe.

She can hear him now, moving around in the kitchen. A chink of a glass hits the kitchen worktop, a drawer slides open.

The one where she keeps the knives?

She hears another noise then as he rustles around inside the kitchen cupboards.

She has no idea what the fuck he's doing out there and she doesn't want to hang around to find out. Escape is her only option.

Staring over towards the front door, she wonders if she can loosen the cable ties, just enough so that if she makes a run for it, if she reaches the door, she'd have a fighting chance of being able to get out. But as she yanks at the cables, she knows it's no use; they're too tight. The rope on her feet is too.

Mark's voice stops her dead in her tracks.

'Good luck breaking out of them,' he says, strolling back into the room with a glass of water in one hand and two large boxes, containing her sleeping pills and painkillers, in the other. Rebecca watches as he places them down on the table in front of her, the smirk on his face as she reads his mind.

'Poor, poor Alex. That's what they'll say when they find your body. She never got over her husband cheating on her and taking her child. The same way your mother went. Just another mad, crazy bitch who took an overdose. That's what she did isn't it?'

He smiles triumphantly then, watching her face pale.

'Oh, I know all your secrets, Alex. I made it my business to find out everything there was to know about you. And you're just like her, aren't you? A murdering fucking psycho. That's what they'll say when they see the note you leave. Confessing to killing Jessica before you cowardly kill yourself.'

He opens the pill boxes, tipping them out on the table and stacking them into a neat little piles.

And she knows that he'll do it. He's not bluffing.

He's going to kill her.

'Please don't do this, Mark. Please?' She's crying now, Unable to do anything else, as she recognises the malice in his eyes. He's really going to do this, and there's nothing she can do to stop him.

'Please, Mark, at least hear me out. I'm sorry.' She's whimpering. A trail of snot hanging from her nose that she can't wipe away with her wrists bound.

She must look pitiful. Pathetic. But she needed him to believe her.

'I never meant to hurt her…' Her words come as a whisper, a mere tremor as they leave her lips. All the colour drains from her face as the memory of the last time she saw Jessica flashes through her mind. And Mark, hanging lifelessly from the front of the car, his body, twisted and broken. Plumes of smoke spiralling out from the bonnet.

He was supposed to be dead too?

She finds her voice again. 'Two bodies? The headlines said they found two bodies?'

'Neither of them were mine.' He tilts his head, as if to dislodge the words stuck to the back of his throat. Stopping mid-sentence, despite himself, leaning in close, close enough for her to see the emptiness behind his eyes.

'There was a man sleeping rough nearby. That's who you hit, Alex. That's what made us veer off the road. Don't you remember? There *were* two bodies, Alex. A man and a child. But I wasn't that man.'

Mark pursed his mouth, letting her take this information in.

All this time she'd thought he was dead, that she'd killed him. Finally, she was learning the truth.

'I lived to see another day. Another painful, shitty, non-existent day, over and over and over again. While you... You were nowhere to be seen. Because you didn't hang about, did you? You left us. You left *her*.' His face twisted with rage. 'I tried to get her out of the car, you know. But it was too late. She was trapped and I couldn't reach her, and the fire was out of control. I had to stand there and watch her burn. Can you even imagine for a second how that felt? How desperate I'd felt, how helpless?'

'I'm sorry...' Her voice breaks as she starts to sob loudly.

There's another pause and he closes his eyes. Fighting back his own tears. Refusing to cry. Because crying is for the weak. He needed to be strong now, to focus.

'She was dead. Gone. And there's nothing I can do to bring her back. But there's everything I can do to seek my revenge now and make you pay.' Gritting his teeth, he forced himself to say what he needed to say without breaking down.

'You killed the homeless man on impact, so I placed my ID nearby.' He laughs. 'I let them all think that I was dead too. Because, technically it wasn't a lie. I *did* die that night, Alex. I died inside. And there would be no punishment the police could have given you that would have been good enough to avenge what you did. So, I vowed to myself that I would find you. No matter what. And I would make you pay.' Another smirk. He was enjoying this.

'And they'd never catch me, would they? When I caught up with you. Now. Because I no longer exist.'

He pauses, smiling at the genius of his plan. 'She died because of you, Alex. You murdered her!'

He stops himself from saying her name.

Even now, he still finds it so hard to say it out loud.

Even to Alex.

The pain still so raw, that most days he fought so hard to block the memories out.

Her little laugh. Her sparkling blue eyes. Her tiny hand tucked into his.

'Jessica died because of you,' he forces the words out now, taking a slow deep breath as the memories make his chest constrict.

He wondered how much thought this selfish bitch had given his daughter over the past few years.

None, he expected. And it sickened him to his core that Rebecca could just carry on and pretend it never happened. That she could start a whole new life. That she got to experience what it was like to have her own child.

'You don't deserve any of this.' Mark gestures holding his hands up to the grandeur of the house. 'And I'm here to take it all from you. I'm here to make you suffer, just like she did.'

Mark is pacing the floor directly in front of her now, enjoying her obvious discomfort as he sits down in the chair opposite her.

His eyes never leaving hers, he slowly drinks her in.

And Rebecca is sitting so still now, as if she's made herself go small.

She's scared. And so she should be.

Fight or flight. The only two options you have when you're faced with real danger. He's glad Alex realises the severity of the situation, because she's in great danger now.

She's not fighting yet, but he'd give her time.

Because the old Alex was still in there somewhere, he's convinced of that. Despite the pathetic act she was putting on. Despite the disguise she'd put on.

One thing he'd learned a long time ago was that Alex was always full of surprises. She always knew how to put on an act.

'I lived in squalor. Not that you care.' He shrugs. 'I slept on the streets. Huddled in a sleeping bag in some damp, stinking doorway of whatever vacant shop doorway I could find that would offer me some shelter.' He stares at her, his gaze cutting right through her. His eyes icy cold. 'That's where I slept the night of Jessica's funeral. The night of my own funeral.' He laughs. The sound harsh, all humour absent as he cleared his throat then.

'I remember lying there and not even being able to cry. Because there was nothing left inside me. No feelings, no emotions, nothing. And I had nothing left to live for. My beautiful, sweet Jessica was gone. She was all alone, without me, buried down there in the dirt.' He shook his head, still tormented by vision of her lying alone in her cold coffin. 'I almost drank myself to death that night. Fuck, I wish I actually had. I remember slipping in and out of consciousness, and each time my eyes flickered opened again, and I caught a glimpse of the hazy night sky, I begged for my life to be taken too.' Ruefully, he shook his head. Incensed at having wanted something so much, to have prayed for his own death, yet life always seemed to have a way of making its own plans and rules. He hadn't been shown any mercy on the night he wanted to die. Nor any since.

Until now.

'When I finally regained consciousness, do you know what I woke up to? The night of my baby girl's funeral. The night I lost everything. Oh, this will really crack you up. I woke up to a group of lads all taking a piss on me.' He spat the words out, the shock and the humiliation that he'd felt that night still leaving a bitter taste inside his mouth.

268

'It was stupid really. They were just a group of young lads. No more than just kids. They couldn't have been any more than twenty years old. And you do stupid shit when you're that age, don't you? They were all drunk and egging each other on. Just lads being lads on the way home from a night out. But I lost it. I don't even remember what or how, but I was on my feet and I was lashing out. And some of them ran off. But one of them wasn't fast enough, and I must have just blanked out. Because all my anger, all my pain, just erupted from inside of me. I remember pinning this poor fucking kid to the floor and I just punched him. Over and over and over again. And I didn't stop until it was already too late. Until the kid was dead. Just lying there, lifeless on the ground. A bloody pulp in place of what used to be his face. And do you know what I did, Alex? I took a leaf out of your book and I just ran.'

He looked her dead in the eye, his expression full of hatred for all that she was and all that she'd made him become.

'And that's what sickens me the most about that night. That I became just like you. You did that to me. You! You made me like that. You made me into a monster. I left that young lad, somebody's son, there on the pavement like a dog, to die on his own. Just like you left my Jessica.' He rubs his eyes, feeling the tension building behind them, his pulse quickening as he spoke. 'I never slept in another shop doorway after that. I made a point of only staying in squats. Old abandoned houses, with all the other junkies and down and outs. Places with no windows or doors that stunk of stale piss. I found a bedsit, eventually. Nothing anywhere near as grand or pretentious as this place. But at least

I could spend my days on my own, not worrying about someone attacking me or trying to rob me… or worse.'

He falters. 'You murdered her and then you left her for dead, Alex. How could you? All you thought about was yourself that night.'

'No!' Rebecca shouts, finally finding the strength to speak, her tears coming fast now. 'I couldn't save her. She was already dead. The crash killed her. And when I managed to get out, I couldn't get to her. I tried, but the car had caved in, she was trapped. And even if I could have got her out, there was nothing I could do for her. She was already gone…'

The blow came from nowhere.

Fierce and stinging, his fist locking with her jaw with a force that snapped her head backwards, a loud ringing echoing in her ears.

But she knows she deserved that and so much more.

'So you just left her there to fucking burn?' he spat. 'Her tiny body trapped in the back of the car. While you saved yourself, like the selfish bitch you are!'

Pacing the room now as his rage tore through him, Mark clenched his fists, fighting every urge inside his body to lash out. He wanted to hurt her. To make her suffer. Just like she'd made him suffer, every single day of his life since.

'I was in shock. I wasn't thinking straight. I wasn't thinking at all…'

'No!' he shouts. 'You don't get to do that, Alex. You don't get to sit here and give me your pathetic excuses. You knew what you were doing. You always knew exactly what you were doing. Don't play dumb with me. I'm not your fucking husband. I see straight through your little act. You tried to take her from me that day. Remember. You packed the car up and you tried to fucking take her from me. She shouldn't have even been with you.'

'I loved her, Mark. Jessica. I loved her too, as if she were mine. And I've had to live with what I've done every day of my life.'

'She was my daughter. Not yours, MINE. You had no right to take her...'

Shouting now, he's back up on his feet, picking up the heavy silver photo frame, the picture of Ella. He hurls it across the room and watches as it slams against the wall, smashing into pieces, jagged shards of glass all over the floor.

'She was *EVERYTHING* to me, and when you took her, you destroyed my life.'

His face is puce, the spittle spraying from his lips, and she's back there again, that night in the car. Only now he's past angry. He's unhinged.

'And now I'm going to destroy yours.'

He holds up the knife he'd tucked into the back of his belt, walking up to the sofa and bringing it down in front of her face. Close. Just inches from her skin.

She was trying so hard to keep deadly still, her breathing was heavy and laboured.

He moved the knife downwards. A sickening gleam in his eyes.

'Now, you're going to do as you're told. You're going to write this letter and you're going to tell them who you really are. You're going to tell them all what you did. Then you're going to take all these tablets.'

Scooping up a pile of pills, Mark shoved them into Rebecca's mouth, before picking up the glass of water and forcing her to drink it down, to show her that he meant every word.

Carefully, so that he wouldn't leave a mark on her skin, he sliced the metal blade through the plastic cable tie, before holding the knife back out in front of her. A promised threat.

'Swallow,' he shouted, moving closer, the blade just inches from her chest. Rebecca did as she was told, wincing as the tablets caught in the back of her throat, but choking them down.

'That's enough for now. I don't want you falling into a deep sleep before you've written the letter.' He pushes the notepad to her now and Rebecca holds the pen, trying not to draw attention to the shadow that she can see moving behind the door in the kitchen.

They are not alone.

There's hope.

But she needs to buy some time.

Chapter Forty

'Thanks for coming over.' Unable to hide the concern in her voice, Lisa leads Officer Blythe into the kitchen, closing the door so that they don't wake Ella, who is asleep in the travel cot in the living room.

'Like I said on the phone, I don't even know where to start, really. It might be nothing but…' She pauses, a small part of her not wanting to get her brother in trouble, but she's also worried about Rebecca.

'Just tell me what you know, and we can go from there,' Officer Blythe says, knowing that if it really was nothing, Lisa wouldn't have called him.

'They discharged Rebecca from the hospital this afternoon, I take it you know that?' She paused then, wondering if she should go on. Officer Blythe nodded his head.

'And you'd have thought Jamie would have been happy about it but he wasn't, at all. He seemed angry almost…' The words pouring out of her now as she tries to make sense of it all. As if somehow saying it out loud will make it resonate inside her head.

'Jamie's been here all day. He said that he just wanted some space. That Rebecca could do with some time on her own too. That he'd just stay a few days, with Ella. Only he didn't want me to tell Rebecca where he was,' Lisa said now, feeling wracked with guilt that she'd lied to her sister-in-law. 'And well, he's my brother, so I went along with it. Only…' Lisa tails off, staring out of the window, still trying to make sense of what she saw on Jamie's laptop.

'He's been acting strangely. Not himself. And I guess after last night, it's understandable isn't it, after Rebecca was admitted to a psychiatric unit. But it's more than that. He seemed cagey, kept skulking off to make private phone calls. And I was starting to think that he might be hiding something.'

Lisa turned to face the police officer, worried that her next sentence was going to place her brother in the firing line. Only her intuition was telling her that she needed to be honest with the police officer. If she was wrong, which she prayed she was, Officer Blythe would soon work it out and put her mind to rest. And then Jamie would be off the hook.

'Rebecca met me a few days ago. She was in a bad way. She wasn't sleeping, or eating, and she looked awful. She told me that she thought Jamie was having an affair. She was convinced of it. They've been having problems for a while now, apparently. Though of course, I had no idea. They always seem so together, you know? The perfect couple. I told her that she was just being paranoid. That having Ella had put pressure on them both, as a new baby would do, no matter how perfect she is. But Rebecca was convinced of it,' Lisa said, cursing herself now for not taking Rebecca's claims more seriously.

'And do you think that he was having an affair?' Officer Blythe asked, hearing the remorse in Lisa's voice.

Lisa nodded.

'I've only just found out now, for certain. I know I shouldn't have, but when he went to make that last phone call, I went through his laptop and looked at his emails. He's got a secret email account set up, just for her. His PA Christ! It's all such a bloody cliché. I met her at the Christmas party a few months ago and she's at least half his age. It's pathetic. Rebecca doesn't deserve this,' Lisa says, unable to keep the anger from her tone, disappointed that her brother would be the type of man that would not only betray his wife, but his newborn baby daughter too. A part of her wanted so badly to believe that Jamie wasn't the bad person in all this. But so far, it didn't look good.

'I clicked on the window that was on the screen and he was watching her. Rebecca. Through the security system. I think he has been all day. And I know it sounds weird, but what if he's been doing it for a while? What if it's been him, watching her? Because Rebecca said that she felt someone was watching her, didn't she?' Lisa's voice was almost a whisper now, as if she was worried that any minute Jamie would come waltzing back through the door and hear her accusations. She felt like a traitor. But she couldn't shake the bad feeling that she had about all this.

If she was wrong, then so be it. The police would prove it, and they could all move on.

'He started to say weird things about her, accusing her of manipulating the doctors. Of her lying to us all? He said that we shouldn't trust her, that there were things we didn't know.' Lisa frowned then, part of her glad to get everything she was thinking out. Hopefully the officer would be able to make sense of it, because so far, she couldn't.

'There's other things that he's hiding too…' She tailed off again, frightened that anything she said next might incriminate her brother, but she knew she had to be honest with the officer, for Rebecca and Ella's sake, if no one else's.

'Other things, like what?' Officer Blythe asked.

'I think he's been having her followed by someone. That he's paid someone to keep tabs on her and report back to him. This new email account that he's set up, it's only receiving mail from two accounts. One is the woman he's having the affair with,' Lisa said, tightly, 'And the other one, well, at first it didn't make much sense. It was just lists. Dates, times, places, that kind of thing. It didn't make much sense at first, but I worked it out. It's a log of Rebecca's movements over the past few weeks. I think Jamie's been having her followed.'

'Do you think it could be something innocent, like Jamie was just concerned about the state of her mental health? Maybe he just wanted to make sure that she was okay with Ella?' Blythe questioned.

'I don't think so. I mean, what about last night? Don't you think it's strange that he didn't tell you any of this? Even if he spoke to you in confidence, without Rebecca knowing. I mean you would, wouldn't you? If your wife was being interviewed by the police after having an intruder in the house, and she was adamant she was being watched and followed the past few weeks, surely you'd have to set the record straight? And wouldn't part of you want to put your wife's mind at ease? She thought she was being stalked and he let her get carted off to a psychiatric unit?' Lisa paused again, realising how bad her choice of words sounded.

The truth was, Lisa *did* doubt him. Her own brother. Her own flesh and blood and the officer could hear it in her voice. 'Even if she was wrong about there being an intruder in the house last night, she wasn't being paranoid or having a breakdown. She was telling the truth. She was being watched. So why didn't Jamie admit it?'

276

There were too many games being played. Too many lies and secrets being told.

'He lied about being at a hotel last night too. He was with Jenna. I read the messages, she asked how Ella was. Jamie made out that he'd been called away in an emergency. He'd told her that Ella was sick. That must have been when he came home and found Rebecca in the garden. Only, it's too much of a coincidence, isn't it? That he left Jenna in the middle of the night, only to come home and find Rebecca right when she needed him the most? More lies. I think he was watching her then too. I don't think Jamie turned up in the middle of the night, right at that moment, by chance. And I know how this all sounds, and shit, I know he's my brother, but what if it was Jamie doing this to Rebecca all along?'

Officer Blythe nodded.

He could see the genuine split of loyalties on Lisa's face.

'You've done the right thing calling me, Lisa. I appreciate how difficult this must be for you. When was the last time you saw Rebecca?'

'I picked her up from the hospital this afternoon. She was distraught to find out Jamie had taken Ella. Shit. I should never have gone along with him and lied to her. She said she was going to have a sleep and I was to give her a call tonight.' Going over to Jamie's laptop, Lisa clicks on the mouse. 'I managed to deactivate the password lock. I thought I better keep an eye on Rebecca, just in case Jamie went back there. He hasn't. Rebecca's in the office.'

Clicking the mouse, the screen lit up, showing the security footage so that the police officer could see for himself. Only now, the office was empty. All the carnage in the office Lisa had seen earlier had been tidied away.

Lisa clicked a few more buttons, alternating the view of each room in the house.

Nothing.

'Maybe she's gone back to bed? There's no cameras in the bedroom. They only covered the main living areas of the house... I don't know. Maybe this is all nothing and I'm overreacting. I just thought I better call you.'

Hearing Ella starting to wake, her low, throaty cry indicating that it was time for her next feed, Lisa excused herself, leaving Officer Blythe to take his time going through Jamie's laptop himself.

Feeling bad that she'd just rang the police on her own brother, but what if it was Rebecca that couldn't be trusted?

She didn't know what to think or who to believe anymore. All she did know was that she couldn't shake the feeling that something much more sinister was going on.

Chapter Forty-One

She's crying now.

Sobbing.

Because she knows Mark is capable of carrying out his threat and if there's any chance of getting out of this alive, she needs to try to stall him.

Eyeing the kitchen door, she thinks someone else is out there.

Someone who might be able to help her, but she can't be sure and she mustn't give anything away. Because Mark would kill her without warning.

For now, she just needed to keep him distracted.

Talking about Jessica only makes him crazy with anger.

She needs to talk about something else.

'How did you find out about my mother?'

Bingo.

He smirks, thinking he has one up on her, but Rebecca knows her past wouldn't have been hard to discover, seeing as it had been all over the newspapers when she'd been a child.

He's distracted now, so she starts talking. Not even caring if he's listening or not as it all spills out of her.

All the while her eyes are fixed on the kitchen door, and the shadowy figure moving around on the other side.

****

There are some memories you can never shut out completely, no matter how hard we want to and no matter how hard we try.

Because our brains hold onto our deepest, darkest fears and they lock them away, deep down inside of our subconscious minds. Just far enough away from our everyday thoughts, so they can't do us any harm.

It's part of our survival instincts.

There are triggers all around us.

A familiar look, a turn of phrase, a smell. *Olfactory memory.* That's what they call it when a scent or aroma triggers sudden memory or nostalgia.

For me it was always that potent sharp stench of whisky as it's poured neat from the bottle.

Or a lit cigarette.

Or hot milk and cornflakes.

Those memories never really leave you. No matter how far you manage to get away from them, no matter how much your life changes.

They are always there.

Physical and psychological abuse. It never leaves us. It lies in wait. Like a potent poison, dripping from an intravenous drip and slowly spreading through your veins.

Constant and silent, until it's completely flushed out the person you used to be. It festers there, the poison. Just underneath your skin, bubbling away inside you as it bides its time.

And then one day you wake up and you realise that your past no longer harbours your demons.

You're not scared anymore.

Because instead, you've become the one thing that you used to hate.

You've become *them*.

That's what they say isn't it? That one-third of victims of childhood abuse become an abuser.

And for me, my whole life has always been just an act, pretending that's not who I've become.

But it's futile, because that's how it works. We mirror the pattern of love we received as a child. That's our way of coping with how we once suffered.

And I am her.

Because it was always her.

My mother.

So damaged and dysfunctional.

That's what they said about us later on. When they finally took me and my sister away and placed us in a children's home. That same fateful night they found my father's body in the shed. He hadn't just upped and abandoned us like my mother tried to have us believe.

My mother had taken a hammer to his head in one of her drunken rages and brutally murdered him. She'd kept him there for days while feigning illness and taking to her bed.

That was the night we'd had dinner at my friend's house when I was just seven years old. That was my last memory of being 'normal.' Sitting around the dinner table and watching another family show us how it should be.

I still remember the numbness I felt when our friend's parents took us home only to find there was no answer when she knocked on the door.

And so, the police were called.

I almost want to laugh at the irony, that the only glimpse of normality I ever experienced as a child happened on the very same night my mother had taken her own life.

They said it was an overdose that took her, that she'd lain in her bed and taken a whole bottle of pills.

And I could picture her for months afterwards, my mother. Every time I closed my eyes. I used to try to remember the familiar smell of her bedroom all the times she'd taken to her bed. Having another of her *funny turns* that went on for days at a time. I'd often go into her room to ask her for something. Food, more often than not.

That smell, it never really leaves me. *Her* smell. A bitter stench of stale body sweat, entwined with the smell from the bottles of Scotch she'd discarded on the floor next to her bed.

My mother was wrong about the way we'd be treated in the children's home.

They treated us well. For the first time in our lives we didn't need to hide the scars and bruises she'd inflicted. We didn't need to shrink so small in our beds late at night, in the hope that we'd become invisible. Or lie in the darkness so still pretending we weren't really there. We were no longer forced to listen to the shrieks and the screams that echoed throughout the house at my mother's violent outbursts, at my father's incessant screams and cries.

Because they were gone. They were both dead.

And for a while it was okay. We were fine.

But then we were separated.

Me and my sister, Ella.

They took her away. They said they'd found Ella a family who would love her.

That she'd have the best chance in life.

They took her from me.

She was the younger sister. The prettiest. The softest.

Unlike me. Hardened. Angry. Bitter, even at just seven years old.

No one wanted me. I was trouble.

'Deeply disturbed,' I overheard one counsellor say.

From that day on, I tried hard to block out all memories of Ella, because it hurt so damn much.

And I started to blame him. My father.

It's funny, because when I was younger, I used to feel heart-wrenchingly sorry for my father.

Only as time went on, my feelings towards him changed.

Instead of pity, I began to place the blame on him for being weak and feeble and full of disappointment.

He wasn't strong enough to stop her.

He just took the pain, took the beatings. The biting and kicking and punches. The constant barrage of verbal abuse she unleashed at him, until there was nothing left. Just a battered, bruised, and broken man.

If he'd have just stopped her, if he'd have just stood up for himself, none of this would have happened. They'd both still have been alive, and Ella would still be here. With me.

Chapter Forty-Two

'Enough of the sob story!' Mark insisted, shaking his head, and staring over towards the kitchen door.

He knew what Alex was doing.

She was chatting shit to buy herself some more time, only her time was running out.

'You can come out now,' Mark ordered, his gaze following Rebecca's, laughing maliciously as he stares at the shadowy movement behind the kitchen door. 'Chivalry isn't dead. Here's the cheating, slippery husband. Cowering away in the kitchen, waiting for his perfect moment to help his damsel in distress!' Mark quips, letting Jamie know that his cover is well and truly blown as he stands up and holds the knife to Rebecca's throat, nodding his head as he instructs Jamie to join them.

'Do come and join us, Jamie. The more the merrier.'

Mark had heard Jamie come in, knew that he'd been standing in the kitchen listening to their entire conversation for the last few minutes.

And Mark had wanted him to hear it all. He wanted Jamie to know what Rebecca had come from.

What kind of upbringing had moulded her into the woman she'd become? Letting her speak meant that Jamie had heard it all, first-hand, straight from the bitch's mouth.

'Let her go,' Jamie said, the nervous tone to his voice betraying him as he stood haplessly in the middle of the lounge, watching the scene unfold before him, a metal pole in his hand for protection.

Which looked almost comical seeing as Mark was holding a blade to his wife's throat.

'Let *who* go? Alex… or Rebecca?' Mark sneers, disappointed that even after everything he'd just heard, he still wanted to help this murdering little bitch. 'Because she's not who she claims to be. You're not even legally married. You can't be, she's not real!'

Jamie's eyes searched Rebecca's for a hint of some truth. What he'd heard had to be lies, surely? This man wasn't right in the head. He was crazy, unhinged. Talking in riddles.

Only as Rebecca looks down, not quick enough to hide her guilty expression, he realises that whoever this man was, he was telling the truth.

'Rebecca?'

'Her real name is Alex.' Mark raised his voice as Jamie paled, shock flashing across his face as he realises that Alex knows this man. That he's not just some random intruder. 'Finally, the dumb fuck gets it. You can't trust this bitch, you know that, don't you? She's a liar and a murderer. Now, why don't you put that down before someone gets hurt,' Mark instructed, nodding at Jamie, indicating for him to put the pole down on the floor and take a seat on the sofa.

Eyeing the fresh cut that's forming on Rebecca's throat, a small trickle of blood running from where the sharp blade is piercing her skin, Jamie doesn't need to be told twice.

'She's not all she cracked up to be, is she? This wife of yours. A murderer. A liar. An Oscar-worthy actress. She had everyone fooled. Me too, once upon a time.'

Jamie scanned the coffee table, his eyes going from the pile of medication in front of him, back to Rebecca, as he wondered how many tablets she'd already been forced to take.

She looked awful. Her eyes, red and puffy from crying, were fixed on him. She was scared. He could see the genuine fear radiating from her.

Whoever this man was, he was trying to kill Rebecca, and he looked capable of going through with it too.

'What is it that you want? Money? Because I have money. I can give you whatever you need.'

'Money? Is that what you think will fix this? You heard the conversation. You saw the newspaper articles I sent you. You should know what she did. It was her. She was driving that car.' Mark shook his head, incredulously, the disgust clear in his voice that Jamie still wasn't getting it. That somewhere inside his skull, his brain still couldn't comprehend that Rebecca wasn't who he thought she was. 'She killed two people.' He bit his lip, his face twisted into an expression of complete hate.

'She killed Jessica. My child died. *MY CHILD*. And this bitch here fled the scene and saved herself. She's been trying to save herself every day since.' Mark was shouting now. Bellowing. Spelling out the obvious to this imbecile in front of him who thought he could just throw some money at him, and Mark would go away.

He wasn't going anywhere.

Not yet.

Not until he'd done what he'd come here to do.

'She's using you. All she ever wanted was a new identity. A new life to hide inside. She used you, just like she uses everyone. And you gave her everything she needed. Yet here you are, like a mug, coming to save a woman who doesn't really give a shit about you.' He turned back to Rebecca then. 'But then that's Alex, exactly as I remember her. She's only ever looked out for number one. Putting herself before others, no matter what the cost. And the cost this time was an innocent child's life.'

Mark stared at Jamie.

Jamie's face had paled. He looked directly at Rebecca now, willing her to tell him that it was all lies. That none of it was true.

Only she didn't speak.

She couldn't.

'Go on, Alex. Tell him,' Mark said. 'Fucking tell him what you did!'

'It was an accident,' Rebecca spluttered, feeling the knife pressing harder against her skin, as Mark riled himself up, his temper taking over, making him unaware of the strength he was using. 'I never meant to kill her. And I didn't want to lie to you, Jamie. But how could I tell the truth?'

'Because you're a liar, Alex. You lied to him. You lied to everyone. Everything about you is fake.'

'No, we were real.' Rebecca turned her pleading eyes to her husband. 'Me and you, Jamie. I never lied about how I felt about us.'

Tears streaming down her face, she gulped, the pressure of the heavy blade against her windpipe making her scared to breathe too hard or talk too loud. She could see the look of disgust on Jamie's face, and worse than that, something else.

Doubt.

He didn't believe her.

And part of Rebecca knew that he'd already started to put two and two together before today.

Because he'd seen the emails.

He would have been piecing everything together.

Only the truth was much worse than Jamie could have ever suspected.

'Her name is Alex Besley. And all of this – this house. This marriage. None of it's real. Even now, what she's saying. It's all lies. Alex isn't capable of loving anyone. You heard her yourself. The life she had before me. Her murdering nut job of a mother; she's just like her. They are two of the same. And now she's sucked you in too, she's using you for her own devices. Trust me. I know her, better than she knows herself.'

Jamie drops his gaze, his eyes fixed at the floor. His body deadly still.

Unable to look Rebecca in the eye.

Because this man, a complete stranger to him, was right.

Their entire marriage, relationship was all based on complete lies.

Jamie didn't have a clue who she really was.

Mark laughs then, victoriously.

'Even your husband doesn't want you now, Alex. How does that feel, huh? But then, he hasn't wanted you for a while, has he?' Mark says with a smirk, his sarcasm clear to them both.

Knowing full well that Jamie would come around to his way of thinking, now that he could see Alex for exactly what she really was.

A lying, child murdering bitch.

Chapter Forty-Three

'Lisa, what time did you last see Rebecca in the office?' Officer Blythe asks as Lisa returns to the lounge holding Ella in her arms.

'I don't know, it was about ten minutes before I called you, I guess. So about forty minutes ago… Why? Can you see her?'

'No, I haven't seen her yet. But I think there might be something up with the recording. You said you saw Rebecca tearing the office apart? But it looks immaculate now?'

'Yeah, I thought that was odd, you know. One minute it was a complete mess. She must have tidied it back up?'

'Well, I've been wondering about that.' Clicking the link, the officer zooms in on the office. Pointing at the clock on the office wall.

Lisa leans in close and peers at the time.

'The batteries have stopped?' she says with a shrug.

'The tapes have been looped. This isn't the real time.' Officer Blythe shakes his head and makes a grab for his radio.

'Why would the tapes be looped? I don't understand… So what we're seeing now isn't real?'

'I'm guessing someone doesn't want anyone to see what's going on inside that house,' Officer Blythe says with urgency, pressing the main button and calling it in, requesting immediate backup.

'Do you think it's Jamie? I mean Jamie wouldn't do anything to hurt her. I'm sure he wouldn't…'

Officer Blythe decided that Lisa needed to hear the truth. 'I don't want to worry you, but I had the tapes from last night analysed by an ex-colleague of mine who owed me a favour, so that we could speed things up a bit. Rebecca was adamant that we took a look at them, and she was right, someone *had* tampered with them. They'd deleted the original footage and placed the old footage on a loop. Just like this.'

'So, Rebecca could be there right now. In one of these rooms. But we can't see her?' Lisa questioned, panic spreading through her. 'But why would Jamie go to such lengths to disguise the footage? What could he be hiding?'

'That's what we need to find out,' Blythe said, having already suspected Jamie's involvement in all of this. He had concerns of his own.

'We don't know anything for certain yet; right now our priority is finding Jamie and making sure that Rebecca is safe.'

'You think she's in danger?' Lisa asked, her voice rising, but Officer Blythe didn't answer her question.

'I'm going to get a family liaison officer to come and sit with you and Ella, okay? I don't want either of you to move from this house.'

Lisa nodded as she watched him hurry out through the front door and wait for back up to arrive, just as Ella started to cry, probably picking up on the fear that rippled through her right now.

Lisa hugged her closely, rocking the baby back and forth to soothe her cries, as she prayed that she was wrong about Jamie.

'It's okay, darling,' she whispered to the child. 'Nothing's going to happen to you, I promise.'

She just wished she could be so certain about Rebecca.

Jamie wouldn't hurt her though, Lisa knew that.

Would he?

Chapter Forty-Four

'Get the fuck off me.' Rebecca's words were lost as she chokes loudly, twisting her head away from Mark's grip as he pinches either side of her face. Her lips were forced apart, as Mark pours a few more tablets into her mouth, his grip too strong.

He forces down more water, clamping her mouth shut with the palm of his hand to ensure that she does what she's told and swallows the medication.

'There's a good girl! Drink it all down.'

'You can't do this,' Jamie blurted out, unable to remain silent any longer.

The knife is on the coffee table now where Mark had placed it down beside him. Just a little too far from Jamie's reach.

The man's threats were still spinning around and around Jamie's head.

He was really going to kill Rebecca.

'Whatever she's done, this isn't going to make it right.'

'*Whatever's she's done*? You heard *exactly* what she's done, and you still don't get it, do you?' Mark said with a sneer, as Rebecca choked down the last of the tablets now that the confession had been written.

'*I killed Jessica. I left her inside the car, and I ran away,*' Mark said mimicking Rebecca's voice as he read the line out loud.

'This isn't about making things right. Nothing can make any of this right. Nothing will bring back my Jessica. This is about making this bitch pay. This is about taking everything away from her that she's ever loved. Think about it, Alex. You won't get to see that precious baby of yours grow up. You'll miss her first word, her first steps. Her first day at school. You'll miss all of it. Just like I've had to…'

Mark was bellowing now, his hands clenched at his sides to stop them from shaking.

'Her last day at school. Her wedding day. You took that from me, you took all of it…'

His eyes don't move from Rebecca's.

She'd gone quiet now, slumped back in the chair, the medication she'd been forced to take starting to take effect on her. Drowsy. As if at any moment she would just close her eyes and go to sleep.

Only, he knew that as soon as she did, she wouldn't wake up again and Mark wasn't ready to let her go just yet.

He wanted her to suffer. To really suffer.

He wanted her to hurt as much as he was.

'How could you do it, Alex? How could you leave her there, inside that car? You should have at least tried to get her out. But instead you ran. Because you're a gutless coward. All you care about is yourself. That's all you ever cared about.'

Jamie found his moment then, aware that Mark was caught up in his anger as he stood up and paced the room, that he was distracted. Jamie knew it was now or never.

He made a grab for the knife, pouncing from the sofa, reaching out his hands until he was just millimetres away.

Only Mark had already anticipated Jamie's move.

And he was on him in just seconds.

'Jamie!' Rebecca managed to scream, trying to warn Jamie as she swung her legs off the sofa, forgetting they were tightly bound, that she couldn't do anything to help.

It was already too late, anyway.

The two men were exchanging blows and although Mark's frame was more slight than Jamie's, he fought ferociously, like a wild, frantic animal, fuelled by years of fury.

Jamie fought back, but he was losing. He didn't look as if he stood a chance as Mark punched him, wrestling him to the floor.

Rebecca screamed loudly as the two men crashed through the coffee table, the wooden legs splintering beneath them, as they obliviously continued to exchange blows.

Rebecca could already feel herself growing tired, the energy draining from her, her eyes just wanting to close.

She needed to get out. Staring over towards the front door, she realised that this was her chance to escape, only her mind was foggy, and she wasn't thinking clearly. Awkwardly, she tumbled onto the floor and scrambled to get back up, only she couldn't. Her whole body felt heavy, as if it was beginning to turn to lead, the tablets had started working.

Move, she told herself silently, only her body was fighting against her now, and a part of her just wanted to just give in to it, to lie down on the carpet and go to sleep. She'd feel better then. She was sure of it.

Only, she kept thinking about Ella.

MOVE, REBECCA. MOVE.

'Where's Ella, Jamie?'

She needed to get out of here. To stay awake. Stay alive. For Ella's sake, if nothing else.

Seizing her opportunity as Mark and Jamie continued to struggle, she wriggled along the floor as best as she could with her legs still bound, turning to keep an eye on them.

Jamie had the knife now. There was hope, only it was diminished quickly.

'Let it go, or I'll break every bone in your hand,' Mark threatened Jamie through gritted teeth, his hand clamped hard around Jamie's, squeezing his fingers with every bit of strength he had, so that Jamie had no choice but to release his grip on the knife's handle.

Rebecca watched in horror as the weapon fell to the floor, wincing as Mark got on top of Jamie again, straddling his body, pinning him to the floor, before unleashing a rain of almighty punches.

Jamie was losing. Mark was overpowering him.

It would be her turn soon, Rebecca knew.

She needed to move faster.

Dragging herself across the floor, her head was spinning, her mind going into overdrive at what Mark would do next.

She couldn't die. Ella needed her.

That was the only thought that spurred her to keep going as she forced her body to keep moving.

She was frantic now, her legs dragging heavily behind her, but she'd almost reached the front door. All she had to do was reach up and grab the handle. A few more steps and she'd be outside, then she could call for help.

Someone would see her. They'd help her.

Turning back to check on Jamie, she flinched at the sight of his lifeless body sprawled out on the floor, already unconscious. She knew Mark wasn't going to stop there and sees him reach for the knife. Rebecca's worst fears come true as he holds it up high above him, before plunging it back down into Jamie's chest.

'No!' Her scream comes out as no more than a strangled whisper, muted by the sickening crunch of the knife as it plunges into Jamie's body. His head lolls to one side, a look of shock spreading across his face as he lies there, helplessly bleeding out.

She can't move. She can't breathe. She's caught in a trance, surrounded by the deathly silence in the room as Mark starts to get back up onto his feet, a thick splatter of blood all over him.

His eyes fix on her now as he realises she's trying to escape. She's so close now. She's almost there, almost at the door, but the room is spinning. Or is it her body? She's not sure.

She's shaking, her vision blurred, trembling violently as the adrenaline surges around her body, a mixture of shock and fear taking over her.

I don't have long, she thinks as she desperately fights to keep her eyes open, knowing her body was shutting down. Soon she'd be completely powerless and completely at Mark's mercy.

ELLA. It's as if a voice inside her tells her to keep fighting, that she has something to live for.

MOVE!

Rebecca is clawing at the carpet now, trying to gather momentum.

The front door is just a few inches away. She's almost there. She's on her knees now, clambering up the wooden panel, her fingers gripping the door handle.

She manages to pull the door open, a rush of cold air on her face. She's out.

'Help!' she shrieks into the cold night air.

SLAM.

The door is slammed shut. She's back inside, and she can feel the strong grip of Mark's hands as he drags her back across the lounge by her bound legs.

And all she can think is that she's never going to see Ella again.

Chapter Forty-Five

Rebecca is crying now, because her fate is sealed.

She can't get away. She can't save herself. Mark is too strong for her to fight against. But she has to at least try.

As he drags her back into the living room, the carpet soaked with Jamie's blood, she feebly grabs at every bit of furniture she passes in the hope that something will give her some leverage. That there's something she can use to fight him with and free herself from his tight grip.

But she knows it's no use. Mark is going to kill her too.

Jamie scuppered all his earlier plans.

Her death won't look like a suicide now. Not now Jamie is laying murdered on the floor.

Is Mark going to stab her too?

'There you go again, Alex. Right until the end, you're always out for number fucking one, aren't you? Always trying to save yourself.' Mark leers. 'Old habits die hard.'

He pulls her harder. Not caring that the carpet burns her face as he drags her body across it. 'Well not this time, Alex. You can make an addition to that fucking letter. You're going to say that you stabbed Jamie too. Because he found out who you really were. And they'll find all the evidence of that on your computer. All the emails he sat agonising over late at night. The emails I sent him that they'll have no way of tracing back to me. I watched him. Sitting there, knocking back drink after drink as he stared at the computer, trying to take it all in. To work out if what he was seeing was true. That his perfect wife had secrets. Fuck, it's no wonder he thought you were crazy, Alex, and that he wanted you carted off to a mental institute. He knew what you were! He knew what you were capable of.' Mark sneered, spittle leaving his lips.

'And they'll say that this is history repeating itself, won't they, Alex? When they find out about your mother and father. That life's one big circle and you're just like her, aren't you?'

'I'm not like her…' She mouths, the room spinning once more. Leaving her feeling sick and dizzy. Her body feeling limp. She tries to roll over but as her eyes rolls to the back of her head, she loses consciousness.

'Oh no. Not yet!' Mark shouts, staring down at the state of her now, unconscious on the floor. 'You're not going anywhere yet. You need to finish the letter. You need to finish this, Alex.'

She recognises the faint note of panic to his voice as he stares at the chaos and destruction in the room around him. The remainder of the pills all over the carpet, mixed with the pool of blood seeping out from the knife wound in Jamie's stomach.

She knows what he's thinking. *Alex is a cunt.* Even now, she's fucking up his plans. Mark had been so stupidly eager to make her take all the tablets that he hadn't factored how quickly they'd start to take effect.

She couldn't die yet.

She needed to finish this properly.

Jessica deserved her justice.

Turning back to her, her head lolling to the side now, Mark grabbed at her shoulders with one hand and smacked her face with the other.

Nothing.

Her body sank back, lifeless.

Mark hurried from the room and was back seconds later with a glass of cold water. He poured it over her, the water cascading down her face and hair, and still she didn't move, just lay there. Her skin pale. Her eyes shut.

She can't be dead.

Not yet.

Bending down, Mark held her wrist and took her pulse, willing it not to be true. She couldn't get away with it again, with no repercussions.

It wasn't fair.

Mark wanted to cry, incensed at the unfairness, he wanted to lash out and scream. To hurt Alex. To really fucking hurt her. But it was too late, she was already gone.

Or was she?

He could feel a pulse. A mild one. A slow rhythmic beating beneath his fingertips.

Then out of nowhere, Alex lunged towards him, catching him unawares with a jagged shard of glass she'd clawed up from the carpet as he'd dragged her across the room.

A large piece of glass from Ella's broken photo frame. She'd been clutching it so tightly she'd sliced through her own flesh, her palm filling with a pool of warm blood as she'd waited so patiently for the perfect moment to strike, summoning the last of her energy. That moment was now.

She dragged the sharp blade of glass across his skin, opening his throat, relishing the flash of complete shock on his face. The horror of what she'd just done to him.

And the fact that she'd duped him.

In his own words, Alex was forever the actress. Just like her own mother.

She smiled.

It was over.

It was Mark's turn to bleed.

Chapter Forty-Six

'Officer Blythe,' a voice way off in the distance calls out. 'She's waking up...' Rebecca's eyes flicker, the sound of Lisa's voice pulling her back from the darkness of her sleep. Though for once, she has no recollection of having any kind of bad dream, which was a first for her.

In fact, she has no memory of her sleep at all.

Just blackness.

The lights are too bright as she slowly opens her eyes, they're blinding her. Instantly she shuts her eyes again, trying to block out the bright hue from the window next to her.

'Rebecca?'

She tries again. Only this time, she opens her eyes slowly, allowing her focus to adjust to the light before she looks around the room.

She doesn't recognise where she is.

She's lying in a strange, narrow bed and the room is cold and feels sterile.

And that screeching noise?

The sound of monitors bleeping all around her, she realises.

For a second, she wonders if she's back in the psychiatric unit. But she's somewhere else.

'I'm in hospital?' she says finally, her voice weak and small. Sounding, even to her own ears, as if it belongs to someone else.

She has no memory of how she got here. No record of what's happened to her.

But she remembers her baby girl.

'Ella? Is Ella okay? Where is she?'

'She's right here, Rebecca.'

Rebecca turns and takes a proper look at Lisa. Standing beside the bed, she's cradling Ella in her arms as the child sleeps peacefully. Lisa crouches low, near to Rebecca, so that she can see her daughter properly, snuggled in her soft, pink, fleece blanket. Her thick lock of red hair peeping out.

Rebecca reaches out to take her, only the movement causes her to wince in pain.

'She's safe, Rebecca. You are now too. You've been through quite an ordeal...' Lisa says, teary now as she places her free hand softly on Rebecca's arm, her voice thick with concern and something else, which Rebecca can't quite distinguish.

'Shit. Why do I feel so weak?' she asks, placing her arms back down on the bed either side of her, her limbs feeling as if they are weighted down.

She's not sure how long she's been asleep for and despite only just waking up, she feels exhausted. Her head is throbbing, her mind foggy.

'Don't you worry. I've got her. You need to get your rest. You'll be right as rain again soon. She needs you strong again,' Lisa says, and Rebecca sees the tears running down Lisa's cheeks as she speaks. Unable to stop herself.

It's only when Lisa reaches out a free hand and wipes Rebecca's face, that Rebecca realises that she's crying too.

'Jamie?' Rebecca says, but she already knows the answer. She knows he's dead.

She remembers it all then… the image of Jamie's unmoving body, bleeding out on the lounge floor, surrounded by a pool of deep red seeping out all around him. The lights in his eyes extinguished, replaced with a vacant empty stare as she'd looked at him.

He was gone.

And now, she can see the raw pain etched in Lisa's eyes too.

But even so, Lisa tries to hide her own pain and console Rebecca.

'There was nothing anyone could do, Rebecca,' Lisa says, her body wracking with sobs, trying to comfort Rebecca. Trying so hard to be strong for her and Ella, despite the fact that she too had lost someone she loved. Her only brother. 'He was already dead by the time the police and the paramedics arrived. But they got to you just in time. When they found you, you were unconscious. The doctors said you were critical. You're a fighter, Rebecca…'

Her words are cut short as a nurse and Officer Blythe entered the room.

'She certainly is. How are you, Rebecca? I'm Nurse Lorraine Rath. I've been taking care of you since you were admitted last night,' the nurse said with a friendly smile, checking the monitor's readings as she pursed her mouth and nodded her head. 'You're making a great recovery,' she added, making a note of the machine's statics on Rebecca's personal chart. 'You're doing well, Rebecca. You're a tough cookie. How are you feeling?'

'Sick. Tired. I don't know,' Rebecca said, shaking her head. 'I feel a bit lightheaded. Can I have some water?'

Rebecca wasn't entirely sure how she felt about anything right now.

Her head was all over the place.

All she really felt was numb.

'Of course, you can,' Nurse Rath said, pouring out a fresh beaker of water before placing it to Rebecca's lips so she could take a few sips.

Rebecca flinches, visions of Mark forcing her to drink down the tablets flooding her mind.

'You're okay, Rebecca,' the nurse said then, sensing how out of sorts Rebecca must be feeling.

She would still be in shock.

Not only had she just lost her husband, but he'd been brutally murdered in front of her, and she'd almost been killed too.

'You suffered quite an ordeal, Rebecca. We pumped your stomach and administrated some liquid charcoal to help lessen the amount of medication you took from getting into your bloodstream. You'll feel a bit queasy for a while yet. And you'll feel very drowsy too. Your body's been through a lot. You need to get some proper rest so you recover fully,' Nurse Rath said, aiming her last comment in the police officer's direction.

'So that means, Officer Blythe, you've got five minutes and then my patient needs her sleep.' The officer smiled and nodded. Nurse Rath was his kind of woman. Her only concern was her patient's welfare and Officer Blythe wasn't going to argue with that.

Rebecca Dawson had been to hell and back the past few days. He had no intention of upsetting her further.

'Thank you,' he said to the nurse, before stepping forward to greet Rebecca.

'Hi, Rebecca,' he said before looking at Lisa and waiting as she nodded to confirm that Rebecca knew about Jamie. 'I'm so sorry for your loss. I wish we could have done more.'

Officer Blythe meant it too. They'd followed all their leads and an investigation was underway, but if he'd have just believed Rebecca in the first place about the tapes, maybe they would have carried on the search for the intruder more thoroughly, instead of just believing that Rebecca Dawson was seeing things that weren't really there.

'There was nothing anyone could do,' Rebecca said with a shrug, unable to find any other words. None of them could have predicted what would happen. None of them, not even her.

'I hate to do this so soon after you've woken up, but I need to take a statement from you, Rebecca. Is that okay?'

Rebecca nodded her head, before asking, 'Is he dead?'

'The intruder? Yes,' Officer Blythe confirmed. 'He died at the scene too. From a large laceration to his throat. Do you have much memory of what happened? I know it won't be easy, but I need you to tell me everything you know.'

Rebecca paused and took a deep breath before nodding her head.

She just wanted this all to be over.

She wanted her life back.

'I was in the office… I was looking for something that might tell me Jamie's whereabouts. Confirmation of a hotel booking or a receipt of some sort. I can't really remember much of what happened, but I remember feeling dizzy, I must have fainted. From the stress of the past few days, I expect. It's all been a bit too much. And I think that when I fell, I must have banged my head. That's when he must have got inside the house. He must have been watching me all along. He knew when to strike, because when I woke up, I was on the sofa, my hands and feet tied up. I thought at first that Jamie had come home… but *he* was there. This man?'

'So, the intruder wasn't known to yourself or your husband?'

'No. Neither of us knew him. I've never seen him before. He told me he'd found me online. That he was a "Ratter"?' she said, shaking her head and closing her eyes tightly, part of her frightened of what the officer might see if she kept her eyes open.

Remembering how Mark had boasted about how he'd found her in the end. *Play your role*, she reminded herself.

You are the victim here.

You are the one lying in this hospital bed.

'He'd been stalking me, all this time. He was the one watching me. He told me he could see me all the time. Though my webcam and my phone. He said he'd hacked into the security system too and accessed all the cameras. He'd been watching me for weeks. And he was in our house the other night. In Ella's room. It was him.'

309

'A Ratter? What the hell does that even mean?' Lisa interrupted, her expression a mixture of confusion and horror, as she looked from Rebecca to Officer Blythe, hoping someone would explain.

'Remote Access Technology, or RAT for short.' It was a term Officer Blythe was only too familiar with. 'There's a network of them out there. Young men, mainly. They are known to hack into unsuspecting victim's computers and phone devices. The motive more often than not is of a sexual or voyeuristic nature. It's rare that they ever venture beyond the realms of technology though. They're normally just kids, hiding behind their computers,' Officer Blythe said, more than aware of the kind of anonymous creeps that were lurking around out there on the web, making the force's job to track them down almost impossible.

'But this went beyond just watching Becks through a laptop? He was following her? He'd gained access into her house. When she was alone at night. Shit. How? Why?' Lisa said, panic rising inside her at the thought of what could have happened to Rebecca and Ella.

The man sounded deranged, as if he was capable of anything. Stalking Rebecca, and breaking into her house? That wasn't the actions of a normal person.

'What did he want from her?' Lisa asked.

'Well, I'm afraid that it can be much more complex than just watching their prey. The Ratters only operate through the Dark Web and mostly it's just a game to them. Teenage boys with a sick hobby, if you like. First, they infect your computer so they can get in and start gaining some control. Recording images and copying information, accessing bank details, calendars. Obtaining control over your whole life. They can find out everything. Your name and address, your passwords, your online banking details; and that's just the start. Some of them take it much more seriously than that. They build a profile of you, to sell on to other Ratters. That's how they make their money. They call them Girl Slaves. We're doing our best to crack down on it, but it's a tough job to trace these people back to the direct source.'

Officer Blythe was well aware of Ratters. It was becoming more and more common as technology progressed, and they were becoming better and better at covering their tracks.

'And that's what happened with Rebecca?' Lisa asked, feeling sick to her stomach. 'Someone collected all her details and sold it on to this fucking psycho? So that he'd own her? And what, he was trying to kidnap her?'

'It certainly looks that way,' Officer Blythe said, sadly. 'Did he say anything else, Rebecca? Anything that might give us a clue about his identity? Did he mention a name, a place? Is there anything that sticks out in your mind?'

So far, they had nothing on the man. No identification. No leads as to who he might have been.

All they had was a body. Their only hope was trying to find out who he was by trailing through dental records. But that could take months.

'No, only that he admitted that he'd hacked into the security footage and played a small part of the recording on a loop. So that you'd all think I was lying about him being there. He said that was half of the fun for him. Fucking with my life. Making me and everyone around me think I was crazy. And that it would make his plan easier.'

'His plan?' the officer asked.

'To take me. He said that he wanted me to take Ella and leave Jamie. For him,' Rebecca said now, her voice cold and hard. 'He kept saying "you're mine". He was acting crazy, deluded. He wouldn't listen to me, just kept talking in rhymes, but none of it made any sense. Then he started getting angry. Saying that he if he couldn't have me, no one could. That he was going to kill me. And if I didn't take the tablets so that it looked like an overdose, he'd kill Ella too.'

Rebecca was crying again, relieved that she'd survived. That she was still here, for Ella's sake.

It could have all turned out so differently.

'Can you lay her next to me on the bed, Lisa,' she whispered. Grateful as Lisa placed Ella in the crook of her arm. Rebecca kissed Ella gently on the top of her head.

'I begged him not to hurt her. I pleaded with him.'

'Did he hurt you, Rebecca? Did he do anything to you? Anything at all?' Officer Blythe said carefully.

Lisa stood next to him, holding her breath, scared of what Rebecca's answer might be. She'd already been through so much; Lisa couldn't imagine what else her poor sister-in-law had been subjected to. She let out a sigh of relief when Rebecca shook her head.

'Jamie must have let himself in through the back door. I don't know how long he was inside the house, or how much he heard. But the man heard him, and everything just happened so quickly after that. Jamie

312

tried to fight. God, he tried to fight so hard to help me. But this guy was like a crazed animal. He just stabbed him. And it was a blur after that. I remember seeing Jamie on the floor and thinking I need to help him. That he was going to die. But I was powerless, and I was scared for my life. My only option was to try to escape, because I knew I would be next, but I could barely move. He'd given me too many tablets, and I knew I was going to pass out. So, I just started crawling. Dragging myself across the carpet with all the strength I could muster. Only the man was on me in seconds, dragging me back across the room by my ankles. That's when I picked up the glass that was on the carpet, from the photo frame of Ella he'd smashed earlier.

'I just tried to protect myself. He was going to kill me. Jesus, there was so much blood. It was everywhere. But I didn't mean to kill him, I was just protecting myself. I just wanted to get him away from me. I was scared. And then I don't remember anything else. Just darkness. I must have passed out. And then I woke up here…' Rebecca tails off.

'I know this is difficult for you, Rebecca, but did you see the man stab your husband?'

Rebecca shook her head.

'No. I don't know.' She was crying again. 'I saw the knife… he was on top of Jamie. Holding it above him, but I was trying to get out. God, I feel so gutless for trying to escape, but I was trying to get help. I couldn't do it by myself.'

Rebecca looked at Lisa then and broke down crying. Knowing how devastated. Lisa would be at learning her brother's awful fate. How Rebecca had tried to save herself.

313

'There was nothing I could have done. How will I live with myself knowing that I left him? You must hate me?'

'Don't, Rebecca.' Lisa said, crying too now. 'It wasn't your fault. You loved him too.'

She was sobbing loudly now as Nurse Rath walked back in the room.

'Okay, Officer Blythe. That's your time done, I'm afraid. My patient needs her rest.' Annoyed with the officer now for upsetting her patient, she cut the conversation short, before making a note of the high blood pressure readings on the monitors which only confirmed Rebecca's obvious distress. 'That's your lot for today, I'm afraid.'

Officer Blythe nodded. 'Thank you. I have everything I need right now.'

It wasn't much else to go on, there was no information they didn't already have. But at least they'd established that the intruder wasn't known to the Dawsons and they now had an idea of his motive. They'd already taken away the computer and the phones from Rebecca and Jamie's house. Hopefully they'd get something from them.

'Don't worry, Rebecca. We're going to do everything we can to find out who this man is. In the meantime, if you think of anything else, any other details, you let us know, okay? No matter how small you think it might be. Thank you for your time, especially under the circumstances. Once again, I'm so sorry for your loss.'

'Thank you, Officer. I appreciate that,' Rebecca said as the nurse ushered him from the room, and Rebecca sank back into the pillows behind her, leaving her and Lisa alone once more.

'Jesus Christ, I'm so sorry, Becks,' Lisa said, full of guilt for ever doubting Rebecca. She hadn't realised the severity of what had been going on right under her nose.

'You have nothing to be sorry for, Lisa. You've done nothing wrong,' Rebecca said giving her sister-in-law's hand a gentle squeeze.

'I knew...' Lisa paused, wondering how much she should say, but quickly deciding to tell the truth.

There was no point in lying now. Not when Jamie was dead.

'I knew where Jamie was when you got home from the hospital. He was at my house. Him and Ella. He asked me to pick you up from the hospital, but he begged me not to say anything to you about where he was. He said he needed to get his head straight. That he'd only stay for a day or two at the most. I felt awful for not telling you the truth. I told him that too. I told him that he should have been at home with you...' Lisa said, realising now that if she'd tried harder, if Jamie had listened to her, he could have been at home. And then maybe none of this would have happened.

Jamie might still be alive.

'You were looking out for your brother, Lisa. I'd have probably done the same,' Rebecca said, too drained to hold any kind of grudge now. What was done was done.

Lisa faltered. Wiping her tears. Rebecca could see by her face there was something else she wasn't saying. So she waited.

'I know this isn't the right time, Rebecca, but I need to tell you something. Jamie had been watching you too. I looked on his phone and his computer when he went to make a telephone call. That night he'd come home early and found you in the garden, you said it was strange how he turned up right when he did? That he'd never come home at that time before from a business trip, in the middle of the night? Well, he'd been at *her* house. Jenna, the girl from his office. I only found out yesterday when I read their messages. He'd been staying there the night.' Lisa paused.

Rebecca frowned.

'You're saying Jamie was watching me too?'

Lisa nodded.

'He'd hired a private investigator to follow you around. He'd been asking questions about your past.'

'About my past? What was he hoping to find out?' Rebecca said, her face a picture of confusion.

'I don't know. He didn't say. All he did say was that you were lying to us. That you couldn't be trusted…' Lisa felt a surge of disloyalty run through her, at betraying her own brother in this way. But Rebecca was family too. And what Jamie had said hadn't made any sense.

And Lisa couldn't forget how he'd gone behind Rebecca's back. Cheating on her and having her followed, when it was Jamie that couldn't be trusted all along.

'He went to take another call and I was going to have it out with him when he came back downstairs. I was going to make him leave. I was going to insist that he went home and talked to you…' Lisa trailed off, almost embarrassed now at how cruel and unsupportive Jamie had been, how she hadn't seen it herself until it was too late. 'Only, when I went to speak to him, he'd already gone. We'd argued before he left. He seemed so distracted and angry about everything. And I was worried that maybe he'd gone to see you, and that something might happen between you both. He was in a strange mood, and I didn't understand why he was having your movements tailed... why he didn't trust you. So I called Officer Blythe and told him everything I knew.' Lisa was sobbing now. Wishing that things had been different. That she and Jamie hadn't parted on such bad terms. 'He should have told the officer that he'd been watching the security tapes. He should have said where he was that night. How could the police investigate what was going on, when all they had to go on was lies? Maybe things would have been different. Maybe Jamie would still be here?'

Rebecca closed her eyes, then opened them again, blinking back the last of her tears.

She wasn't going to cry anymore. She needed to be strong, to focus on getting better so she could look after Ella.

'None of this was Jamie's fault, Lisa. He wasn't to know. We all saw the tapes. There was no sign of an intruder on them. Jamie had every reason to worry about my state of mind. He had every reason to believe he couldn't trust me. That's what this nutter set out to do. He wanted to make me look as if I was crazy, and it worked. Christ, even *I'd* started questioning my sanity at that point. I felt as if I was going stark raving mad. And that's exactly what this man wanted everyone to think. That had been his plan all along, to make everyone around me believe I'd lost my mind. You can't blame Jamie for the way he acted. He didn't know any better,' Rebecca said, the conversation ending when Nurse Rath walked back in the room.

'Right, how about I show you to the day room, Lisa? You can get yourself a coffee and I'm sure some of the nurses down there would love to coo over this young one. Rebecca needs to get some rest. The sooner she makes a full recovery, the sooner she'll be discharged,' Nurse Rath said, ushering Lisa and Ella from the room, before any of them could protest, though Ella had already started crying.

'It's like a sixth sense isn't it,' Lisa said to Rebecca. 'They pick up on everything. Don't you worry though, Becks. I've got her. She's in safe hands. I'll see if she needs a feed. You get some sleep, yeah?' Lisa said, hoping to give Rebecca some reassurance. 'We'll be back before you even know it.'

'Can you hear that, Rebecca?' Nurse Rath said, turning back to Rebecca and shooting her a smile once they'd gone. 'Silence. You make the most of that for the next hour or two and get yourself some rest, lovey. Because I can see your little one has the same fighting spirit in her as you do.'

Rebecca nodded.

Turning her head to the side, she closed her eyes, unable to get the image of Jamie and Jenna together out of her mind.

And the fact he'd hired a private detective, that he'd seen those articles online.

That he'd been so close to finding out everything about her.

All her buried secrets.

She'd been right about him all along. It had only been a matter of time until Jamie had found out everything.

Her only conciliation now was that the dead couldn't talk.

318

No one need find out a single thing.

She shouldn't feel bad about what she did. Not anymore.

She'd protected herself and Ella.

She'd done the right thing.

Chapter Forty-Seven

Fastening my seat belt, I start the engine before turning to look at Ella, all snuggled safely, cocooned in her car seat.

I glance back at the house one last time, taking one last final deep breath as I pull away.

I watch through the rear-view mirror as my once perfect home, my once perfect life, get smaller and smaller as I make my way into the distance.

Until that life is gone completely from my sight.

I concentrate on the road ahead, knowing that in time it will feel as if none of this had ever happened.

Because I've done this before, started from scratch, so I know I can do it all over again.

Except this time, I have Ella.

And although I have no idea where we're heading, at least we're together.

Me and my beautiful girl.

I think of Jamie then, all the things he'll miss out on. All those memories yet to be made. And memories are all I have left of him too.

It feels like a million years ago now, when I first saw him at that hotel bar. Dining with some clients, as I sat at a far corner table all on my own. Invisible to the likes of him. And he would have been invisible to me too, if it hadn't been for the spectacle of the entire waiting team practically falling over themselves to keep him happy and all their *Yes sir, no sir, three bags full sir.*

It had been entertaining to watch. How this one man seemed to have everyone in his power. I could see the appeal.

An attractive man with an air of importance about him. He looked like he wouldn't take any bullshit. And well, I always did love a challenge.

It didn't take much to find out who he was, the maître D had only too gladly corrected me when I pretended to mistake him with someone famous.

'No, no. That's Mr Jamie Dawson. The director of one of London's most successful recruitment companies. He's a regular client.' Then, lowering his voice, he quipped as he winked at me. 'A bit of a bachelor by all accounts.'

Of course, I took the bait and looked him up online. An eligible bachelor with money and power and everything already in place for me to start again in a whole new life. I studied him hard for two whole days, from the confines of my bleak hotel room. It wasn't as if I had anything else to do. I was still hiding away, trying to camouflage myself into my new identity.

Recovering from the whiplash I'd suffered.

The news of the car accident, of Mark and Jessica's death, had been all over the news. Reported as a hit and run.

I was desperate. So, I made it my business to find every article I could about this Jamie Dawson on the Internet, devouring articles about his company. About the charities he sponsored. The fundraising events he'd been to. And I found a few personal posts on Twitter too: A reference to a book he once read and loved. George Orwell's *Nineteen Eighty-Four*. A photograph of his favourite bottle of drink. The same vile Glenfiddich my mother drank.

I had all the knowledge I needed to impress him.

And I used it with vigour.

Jamie Dawson fell for me, hook, line, and sinker that first night he'd approached me at the hotel bar. It went much quicker and smoother than I ever could have hoped. Because I gave him the illusion of everything he thought he wanted me to be.

A clone of him, in effect. I fed his insatiable ego.

Over the first few weeks of us dating, I morphed into exactly the woman Jamie wanted me to be. If Jamie didn't like spicy food, I didn't like spicy food. If Jamie had a favourite movie, I had the same favourite movie.

He never suspected. He never clicked that I was just impersonating his perfect ideal.

And then I got pregnant with Ella. My sweet, darling Ella.

She'd been the one real flaw in my plan.

Because I never wanted to get pregnant. I never wanted a child. Not after what happened to Jessica. And from the minute Ella was born, I've lived with the constant fear that when I wasn't looking, karma would come and snatch her away from me.

And Mark almost managed it.

Poor, pathetic Mark.

I remember the first time I ever hit Mark. He just took it. Believing me when I begged him to forgive me, promising him it would never happen again.

I did what was expected. What I'd witnessed my mother do time and time again when I'd been growing up.

And it had worked. He believed me.

But gradually over time, I got worse.

My demons became too overpowering and I started drinking to ease my throbbing head, all those vicious painful flashbacks. Anything to block out those awful memories.

And then I started to hit him when I hadn't had any drink at all. Completely sober, but full of jealousy and rage. Because I was losing him, and that's what you did, wasn't it? When everything started to slip. You fought to stay in control.

My mother did that too, the experts said later. When they'd printed their contemptuous profiles about her in the press.

How she'd kept us all living in fear of her for years, because she believed that was the only way to make people stay.

Because she believed it was the only way you could stop people from leaving you.

Mark tried to hide his affair from me at first, but I knew something had changed. He started being careless, as if he wanted me to work it out. As if he wanted me to know.

Because he wanted it to be over. He wanted to leave me. That's the truth.

I only realised that when I finally confronted him.

I expected him to deny it, I expected him to plead on his hands and knees to forgive him.

Only he didn't do any of that.

He told me that he'd found someone who genuinely loved him, not someone like me; someone who wasn't capable of real love.

And in that moment, I just wanted to kill him.

So I waited for a few days after our row, then loaded up the car with all of my stuff.

I was going to leave him.

But I was going to make him pay.

I was taking Jessica with me.

She might have been his daughter by blood, but I'd helped to raise her too.

I'd wiped her tears when she cried and hugged her tight when she'd had a bad dream.

I loved her like my own.

Even now, I can still remember every tiny detail about her, though I try my hardest to block that all out. Her dainty plump white hands. Her mass of bright blonde curls. The way she used to belly laugh whenever we said or did something funny.

She was just four years old and she trusted me.

She loved me too.

So, of course she didn't protest when I strapped her into the car and told her about us going on a little adventure.

But Mark had to go and ruin all my plans. Clearly suspicious, he'd come home from work early that day, before I'd had time to get in the driver's seat and start the engine up, and I wasn't fast enough. I wasn't prepared.

By the time I'd started the engine, he'd yanked open the passenger door and had jumped into the seat next to me. And I just panicked. I put my foot down and drove.

Aimlessly at first. Recklessly. Fast.

It was getting dark, but I didn't notice the rain, not until later.

Until afterwards.

We were shouting.

And I told him that he couldn't leave me. He couldn't take Jessica away from me.

And he shouted back.

That it was over. That he didn't love me. That Jessica was his.

I told him all the things I wanted to do to him. All the ways I'd make him suffer.

And then he hit me.

The back of his hand locking with my cheek.

The shock stinging me far more than the actual blow.

It was the first and only time he'd ever lain a hand on me.

I saw red. I remember thinking that there was no going back from there.

We couldn't just go home.

We were done. He was going to leave me, and he was going to take Jessica away from me.

When we went off road, I drove at those trees, aiming for the one on his side. And in my head, my plan was going to work.

I'd turned and checked that Jessica was strapped in. Ignoring her terrified cries as her father and I continued to scream and shouted at each other.

We'd be okay. I could feel it.

The car sped up, plummeting towards the tall oak tree in front of us. And with seconds to spare, I put my hand out and unclipped Mark's seat belt. Slamming my foot down on the accelerator, hard.

And it would have worked. I'm convinced of it. I would have hit the tree nearest to him and killed him instantly. But we hit something else beforehand.

Someone else, I now know.

The car veered off. Sailing through the air, Jessica screaming in the back.

There was a piercing screech, and then an eerie silence, a deathly quiet that went on to haunt my dreams for years to come.

I knew she was dead. That I'd killed her.

So I did whatever I could to get away. To save myself. I crawled from the wreckage and I never looked back.

It was the only way I'd have any chance of survival. I had to block it all out. Pretend it had never happened. Pretend I didn't kill Jessica. Pretend it wasn't me.

Because I was going to become someone new. Someone different. Someone good.

And Jamie Dawson had been that chance... until he'd betrayed me too.

Chapter Forty-Eight

He's still breathing, but shallowly, his chest heaving as he chokes back the blood that bubbles in his throat.

Jamie is splayed out on the floor, next to Mark's dead body, the two of them side by side in one thick puddle of pooling blood.

Jamie raises a hand to me. Holding it up, in a plea for help, unable to find his voice.

I crouch at his side, now that I've cut the ties from my ankles, and stare deeply into his eyes.

I see the flicker of confusion there at my lack of urgency to call for an ambulance, a silent plea in his eyes for me to help him.

Instead, I just look down at him.

He sees me then, finally, for the very first time. The *real* me.

And he knows then, too late, that everything Mark had said about me was true. I wasn't some victim of domestic abuse. I wasn't hiding from Mark.

I was hiding from myself.

From what I'd done.

Damaged and dysfunctional me, doing what I've always had to do in order to survive.

'You took Ella from me,' my voice is a whisper and my words are filled with sadness as I shake my head. 'Don't you know that the most dangerous place you can ever stand is between a mother and her child.'

He's listening. I can see his eyes flickering with fear as he takes in my every word.

And he knows. In that one sentence, that one statement, that I can't let him live.

Because he knows all my secrets, he knows all about me now.

And if he's taken Ella once, I know he's capable of doing it again.

Only this time she'll be taken from me for good.

And I recognise the look of terror on his face when I withdraw the knife from his stomach and hear that final gasp of breath that leaves his body, as the knife plunges back down into his chest, the blood bubbling inside his throat.

And it's this second stab wound that kills him.

I watch him take his final breath before I place the knife in Mark's hand.

I burn the letter Mark forced me to write. I let it sit in the vase that was now on the floor, surrounded by the debris of the broken coffee table. I watch as it turns to ash, all the while praying that the police will believe my story.

The poor, distraught, grieving wife.

I feel my body shutting down. Slumping to the floor, my eyes close.

The sound of hammering on the front door sounds so faint, so way off in the distance.

Officer Blythe is anything but stupid, and once he finds the emails Jamie was sent from Mark about the car crash, he'll start digging for me.

He'll figure out that my hospital records never went missing, and that I used a forged copy of a birth certificate for the wedding.

He'll find out that Rebecca Dawson doesn't exist. That she never existed.

So, I can't risk staying any longer than I have already.

My only regret will be leaving Lisa behind.

Because she was like the sister I once had. Loyal to me to the very end.

She had been real.

I know I'll miss her forever.

But I need to make sure Ella is safe and that no one can take her from me.

And as I drive away from my old, pretend life, I know that finally I'm free.

Acknowledgements

Many thanks to my fantastic (Fairy-God) editor Keshini Naidoo for her amazing editorial skills. I truly value all of your advice, support, and friendship. It's been an absolute pleasure to work alongside you on MINE. Huge thanks also to the brilliant Emma Mitchell over at Creating Perfection for your publishing services and proof reading. You did a fantastic job! Special thanks for all the sweary notes that made me chuckle whilst doing the final read through. And to Stuart Bache at Books Covered for the fantastic cover art.

A big shout out to everyone who's kept me sane on this crazy writing journey. To all of those at the scene of the crime, you know who you are!

Special shout out to some of my fantastic writerly friends, whose friendship and support is more appreciated than they could ever know. Emma Tallon, Emma Kennedy, Noelle Holten, Kerry Barnes, Dreda Say Mitchell, Mel Sherratt, Louise Ross, and Pete Sortwell. (Pete, Frank says hi!).

HUGE thanks to YOU! All the fantastic readers and book bloggers who choose to read my books, and an extra special thanks to those of you who take the time to leave a review. I read and appreciate every single one! Reviews really are the best gift to leave for an author.

I love receiving your emails and messages, so please do keep them coming!

Some days, they literally are the very thing that keeps me going while I'm slogging away over my keyboard!

As always, I'd like to thank my extremely supportive friends and family for all the encouragement that they give me along the way.

The Coopers, The Ellis, and The Kellehers.

All my fab girlies. Special mention as always to Lucy! Who waited so patiently to read the very first copy of MINE before devouring it in record time as always. And to the 'Girls Gone Wild' ladies who might spot a few familiar names in this book!!

Finally, a big thank you to my husband, Danny for your endless support and encouragement. You are my absolute rock and I could not do any of this without you!

Last but never least, our three sons, Ben, Danny, and Kyle.

And Sassy and Miska – the best little writer's assistants ever!

x x

If you want to be the first to hear about my next release, you can sign up to my newsletter here: www.caseykelleher.co.uk

Facebook: www.facebook.com/officialcaseykelleher

Instagram: @caseykelleher

Twitter: @Caseykelleher

Printed in Great Britain
by Amazon

37978477R00190